PROTECTING THE THIEF

ELOUISE EAST

A Novel in the
SAMANTHA COLE'S SUSPENSEFUL SEDUCTION WORLD

Protecting the Thief

This book is a work of fiction. Names, characters, businesses, organizations, places, events, and incidents either are the product of the author's imagination or are used fictitiously. Any resemblance to actual persons, living or dead, events, or locales is entirely coincidental.

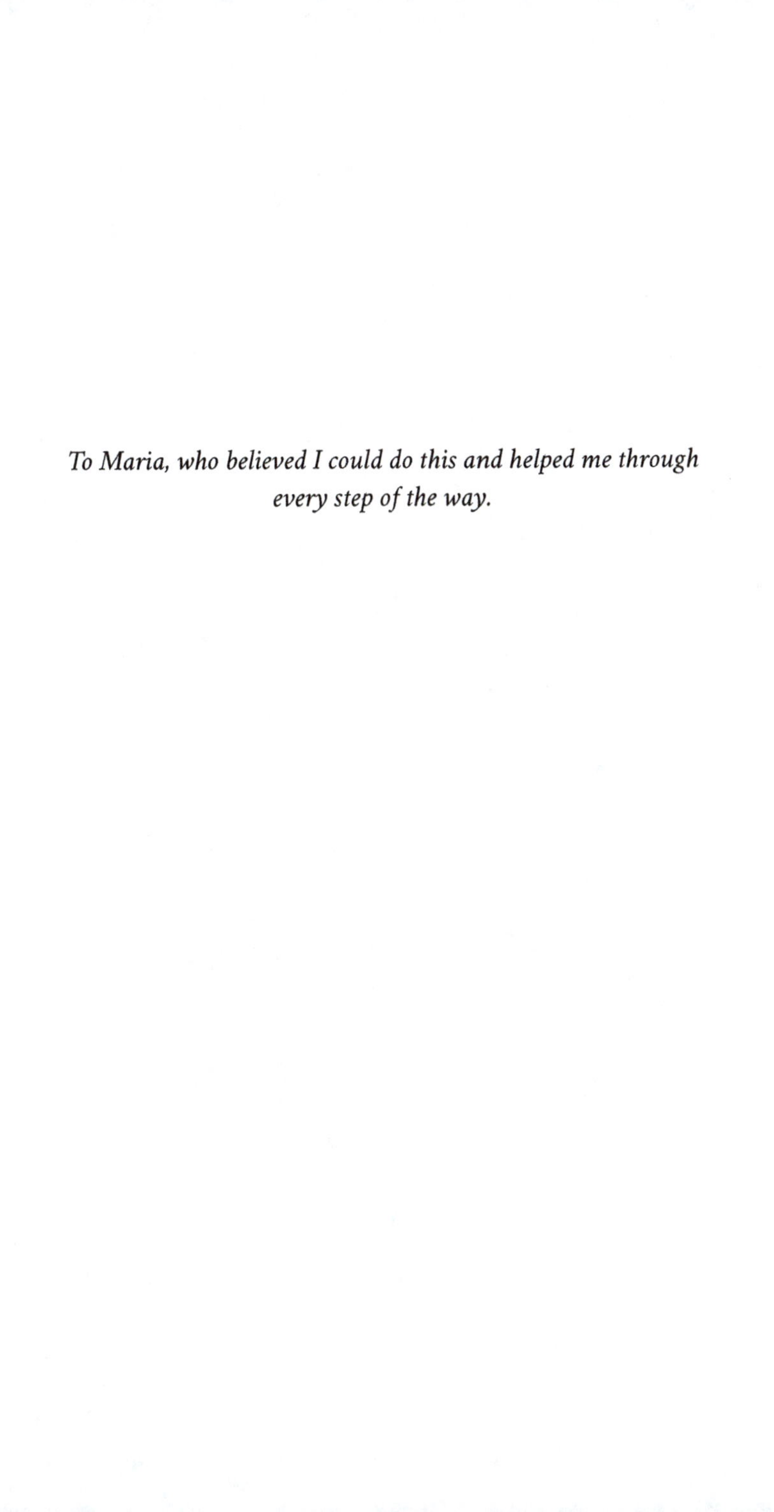

To Maria, who believed I could do this and helped me through every step of the way.

# ACKNOWLEDGMENTS

A huge thanks to Samantha A Cole who allowed me to write within her awesome world. Her universe and characters are so well created that I felt as if I was physically in the world itself. So, thank you for taking a chance on me.

Maria Vickers, I owe you so much. You have been with me throughout my author journey and continue to support me. I don't think I could do this without you.

A big thanks to my PA, Renee Botbyl, who puts up with me and my hectic schedule and always asking for advice. She never lets me down.

And finally, to Emma Brown, who helps me to make my characters shine and tells me when things need changing or don't work. I appreciate everything you have done for me.

INTRODUCTION

Dear Readers,

The authors of this book have borrowed (with my permission) one or more of my characters from the Trident Security series and/or the Doms of The Covenant series. Some are minor characters who are now getting their own story, while others are major characters who are being mentioned to connect the story to my series. This book has been published under a contractual agreement between the authors and me.

While I may have provided some suggestions for including my characters in the storyline, this book is the sole work of the authors who wrote it. I was not involved in the writing or editing process. However, several beta readers familiar with my characters helped review the final product. While the BDSM lifestyle is included in many of my books, it may or may not be included in this story.

If you're unfamiliar with my series and characters, there is a list at the end of this book.

Thank you for supporting the authors and me, and I hope you enjoy this extension of my Trident Security and/or Doms of The Covenant series.

Love,
Samantha Cole

WHO'S WHO AND THE HISTORY OF
TRIDENT SECURITY & THE COVENANT

***While not every character is in every book, these are the ones with the most mentions throughout the series. This guide will help keep readers straight about who's who.

Trident Security (TS) is a private investigative and military agency, co-owned by Ian and Devon Sawyer. With governmental and civilian contracts, the company got its start when the brothers and a few of their teammates from SEAL Team Four retired to the private sector. The original six-man team is referred to as the Sexy Six-Pack, as they were dubbed by Kristen Sawyer, née Anders, or the Alpha Team. Trident had since expanded and former members of the military and law enforcement have been added to the staff. The company is located on a guarded compound, which was a former import/export company cover for a drug trafficking operation in Tampa, Florida. Three warehouses on the property were converted into large apartments, the TS offices, gym, and bunk rooms. There is also an obstacle course, a Main Street shooting gallery, a helicopter pad, and more features necessary for training and missions.

In addition to the security business, there is a fourth warehouse that now houses an elite BDSM club, co-owned by Devon, Ian, and their cousin, Mitch Sawyer, who is the manager. A lot of time and money has gone into making The Covenant the most sought after membership in the Tampa/St. Petersburg area and beyond. Members are thoroughly vetted before being granted access to the elegant club.

There are currently over fifty Doms who have been appointed Dungeon Masters (DMs), and they rotate two or three shifts each throughout the month. At least four DMs are on duty at all times at various posts in the pit, playrooms, and the new garden, with an additional one roaming around. Their job is to ensure the safety of all the submissives in the club. They step in if a sub uses their safeword and the Dom in the scene doesn't hear or heed it, and make sure the equipment used in scenes isn't harming the subs.

The Covenant's security team takes care of everything else that isn't scene-related, and provides safety for all members and are essentially the bouncers. With the recent addition of the garden, and more private, themed rooms, the owners have expanded their self-imposed limit of 350 members. The fire marshal had approved them for 500 when the warehouse-turned-kink club first opened, but the cousins had intentionally kept that number down to maintain an elite status. Now with more room, they are increasing the membership to 500, still under the new maximum occupancy of 720.

Between Trident Security and The Covenant there's plenty of romance, suspense, and steamy encounters. Come meet the Sexy Six-Pack, their friends, family, and teammates.

The Sexy Six-Pack (Alpha Team) and Their Significant Others

- Ian "Boss-man" Sawyer: Devon and Nick's brother; retired Navy SEAL; co-owner of Trident Security and The Covenant; husband/Dom of Angelina (Angel).

- Devon "Devil Dog" Sawyer: Ian and Nick's brother; retired Navy SEAL; co-owner of Trident Security and The Covenant; husband/Dom of Kristen; father of John Devon "JD."
- Ben "Boomer" Michaelson: retired Navy SEAL; explosives and ordnance specialist; husband/Dom of Katerina; son of Rick and Eileen.
- Jake "Reverend" Donovan: retired Navy SEAL; sniper; husband/Dom of Nick; brother of Mike; Whip Master at The Covenant.
- Brody "Egghead" Evans: retired Navy SEAL; computer specialist; husband/Dom of Fancy.
- Marco "Polo" DeAngelis: retired Navy SEAL; communications specialist and back up helicopter pilot; husband/Dom of Harper; father to Mara.
- Nick "Junior" Sawyer: Ian and Devon's brother; retired Navy SEAL; husband/submissive of Jake.
- Kristen "Ninja-girl" Sawyer: author of romance/suspense novels; wife/submissive of Devon; mother of "JD."
- Angelina "Angie/Angel" Sawyer: graphic artist; wife/submissive of Ian.
- Katerina "Kat" Michaelson: dog trainer for law enforcement and private agencies; wife/submissive of Boomer.
- Millicent "Harper" DeAngelis: lawyer; wife/submissive of Marco; mother of Mara.
- Francine "Fancy" Maguire: baker; wife/submissive of Brody.

Extended Family, Friends, and Associates of the Sexy Six-Pack

- Mitch Sawyer: Cousin of Ian, Devon, and Nick; co-owner/manager of The Covenant, Dom to Tyler and Tori.
- T. Carter: US spy and assassin; works for covert agency Deimos; Dom of Jordyn.
- Jordyn Alvarez: US spy and assassin; member of covert agency Deimos; submissive of Carter.
- Tyler Ellis: Stockbroker; lifestyle switch—Dom of Tori; submissive of Mitch.
- Tori Freyja: K9 trainer for veterans in need of assistance/service dogs; submissive of Mitch and Tyler.
- Parker Christiansen: owner of New Horizons Construction; husband/Dom of Shelby; adoptive father of Franco and Victor.
- Shelby Christiansen: stay-at-home mom; two-time cancer survivor; wife/submissive of Parker; adoptive mother of Franco and Victor.
- Curt Bannerman: retired Navy SEAL; owner of Halo Customs, a motorcycle repair and detail shop; husband of Dana; stepfather of Ryan, Taylor, Justin, and Amanda. Lives in Iowa.
- Dana Prichard-Bannerman: teacher; widow of retired SEAL Eric Prichard; wife of Curt; mother of Ryan, Taylor, Justin, and Amanda. Lives in Iowa.
- Jenn "Baby-girl" Mullins: college student; goddaughter of Ian; "niece" of Devon, Brody, Jake, Boomer, and Marco; father was a Navy SEAL; parents murdered.
- Mike Donovan: owner of the Irish pub, Donovan's; brother of Jake; submissive to Charlotte.
- Charlotte "Mistress China" Roth: Parole officer; Domme and Whip Master at The Covenant; Domme of Mike.

- Travis "Tiny" Daultry: former professional football player; head of security at The Covenant and Trident compound; occasional bodyguard for TS.
- Doug "Bullseye" Henderson: retired Marine; head of the Personal Protection Division of TS.
- Rick and Eileen Michaelson: Boomer's parents; guardians of Alyssa. Rick is a retired Navy SEAL.
- Charles "Chuck" and Marie Sawyer: Ian, Devon, and Nick's parents. Charles is a self-made real estate billionaire. Marie is a plastic surgeon involved with Operation Smile.
- Will Anders: Assistant Curator of the Tampa Museum of Art; Kristen Anders's cousin.
- Dr. Roxanne London: pediatrician; Domme/wife (Mistress Roxy) of Kayla; Whip Master at Covenant.
- Kayla London: social worker; submissive/wife of Roxanne.
- Grayson and Remington Mann: twins; owners of Black Diamond Records; Doms/fiancés of Abigail; members of The Covenant.
- Abigail Turner: personal assistant at Black Diamond Records; submissive/fiancée of Gray and Remi.
- Chase Dixon: retired Marine Raider; owner of Blackhawk Security; associate of TS.
- Reggie Helm: lawyer for TS and The Covenant; Dom/husband of Colleen.
- Alyssa Wagner: teenager saved by Jake from an abusive father; lives with Rick and Eileen Michaelson.
- Dr. Trudy Dunbar: Psychologist.
- Carl Talbot: college professor; Dom and Whip Master at The Covenant.

- Jase Atwood: Contract agent/mercenary; Lives on the island of St. Lucia; Dom of Brie.
- Brie Hanson: Owner of Daddy-O's in St. Lucia; submissive of Jase.

The Omega Team and Their Significant Others

- Cain "Shades" Foster: retired Secret Service agent.
- Tristan "Duracell" McCabe: retired Army Special Forces
- Logan "Cowboy" Reese: retired Marine Special Forces; former prisoner of war. Boyfriend/Dom of Dakota.
- Valentino "Romeo" Mancini: retired Army Special Forces; former FBI Hostage Rescue Team (HRT) member.
- Darius "Batman" Knight: retired Navy SEAL; husband/Dom of Tahira.
- Kip "Skipper" Morrison: retired Army; former LAPD SWAT sniper.
- Lindsey "Costello" Abbott: retired Marine; sniper.
- Dakota Swift: Tampa PD undercover police officer; submissive girlfriend to Logan.
- Tahira: Princess of Timasur, a small North African nation; wife/submissive of Darius.

Trident Support Staff

- Colleen McKinley-Helm: office manager of TS; wife/submissive of Reggie.
- Tempest "Babs" Van Buren: retired Air Force helicopter pilot; TS mechanic.

- Russell Adams: retired from Navy; assistant TS mechanic.
- Nathan Cook: former computer specialist with the National Security Agency (NSA).
- Conrad "CC" Chapman: retired Air Force pilot; current pilot of TS jet.
- Clinton Howe: retired Air Force pilot; TS jet co-pilot when needed.

Members of Law Enforcement

- Larry Keon: Assistant Director of the FBI.
- Frank Stonewall: Special Agent in Charge of the Tampa FBI.
- Calvin Watts: Leader of the FBI HRT in Tampa.
- Colt Parrish: Major Case Specialist, Behavioral Analysis Unit.

The K9s of Trident

- Beau: An orphaned Lab/Pit mix, rescued by Ian. Now a trained K9 who has more than earned his spot on the Alpha Team.
- Spanky: A rescued Bullmastiff with a heart of gold, owned by Parker and Shelby.
- Jagger: A rescued Rottweiler trained as an assistance/service animal for Russell.
- FUBAR: A Belgian Malinois who failed aggressive guard dog training. Adopted by Babs.
- BDSM: Bravo, Delta, Sierra, and Mike, two Belgian Malinoises and two German shepherds, the guard dogs at the Trident compound: Ian named them using the military communication's alphabet.

JESSE

The moon hid behind the clouds as if it didn't want to witness what Jesse Flint was doing that evening. It made Jesse's job easier because it concealed his approach to the mansion; therefore, allowing him to slip in through the side door without so much as a click. Pausing inside, he breathed silently, straining his hearing for the tell-tale signs of footsteps or the brush of fabric giving away the position of the guards.

Sensing nothing, Jesse grinned beneath his balaclava, unable to tamp down on the elation surging through his veins. He kept close to the wall, drifting soundlessly down the long hallway.

A guard veered around the corner, and Jesse pulled back into a closed doorway until he merged with the shadows. He narrowed his eyes, reducing the amount of white showing but kept his gaze on the soldier coming closer.

Jesse's muscles vibrated as he readied himself to fight if necessary. It would ruin his surprise, but he would if there was no other option. The guard glanced from side to side while he marched down the hallway, staring straight at Jesse for a pulse-racing moment before continuing on his way and disappearing around another corner.

Jesse blew out a breath and resumed his trek. He knew he didn't have far to go because he'd studied the layout for many an evening. The tingling of the adrenaline flooding his veins had him eager to bounce and jump around, but it would prove too noisy, so it would have to wait until he got back out.

The door he needed was closed as he'd expected, and he twisted the handle with the utmost care, slipping inside and shutting it behind him. His gaze roamed the large, library-style room, although instead of books on the shelves, there were dozens upon dozens of expensive artifacts. Jesse could have had a wonderful evening perusing the shelves and figuring out which would be most advantageous for him to "obtain," but he had one in mind for tonight, and that was his sole focus.

The carpet masked his steps when he shifted closer. He had been unable to determine where the vase he needed to take was, so he searched every shelf until he found it. Nestled between two statues with similar designs, the vase fit in with its surroundings, but Jesse trembled and pursed his lips. Despite the artifact being the reason for his visit to the mansion, he'd hoped his information had been wrong.

Pulling out a small black pouch from his pocket, he opened it and slid out a five-inch metal plate and replaced the pouch. Standing in front of the vase, he eyed the shelf, checking for any electronic devices or sensors he hadn't been made aware of. Unable to see anything out of the ordinary, he lifted his gloved hand to the vase and placed the plate at its base.

Jesse tilted the vase a minuscule amount and slipped the plate between the base and the shelf. Footsteps stomped outside, and he hesitated, swallowing hard. All it would take was for his hand to move, and alarms would blare throughout the mansion.

When the noise receded, he paused a second longer, then resumed his careful movements. The metal plate sliding against the ceramic of the vase and the wood of the shelf sounded extremely loud in the silence surrounding him, but he ignored it and continued until the plate was fully situated beneath the vase. Now was the moment of truth.

Jesse inhaled and held his breath when he lifted the vase from the shelf. Holding it above the plate for several seconds, he released the air in his lungs when no sounds were heard. There might have been silent alarms, but his research had not shown it.

Moving away from the shelf, he wrapped the vase in some fabric and slipped it inside a bag, hooking it over his head. He grinned and tip-toed a victory dance right there before pulling out a small plastic statue—his calling card— and placing it on top of the metal plate. Retracing his steps, he listened at the door and, hearing nothing, slipped into the hallway. By the time he reached outside, he swallowed down his glee, wanting nothing more than to see the face of the person he had taken the vase from when the man figured it out. It couldn't happen, but the thought was enough to make the weight on his shoulders lighten.

Using the shadows as his friend, he hightailed it back the way he came, stopping when he heard voices.

"—ends appear chewed. I bet a fox or something has chewed its way through."

"Are you sure that's all it is? Could a person have done it?"

"I don't think so with how these wires look."

Jesse didn't stop to hear anymore and changed direction, following the sound of the wind rustling through the trees to the rear of the property. It wasn't the best exit point because it meant he had further to travel to get back to his car, but it was better than being caught.

He couldn't see far in front of him, but the shadows of large bushes and plants gave him some guidance as to where he was. The crackle of a radio paused him in his tracks, and he hunkered down, watching a guard stroll along the fence, not ten feet in front of him, smoking a cigarette. Jesse shook his head, not having heard the security guard in the grass. Not acceptable.

Waiting until the scent of tobacco left on a breeze, Jesse slipped to the fence, pulling some cutters from his pocket. They were specially made to cut through wire fencing and to make it appear as an animal had chewed through them. By the time anyone had figured out the holes in the fence were related to the missing vase, Jesse would be long gone.

Making a hole big enough for him to stomach crawl through, he took the bag holding the artifact off his head and pushed it through first, then followed. Rocks and hard lumps of soil dug into his skin through the silk fabric of his clothes, but he didn't care. He was used to it. The benefits of wearing silk clothing outweighed the negatives.

He pushed the wire so it seemed like something had entered the property instead of exited and slid the bag over his head once more. He wasn't looking forward to the three-mile walk, but he'd get through it thinking about how much the mansion's owner would fume once he found out what had happened right under his nose.

Jesse chuckled, pulling the balaclava off and tucking it into his pocket. He released his hair from the band and ruffled his hands through it, enjoying the slight breeze cooling his scalp.

A job well done if he did say so himself.

～

Jesse leaned against the breakfast bar that also doubled as a kitchen table due to the small floor space of the apartment he had rented in Tampa, Florida. He held the phone to his ear and listened to what the caller said.

"I understand the urgency, Mr. Pearson, but you knew the process when I first signed up to complete this job for you. The artifact, although obtained, will be kept in a secure place until I believe it is safe for the item to be delivered to you."

Jesse tried not to roll his eyes at the impatience of the man, but it was tricky. Mr. Pearson was his client, but despite the misnomer that customers were always right, he wasn't. The man was eager to regain the vase because it had been stolen from him several months prior. It had taken Jesse several months of research before being able to figure out who had taken it and sold it on. Then another month of figuring out how to get the item back so he could send it to the rightful owner.

Once he had delivered the vase to Mr. Pearson, he would receive his payment and be able to send some of it to where it belonged.

Jesse's job was to find artifacts that had been stolen or sold and bring them back to the rightful owners. Sometimes, this was an heirloom a family wanted back with them but had been sold generations ago, and Jesse had to research and delve into the story of the item to find where it went. Sometimes, the item had been stolen. Either way, Jesse "obtained" the item in whatever way he saw fit and delivered it to the owner.

He made sure to research the person requesting the item, too. When he had first started with the job, he'd made the mistake of trusting the client. It worked against Jesse, and he found himself in trouble with the law when he'd retrieved an item and delivered it to the client before realizing the client was the one who wanted it stolen from its rightful owner.

Jesse had rectified his error, but it had stuck with him. Now, his investigation into the artifact also contained a study of the client. He refused to be used as a pawn again.

"Yes, I understand. Sorry. I'm eager for the vase to be returned to its rightful place," Mr. Pearson said.

"And it will be. A few more days or weeks will surely not matter."

Mr. Pearson scoffed. "Weeks? It won't take long, surely?"

Jesse did roll his eyes at that. "I don't know, Mr. Pearson. Everything depends on how tenacious the person is at wanting the item back."

"Who had it?"

"You don't need to know. I will be in touch when I have confirmation of a delivery schedule. Please be patient."

Jesse hung up, wishing he didn't have to deal with the clients directly, but since he'd progressed onto working for himself, he didn't have a middle man to handle all the crap he now had to deal with.

Cracking his neck from side to side, he swiped through his contacts, smiling when he found Lincoln's number. He put the phone on speaker and rested it on the counter while he bustled around making dinner.

"Yo, Jesse! Long time, no speak. Where the hell you been, man?"

"I've been around, Linc. You know me, always quiet."

"You ain't been quiet since we met in school. You're only fooling yourself."

Jesse snorted. "Yeah, maybe. I can dream, can't I?"

"Dream away, man. Just don't get all flutey-tooty now you're based in the States."

"I'm not based here, moron. I have one job to do, then I'll be home. You know England is where I belong."

"I'll believe it when I see it." Linc howled. "Where are you anyway?"

Jesse had no idea what to think of Lincoln when he'd first arrived at their school when they were twelve. The boy had been larger than life and had lived in London before being relegated to the center of England in a small village with his grandparents after his parents had died. The moment they'd met, they'd hit it off, and the rest, as they say, is history.

"You know I can't tell you. Plausible deniability and all. There is plenty of sunshine, and I'm not far from the beach. That's all I'm telling you."

"I can't believe you flew across the Atlantic to find something for someone else, and you don't get to see much of where you are. You need pictures, man! Something to remember your jaunt across the ocean."

"Jesus Christ, Linc. You're starting to sound like…I don't know what, but not yourself, anyhow."

"You love me," Linc said.

"You know it."

"When are you flying back across the pond?"

"I don't know. Might be a few weeks."

Linc groaned. "You've been there for three months already. What's taking so long?"

"You know me. You've said so yourself many times. I won't leave without doing a thorough job, and that's what I'm doing."

Linc growled and grumped through the phone for a few more minutes before Jesse managed to turn the conversation onto Linc's latest love interest. As he listened to his best friend bemoan the people around him, Jesse made spaghetti bolognese and sat at the breakfast bar to eat it.

"Oh, shit! I gotta go. I'm gonna be late!"

Jesse glanced at the clock, realizing the time difference meant by the time Linc arrived at the club, he would get into shit with his boss for being an hour late.

"Sorry, I didn't check the clock."

"No worries. Speak later."

Linc hung up, and Jesse imagined him running around their apartment back home, trying to climb into his clothes as well as brush his teeth. Linc was never on time, but this was late even for him. Jesse would ring Linc's boss and apologize on his behalf later.

The silence was deafening. He clicked on the TV, changing it to a news channel to see what was happening in his neck of the woods. Nothing brought flags up for what he'd been up to the previous evening, so he flicked it over to a film and let it run while he finished eating.

As usual, he ran through the job in his head, checking his entry and exit and all things in between, going over what he'd seen and heard. He couldn't see anything wrong with the process; therefore, he let it go.

The man who lived in the mansion, one Robert Baker, was a millionaire from what Jesse could gather. In some ways, he wasn't at fault for buying the vase, although he could've chosen better means than who he'd bought it from, knowing how underhanded the person usually was. Jesse had heard about Vincent Verdon through the grapevine, and he wasn't a nice man. Luckily, he didn't have to deal with Vincent because it had already been sold, which made Jesse's life easier.

Leaving his calling card had been stupid, possibly, but he couldn't resist. His handle was "Robin" in the world he was enmeshed with, and he'd gladly accepted the mantle of Robin Hood, hence leaving a statue of the idol holding a bow and arrow. Around the UK and Europe, he was widely known, but here in the US, he doubted people knew who he was.

No one knew both of his identities. His friends and family knew him as Jesse Flint; his acquaintances knew him as Robin. Never the two should meet.

Jesse rinsed his dishes and pots, dried and put everything

away. He sat on the sofa and switched the TV back to the news, taking his time to go through each specific news channel, both local and national, to see if anything stood out as unusual.

Nothing stood out, although he'd heard more than enough about the new politician who was making waves in Florida. The guy was singing to the people's tune and promising things Jesse didn't think he had a right to promise. Jesse shook his head and switched it off. It wouldn't affect him because he would be leaving in a month at most if everything went to plan.

Sliding his notebook closer to him, he opened it at the last entry, which was the day before yesterday. Taking the pen from its hook, he shuffled into a cross-legged position and began to write notes.

The property was guarded, although plenty of weak spots. A wide expanse of grass surrounding the property from all sides. An unalarmed door at the entry point. Shelves full of priceless artifacts, surprising as the door was unlocked. Unable to confirm whether sensors beneath the item were present because a metal plate inserted as a precaution. Two guards found near the entry point, one was leaning toward a wild animal chewing through, the other was unconvinced. Neither sounded an alarm.

He finished his entry by detailing his thoughts and feelings during the job, then closed the notebook and put it back in its place on the table. It was a routine for him to get his thoughts down on paper because sometimes things didn't work out as planned, and he was able to scrutinize it and see where his research had failed him or if information had been given to him incorrectly. Having done the job for ten years already, he was getting to be an expert.

Sitting back on the sofa, he closed his eyes and breathed deeply. His body was invigorated, but he needed to sleep. Standing, he wandered to his bedroom and hit the shower. Once the warm water had done its job to relax him further, he slid, naked, under the covers and tucked them around his shoulders. He hated being cold when he slept, but he couldn't sleep in clothes.

He didn't bother to set an alarm because there was no place he needed to be for the next few days. All he needed was his kindle, his laptop and his phone, and he was sorted for the foreseeable future.

2

———

GEORGE

George Valmonte sank into a chair at the table in the war room of Trident Security, wondering what they'd been called in for first thing on a Monday. He was the first to arrive and rocked his chair back and forth while he waited for the others.

He didn't feel like he had earned his place at the table yet, having only been there four months, but he was willing to do what he was told to ensure they deemed him suitable. Granted, his experience as a corpsman was beneficial to the company, but they could easily find someone else if they found George wasn't a good fit.

"Morning, Nipper."

George clenched his jaw against the nickname he'd been given as the newest member of the team. It wasn't the name used when he was in the military—that had been Wash—but he expected nothing less of fellow former military. He smirked at the black-haired man, whose body had been likened to a Roman God.

"Marco."

Marco DeAngelis, nickname Polo, had been with the

team for many years and was an expert in communications. He was also their backup helicopter pilot.

More people entered the room until Boss-man closed the door behind him. "Good morning, everyone." When Ian Sawyer spoke, everyone listened. He was a former Navy Lieutenant, and George would prefer never to be on the receiving end of his interrogation expertise.

"I received a phone call early this morning from one Robert Baker. From what he told me, which Brody needs to confirm, he is a self-made millionaire through buying and selling various items, including artifacts, art, cars. Basically, anything someone wants him to source, he finds it, buys it and sells it at a profit."

"What did he want with us?" Jake Donovan was the giant of the room at six-foot-five and had married Ian's brother Nick, who was another member of the team.

Ian leaned back in his chair, the creak sounding ominous, and linked his fingers across his stomach. "He's had an artifact stolen from his property."

George frowned. "What's it got to do with us?"

"The artifact is worth $800,000. He wants us to find who stole it and retrieve the item before delivering it back to him. He believes we have the skills and security measures to ensure the artifact is not 'lost' on its way back to him."

Devon Sawyer, Ian's other brother, rested his elbows on his knees. "Does he have any clues who did it?"

A small smile curved Ian's mouth. "Yes. A novelty statue of Robin Hood was put in place of the vase."

"Robin Hood?" George raised his eyebrows. "As in the English legend?"

"Yes."

"Did he have anything else on the person?"

Ian shook his head, sitting upright once more. "He says that's all his security team has to go on. The guards found two possible entry or exit routes in the perimeter fence, although they appeared more like a wild animal had gnawed through them than someone using it to get onto the property."

"Doesn't he have his own men who can investigate it? Why us?" Devon tilted his head.

"He's interested in seeing how we work together. He said he may have more work for us if this goes well."

The room digested the information.

"When did it happen?" Brody Evans, the team's computer expert, opened his laptop and typed away, although George knew his focus was on Ian.

"Overnight last Thursday into Friday. They have no security footage showing anything amiss, either inside or outside. The person is a ghost."

"Or a legend," George muttered.

"Polo, Nipper, check out Robert Baker and his social circle. Egghead, have a check for anything related to Robin Hood and the statue. Baker sent me a photo. Revered, Junior, I want you to come with Devon and me when we go and see Baker. You can check out the outside and speak with their security team while Devon and I check the inside. Boomer, you're coming as well. I want you to check the statue for any potential threat. We'll touch base again later today."

After several "Yes, Boss-man" responses, George exited with the team and strode to his desk. He wasn't as good at computer research as Brody, but he could hold his own.

When he had little more than news articles and charity events listed, he stood and stretched, his bones clicking as they realigned.

"There has to be more to this," he muttered to himself, shoving his hands deep into his pockets and staring out of the window to the compound.

The Trident Security buildings were based on the

outskirts of Tampa, Florida and consisted of several warehouse units converted into different offices, rooms and apartments with the surrounding areas used for training and a space for the helipad.

Outside the inner gate was where The Covenant stood, Ian and Devon's secondary business, a BDSM club. It wasn't George's thing, but as far as he was concerned, everyone was entitled to their own kink. It was one of the topics of conversation Ian brought up before George had been offered a job. George had tried certain aspects of the BDSM lifestyle before, but it had never intrigued him enough to continue. He knew many of the other members of Trident were part of it.

A knock sounded, and Marco hustled in without waiting for an answer. "Nipper, have you found anything?"

George blew out a breath. "No, nothing bar charity events and the occasional date night, it seems."

Marco frowned. "Yeah, same here. Something doesn't feel right about this."

"I thought the same thing. He seems too clean-cut." George wandered back to his chair and sat, picking up his pen and twiddling it in his fingers. "I wonder if there have been any members of staff or his security team that has recently left or been fired?"

"They'd certainly know the lay of the land and have a lot of information about the inner goings-on."

George dropped the pen and clicked onto a different browser. He had no clue how to search for previous employees, but he typed in a few search words and sighed when nothing useful showed up.

"I'll keep checking. Brody is better than either of us at this. He'd have the information in no time." Marco's words were barely audible grumbles as he left the room.

George spent several hours exhausting every avenue he

had. Being new to the area, he had no sources on the ground he could use to find out more, but that was no doubt being covered by one of the others.

"Meeting room."

Marco's words made George's stomach clench, but he showed no outward flinch when he rose and followed him.

"All right. We have limited information because Baker had nothing for us. The security team, whilst appearing well-trained, couldn't give us anything about how it happened or when it happened. The property cameras were black for one hour, but it was regular maintenance, nothing untoward." Ian sighed.

"You're telling me, somehow a thief knew when the camera maintenance was taking place, entered not only the surrounding land, but the house itself, stole a vase and escaped without any kind of detection. Is that what we're saying?" Jake sounded as incredulous as George felt.

"Basically, yes. Marco, Nipper, what did you find?"

Marco leaned forward. "Nothing of consequence. As far as the media is aware, Robert Baker is a man who supports endless charities and takes his dates to expensive restaurants."

"I tried searching for previous employees, but nothing showed up. I'm sure if Brody had a chance, he could probably find out more from his sources." George hated showing incompetence but knew he had nothing to work with.

"Brody?"

"Robin Hood is an English legend who is said to have robbed the rich to give to the poor. On the surface, nothing showed up. I dug a little deeper and investigated where these statues were sold. Initially, it sent me on a wild goose chase, but I managed to locate several places in the continental US that sell them. They are novelty gifts, though why they sell them here, I'm not sure."

Brody clicked a few buttons on the computer, and the screen behind Ian lit up. Ian swiveled in his chair, and they focused on the map.

"These are the places that sell the statue. When I checked, none of them had sold any of them within the last six months."

"What are you thinking?" Devon crossed his ankle over his knee.

"I wondered if the reason for the Robin Hood moniker wasn't *just* because of the robbing the rich thing. What if they were English? I checked where these statues were sold in the UK, which isn't as many as I expected, and found one place that had an order of ten delivered to a place in Nottingham, England four months ago."

"It's a long shot. Why would someone from England fly across the pond to steal a vase?" George furrowed his brows and rested his elbow on the table.

"I'm getting there." Brody clicked a few more buttons, and a new map came up. "I checked a little deeper on the web and found several mentions of a Robin Hood statue. These pins here show the places where a similar statue to the one in Baker's house have been found."

"Have you cross-referenced any other factors?" Ian glanced at Brody.

"Yes. In each of those six places, something had been removed or stolen."

George crossed his arms over his chest. "This person is stealing from the rich?"

"Pretty much. I've no idea how the giving to the poor thing comes in, but regardless, each of the items stolen was worth money. I did find one curious aspect. Each artifact had been previously mentioned as having been stolen from a different place."

Ian swiveled his chair back. "Explain."

"Okay, take this chest. In 2001, it was listed as having been stolen from Gerald Winters' house. It was never found, and Mr. Winters died several years later. In 2016, the chest was reported as having been stolen from Edward Anderson. Again, it wasn't found initially. In 2018, Andrew Winters, who is Gerald Winters' grandson, publicly thanked an unknown person for returning the chest to the family. Police investigated and found Edward Anderson had bought it from a so-called reputable company. He had no idea it had been stolen."

"What does this have to do with our case?"

"What Edward Anderson hadn't made public was that a Robin Hood statue had been left in place of the chest."

Ian rubbed a hand across his mouth. "Whoever stole it from Edward was returning it to its rightful owners?"

Brody held his hands out. "It would seem."

"Why wait so long to return it?" George could see the idea behind it working, but he was reluctant to think it was happening here.

"Maybe the thief needed to let the media circus die down," Brody said.

Ian sighed. "All right. Sleep on it, and we'll meet back here tomorrow. One of us might have an epiphany."

"GEORGE, I need you at the compound, please."

Ian's voice brooked no argument. George grabbed his things before leaving his apartment. As he climbed into his car, he frowned, wondering why Ian had called him George when none of them used his name.

By the time he pulled up to Trident, he had persuaded himself he was being fired. Despite the thought, he didn't hesitate when he parked the car and strode toward Ian's office. He'd face it head-on as he always did.

He knocked and waited for Ian's command before entering. It was only his honed skills that stopped him from freezing and staring at the second man in the room. George closed the door behind him and stood at ease, though tense.

"I hope you're behaving under Lieutenant Sawyer's command."

George bristled at the accusation in his father's voice but dampened his response, knowing his father wasn't aiming the statement at him. His cheeks and neck heated.

"He has been impeccable, sir. Beyond reproach." Ian's words surprised George, but he didn't let it show.

"I've heard high recommendations about your company. I'm glad my son isn't bringing it down. He tends to break from the mold his ancestors made for him. Your company might be the making of him."

George's gaze was on the far wall behind Ian, but he heard every word as if it was a spike through his body. He had never been deemed good enough despite doing everything his father had ever asked him to. The one and only time he had "broken the mold," as his father said, was when he chose to become a corpsman instead of a pilot like his father.

"We take the best here. George fits in well. In fact, he is currently the point man for our latest—confidential—client. I have no problems with his work ethic."

Out of the corner of his eye, he noticed his father glance in his direction upon hearing the words, and George wanted to ask Ian what he was doing. Making him appear more important to his father would not work in the long term.

"I'm glad to hear it." His father spun to him. "George, please walk me to my car."

"I apologize, Captain, but I need George here for the

moment." Ian picked up his phone. "Nick, can you come to my office, please?"

"An escort is not necessary."

"I know, but it's my duty to make family feel welcome, and I'm sure you would like a tour? Ah, Nick. Sir, this is my brother Nick. Nick, this is Captain Isaac Valmonte, George's father."

There was a slight note in Ian's words that George didn't understand, but Nick did, smiling brightly at his father.

"Nice to meet you, sir. Would you like a tour?"

His father marched toward the exit. "Your mother is upset. Call her."

George continued to stand at ease, though he wilted inwardly at his father's parting words. He didn't call his mother because she had asked him not to, saying it upset his father when he did. It was a battle he was never meant to win.

As the door closed behind the two men, George didn't move, breathing through his nose to calm his pulse and trying to swallow the lump in his throat.

"He's a nice man."

Ian's words had George snapping his focus to his boss. Seeing the raised eyebrow of sarcasm, George relaxed his stance.

"He's wonderful," George deadpanned and rubbed his hands over his face before dropping into the visitor's chair. "I'm sorry he came. I didn't think he would have bothered."

Ian sat back in his chair, resting one elbow on the arm and his chin in his hand. "Men like him need to be handled carefully."

"Don't I know it. He will be expecting me to regale him with details about *my* so-called operation. You didn't need to lie."

"I didn't." Ian chuckled. "I had planned to make you team

leader on a case soon, but this one is as good as any other. You may as well start now."

George faltered. "So, you did lie, then changed your plans, and it wasn't a lie."

Ian smiled. "Spot on."

"Understood. What do—"

"I found him!"

Brody came racing into the doorway, then twisted around and ran back the way he came with him and Ian following. They entered Brody's office, which seemed more like a computer warehouse than anything else, and he immediately started talking.

"I investigated deeper into various areas and asked about on the web. It took some doing, but I've found out who Robin Hood is."

"And?"

"Jesse Flint. A thirty-year-old British man who has no convictions, arrests, warnings or anything that flags him for any reason."

"How do you know it's him?"

"Too many details to explain, but I followed the trail, and it led me to him."

Brody brought up a picture on the screen of a young-looking man with shoulder-length, curly brown hair, hazel eyes and laughter lines around his face. George's heart kicked at what could be the face of an angel.

"Flint lost a brother to cancer thirteen years ago, and though his parents are alive, they are heavily in debt. During their son's illness, they paid for experimental treatments that were not funded by the government."

"It's a motive for stealing priceless artifacts." Ian leaned closer. "Where is he?"

"Right on our doorstep." Brody grinned. "A small student

apartment complex here in Tampa." He tapped his hand on the table.

"Seriously? He stayed where he did the crime?" George was dubious.

"Yeah. He's a cocky shit. Granted, his identity is well-hidden on the web. Very well-hidden. But if I could find it…"

Brody didn't need to say more. If Brody was able to find it, anyone who had access to a 'Brody' could find the guy, too.

"I think he needs a visit." Ian glanced at George. "What do you say, Nipper?"

"Agreed."

"You, me, and Devon with Jake across the street. Let's see what he has to say for himself."

George smiled, unwilling to vocalize how grateful he was at Ian's easy acceptance of his father.

3

JESSE

A knock sounded. "Delivery!"

Jesse sighed. "I haven't ordered anything!"

"Well, tough shit. It has your address on it."

He growled and pulled himself off the sofa, dropping the remote to the coffee table. The delivery guy banged on the door again. "Yeah, hold on!"

"I have other places to be!"

"All right, all right."

When he opened the door and faced a man with a gun, he remembered deliveries weren't given directly at the doors of the complex. They were left in the main area.

Jesse considered his options but knew he had little choice. He closed his eyes and shook his head. "Too cocky for your own good, Jesse Flint," he mumbled to himself.

"May I come in?"

Jesse snorted. "Like I can stop you." He stepped away from the door and stood in the middle of the floor, away from anything to show he wasn't trying to reach for something. The tall, black-haired man drifted through the door, and two men Jesse hadn't seen followed him in and shut the door, closing them into the small apartment.

"How can I help you?"

The man with the gun—the one who had a gun pointed at him at least—indicated for Jesse to sit on the sofa after one of the other men had checked there was nothing in the cushions. Once he did, the man sat on the coffee table opposite, and Jesse noticed how similar they all appeared. They could be brothers, although one had a slightly stronger jawline and harder eyes.

That guy strode over the window and stood to the side with his arms crossed over his chest. The other stood by the front door. Jesse focused his attention on the original man, who braced his elbows on his knees, the gun held loosely in his hands. Jesse wasn't fooled. This man was highly trained. He wondered how he'd been found after being so careful all these years.

"Jesse Flint. You are a hard man to find."

"It's not a bad thing." Jesse smiled self-deprecatingly.

The man nodded once in agreement. "We've been hired to find the vase you stole last week. If you return it, everything will be swept under the rug and forgotten."

Jesse sniffed. "I doubt it very much."

"You have my word."

"I don't know you. I have nothing to gauge whether you are telling the truth or not."

"True, but what choice do you have?"

Jesse didn't answer. The only choice for him was to try and reason with these guys. "The vase had been stolen from its rightful owner. I was...reacquiring it to return it."

"Reacquiring? Nice choice of words."

He heard a hint of humor in the man's tone. "Who are you?"

"We are part of Trident Security. We've been hired to deliver the vase back to Mr. Baker."

"Not gonna happen."

"Why?"

"Because it's not his, and I need the money I'll be paid on its return to my client."

"We can send all the information we have obtained about who you are and the items you have stolen over the last ten years to those who would be interested in knowing about it. It's a sizable number when you collate it together."

Jesse narrowed his eyes. "If that was the case, why haven't you done it already?"

"We wanted to see whether it was necessary or if we could come to some agreement."

"My job is to reacquire pieces that have been previously stolen or lost from their original families. Occasionally, this means I steal it back." He didn't see the point in denying his work. "Most of the time, I buy it back."

"The ones you steal are the ones you replace with a Robin Hood statue?"

"There's a reason I'm called 'Robin' within the community." Jesse smirked.

The man's mouth twitched.

"There's no way you're doing this for anything but the money."

Jesse's gaze found the man standing by the window. "Who said I wasn't? The money isn't for me."

"Who is it for?"

Jesse glanced at the floor, wishing he didn't have to relive his story. "The only part of the money I take from my payment is what it cost to do the job and to make sure I eat and have a roof over my head. Every penny—or cent in this case—gets given to a charity that pays for experimental treatments for cancer patients in the UK. Those treatments are not funded by the NHS, and the cost weighs heavily on people's shoulders." He gave a small smile. "I try to help alleviate some of the burdens."

"Hmm."

Jesse couldn't stop the glare he sent to the man. "You said you work for Trident Security. Who are they?"

"We are a security firm, usually dealing with protection. In this case, we will be protecting the vase."

The man opposite him hesitated, tilting his head to the side slightly as if listening. He must be wearing an earpiece, so Jesse kept quiet. He didn't want to antagonize anyone enough for them to kill him, and they might be receiving information that could help him. Or they might be receiving the go-ahead to kill him. Either way, he wasn't taking any chances.

The man glanced up at the one near the window—Jesse wished he knew their names. "Thoughts?"

The question wasn't aimed at him, and he peered at the other man, awaiting his answer.

"I'm not convinced he's innocent."

Coffee table man stared over at the one by the door.

"It has potential. He's never usually wrong."

Coffee table man placed the gun behind his back, and his hands came back free. Jesse assumed it was now in his waistband.

"My name is Ian. George, Devon." Ian pointed to the men by the window and door, respectively.

"Why are you telling me?"

"We've received some new information and want to clarify some things with you."

Jesse nodded. "Sure."

"What do you know about Robert Baker?"

"Only what I've studied and researched." When Ian made a 'go on' motion, Jesse collected his thoughts. "Robert Baker, fifty-nine-years-old, self-made millionaire through acquiring and selling items. Not always through lawful means, I might add. He shows up to support several charities throughout the year, doesn't have a partner but goes on several dates every month, sometimes with the same woman. That's pretty much it for the person himself."

Ian sighed. "My computer expert has uncovered Robert Baker does a lot of his business on the dark web and deals with many unsavory characters. He sells black market items to ensure he continues to live his expensive lifestyle, it seems. Most of his acquisitions are unlawful."

"I knew he wasn't on the up and up." Jesse grinned.

"The problem you now have is if Baker conducts business on the dark web and knows the people he does, dangerous people like we think, you are in more danger than before."

"Why?" Jesse frowned.

"Because if we can find you, he can, too." George stepped closer.

Jesse digested that bit of information, and his stomach churned. "I'll be fine."

He contemplated his options for grabbing the vase and being able to leave the US when people were watching for him. It didn't seem possible, but he'd contact Rio, and hopefully, he'd help him out.

"I'd like to offer our services to you."

Jesse whirled his gaze back to Ian. "What? Why?"

"You need protection. We protect."

"I don't know if it's a good idea. I do better when I'm alone. Thanks, though."

Several emotions flickered over Ian's face before he nodded once and stood. "I would recommend leaving the US as quickly as possible in that case." He held out a card. "In case you change your mind."

Jesse took the card but said nothing. The three men left

the apartment, and Jesse finally breathed fully. Those men were larger than life, especially the one called George. There was something about him that was like a live wire.

His life had become ten times more difficult. Despite the visit from Trident, Jesse tried to persuade himself he had been doing the job for ten years now, and no one had found him before. Those thoughts worked long enough to settle down and watch a movie. *Love, Simon* was in the final scenes of the film when his phone rudely interrupted him with an unknown number.

He rolled his eyes, thinking it was Trident again and tucked his slippered feet under him when he answered. Seconds later, he wished he hadn't.

"You need to return the item immediately, or your life is forfeit in its place. You have forty-eight hours."

The distorted mechanical voice sent shivers down his spine, and he swallowed hard against his dry mouth. It was either Trident trying to make a point, or Robert Baker had found him. He hated to admit he was scared, especially with everything he'd been through in his life, but he was.

Licking his lips, he breathed deeply and slid the business card closer. Fingering the corner, he dialed.

"Hello?"

"Please tell me you called me to scare me into using your company to protect me?"

"Jesse?"

"Uh-huh."

"It wasn't us. Who called?"

"A wobbly, computerized voice telling me to return the item within forty-eight hours or I'm dead."

A sigh came across the phone. "Will you allow us to help?"

"Yes." *Hell, yes.*

"I'll be sending a man over within the hour. Be ready to move locations."

The line went quiet, and Jesse pulled it from his ear, seeing Ian had ended the call. "Fuck."

He gave himself five minutes to freak the fuck out, then shuffled to his bedroom to pack his belongings. He didn't have much, enough for one large backpack; therefore, it didn't take him long.

When the knock came at the door forty-five minutes later, Jesse's heart pounded. He checked the peephole, seeing the George guy standing there.

"Open, Jesse."

He did, ignoring his shaking hands, and tried for a smile. "Hey."

"Are you ready?"

Jesse nodded, slipped on his coat, and picked up his bag. "All set."

"Give me your phone." Jesse did, and George placed it on a table, leaving it behind. "Follow me. Stay close."

"Should I be worried about someone following us?"

"No." The single word helped ease his mind until George followed it up with, "That's my job."

George led the way to a black car, smaller than Jesse would've thought a six-foot-odd man would drive, and they both climbed in. Jesse stowed his bag between his legs and fastened his seatbelt while George pulled out into the traffic.

Jesse transferred his gaze from George to their surroundings repeatedly, expecting some sort of communication from the guy. "How long is the journey?"

"A couple of hours."

"Where are we going?"

George's fingers clenched on the steering wheel. "Doesn't matter. You'll be safe while we distract Baker."

"How are you going to do it?"

"Not my concern."

Jesse raised his eyebrows and rolled his lips inward while

he stared out the window. Apparently, he was the conversationalist out of the two of them. Funny enough, he didn't have much to say at that point.

The miles passed, and the scenery changed several times. They drove through towns and rural areas and past lakes and rivers. Jesse lost all sense of direction because he didn't know the area well enough to figure out their destination. In the end, he rested his head against the window and closed his eyes.

He was nudged awake with a gruff voice telling him they'd arrived. Jesse yawned and rubbed at his eyes before staring around him, his mouth falling open. Despite the fact that dusk had fallen, there were shimmers of light reflected off a sizeable lake in front of him. To his right was a large wooden cabin that was well-used but sturdy and able to hold probably ten people, if not more.

As he climbed out of the car, following George's lead, he glanced behind him, seeing nothing but open space for a large distance where huge trees formed a barrier to everywhere else. Or so it seemed.

He inhaled. The mix of grassland and lake water had him smiling and relaxing. If it had been a different situation, this would have been a wonderful place to recuperate for a while.

"Come on."

George pulled some bags from the car Jesse had not seen before, and he hustled to catch up. His protector unlocked the door and pushed his way in, Jesse following and sealing them into what would be their home for the next day or so. At least, Jesse hoped it would only be a day or two.

He grinned while he examined his surroundings. The place reminded him of a cabin from the movies: wooden furniture, colorful throws, stuffed animal heads on the walls. It was the epitome of rustic, and he loved it. He could easily see himself sitting on the porch, drinking beer and watching as the sun went down.

"You have a choice of bedrooms. Drop your bag in the one you want."

George removed food from the bags, and Jesse watched as he placed the items in different cupboards as if he knew where things were kept.

"Whose place is this?"

"A friend of a friend."

Jesse waited for more information, but nothing came. He sighed and wandered down the hallway to the rooms. Opening each of the doors, he came across much of the same for each room: a standard double bed with various covers and blankets, dressers and wardrobes. Deciding to choose a room based on the view from the window, he retraced his steps, the muffled noise from the kitchen growing louder. Entering the first room he had peered in, he stood at the window, seeing the lake's surface glistening. He smiled and dropped his bag onto the bed, deciding to embrace the time he had been given instead of fearing what had made it possible.

Ever the optimist.

Slipping off his shoes, he rummaged through his bag for his slippers. There was no way he'd go anywhere without them.

"Ah-ha!"

Victorious, he slid them on and slipped off his coat, hooking it over the back of a chair in the room before returning to the main area.

"What. Are. They?"

George's tone implied a sort of horror while his gaze focused on Jesse's feet.

"They're my slippers." He lifted a foot and wiggled it around.

"What...I...Seriously?"

"What's wrong with them?" Jesse peered down at his rainbow unicorn slippers, complete with wings and a tail, and back at George.

George said nothing, only closed his eyes and shook his head before returning to what he'd been doing.

"You should see the ones I left at home." He drifted closer. "Is it dinner time?"

George snorted, the first unexpected reaction Jesse had witnessed. "I think it's closer to a midnight feast." He sighed. "Are you hungry?"

"Starving."

"Croque monsieur?"

"Say what?

George glanced at him, his mouth twitching. "Basically, a cheese and ham toasted sandwich."

"Oh. Sure. Thanks. Do you need any help?"

"You can slice the cheese."

Jesse had been sure George would brush him off and was surprised with the offer. He grabbed the cheese from the fridge and shuffled back to the table where a knife and board were waiting for him. Flashing a grin in George's direction, he took to his job.

"Is there a radio or anything here?"

"I would've thought so."

"I thought you'd been here before."

George shook his head, slicing some bread expertly. "I said it belonged to a friend of a friend. I never said the friend was mine."

Jesse snorted. "You're a man of many words, George." He chuckled. "If I had my phone, I'd be able to listen to my playlists."

"It's not safe to have it. It could be tracked."

"Whatever will we do to keep ourselves occupied?"

He passed a plate of sliced cheese to George, who made the sandwiches. Jesse leaned his hip against the table and crossed his arms while George removed a pan from a cupboard and began heating it on the stove. The man's movements were methodical and sure as if he'd done it a thousand times.

Jesse bit his lip, watching the play of muscles across George's back. It had been a while since he'd scratched that particular itch. It wasn't something he went out of his way to do unless he needed to, but seeing the way George moved, sparked a fire that had been banked for months.

George reached for the plate of sandwiches, raising his eyebrows when he caught Jesse staring but said nothing.

As the hiss of the frying pan grew louder, the scent of melted cheese filled the air, and Jesse's stomach growled in response. Seconds later, a smirking George handed him a plate, and Jesse practically salivated when he sat at the table. He picked up the sandwich, alternately removing his hands when it was too hot, but he refused to put it down. Taking a small bite, he groaned. The saltiness of the ham mixing with the cheese and bread made something amazing.

"This is fantastic! Thanks." He covered his mouth as he spoke around the food.

George sat opposite him, a small smile on his face. "You're welcome."

There was no talking until all the food had disappeared, and George told him to get some sleep. Jesse had no idea how he would be able to sleep when he was so wired, but he did what he was told with thoughts of what it would be like to wrap his legs around George's body floating through his mind.

4

GEORGE

"We're here."

"Good. How's he coping?"

Ian sounded distracted while he asked the question, but George answered it anyway instead of asking what was wrong. His boss probably wouldn't tell him anyway.

"Surprisingly well for someone who had his life threatened."

"You don't believe his story?"

George repositioned the curtain to squint into the darkness surrounding them, trying to see anything moving before checking the lock and moving to the next window. "No. I don't see how he can be so calm about this. Most other people would be freaking out that someone gave them a death threat. He's not concerned. Or at least he doesn't show it."

"That right there is the reason I sent you and no one else."

Ian's words paused George's actions. "What do you mean?"

"I needed someone who would see through the bullshit, Nipper. You could from the moment we got to his apartment. Whether or not he is hiding something is irrelevant unless it concerns us, but you won't be swayed by his appearance or behavior. It's why you got this job."

"I thought…"

"I was doing it because of what I told your father. Yeah, I can see that. But no. Look after him; he may have more information than he thinks he does. In the long run, it would benefit us if we can take down some of Baker's business."

"Is that what you're planning?"

Ian sighed, and George heard the creak of his chair and imagined him leaning back in it. "It all depends on what Brody finds. We'll get help to take him down if he needs it. It's why you need to get more information from Jesse and try and find out where he put the vase."

"Yes, Boss-man."

"Get some rest, Nipper."

George blew out a breath and checked the final locks throughout the house. The only room he hadn't checked was Jesse's, and he debated whether it was a good idea to sneak in and check it while he was sleeping. However, George wouldn't be able to sleep, knowing the window might be unlocked, and he knocked gently on the door and waited to see if Jesse responded.

"Yeah?"

"I need to check the window lock."

"Come on in."

George opened the door and tried to ignore the smooth expanse of skin showing from above where the covers pooled on the bed. He stalked over to the window, checked the lock, drew the curtains and retraced his steps.

"Night, George."

The quiet words were whispered before he closed the door, and he hesitated. "Night, Jesse." He wasn't above being polite.

He shut the door, staring at it for a few seconds before wandering across the hallway to the room he'd chosen. Luckily, Jesse had chosen the bedroom George had wanted him to because it made it easier for George to get to him should anything happen. Jesse's window was more difficult to get into from the outside, but it would be fine if they had to get out from the inside.

Jesse was surprisingly talkative, although it was about everything *except* what they needed to talk about. George knew he'd have to broach the subject the following day, but he hoped they'd be able to get some sleep first. As quickly as they'd managed to get Jesse out of Tampa, George wasn't expecting trouble for at least a day, but he needed to be ready in case there was.

He rested his gun on the bedside table and undressed, debating whether to take a shower or wait until the morning when he knew Jesse was alert enough to keep an ear out for noise while George was busy. Settling on having one tomorrow, he kept his boxers on and laid on the bed, one hand behind his head as he stared at the ceiling. Apart from the occasional creak of the cabin, there were no sounds, and George was unsettled. He was used to the hustle and bustle around him, be it at a Naval base, on assignment or the streets of Tampa. The silence, though good because it would be easier to hear if someone approached, was deafening.

He blew out a breath and rolled to his side, staring at the shadow his gun made. It settled him, and he closed his eyes.

He snapped his eyes open and aimed his gun at the doorway to his room, annoyed he'd missed other signs of noise.

"Ah!"

"Fucking hell, Jesse. What were you thinking?" George lowered his gun, replacing the safety and flicking on the bedside lamp. They both winced.

"Sorry! I couldn't sleep. I didn't think you would be sleeping. Why I thought it, I don't know. Maybe you would stay awake for the next however long it takes for this to be over, but then you'd be super tired and no good for anything but a Sleeping Beauty sleep. Yeah, that line of thinking was wrong, but how was I to know for sure? I wanted to ask if you wanted a hot chocolate or something."

If George hadn't been pissed at himself for missing the signs Jesse had been moving around the cabin, he might've been amused by Jesse's verbal vomiting skills. He was pissed, though, and he took it out on Jesse.

"Of course, I'm trying to get some sleep. I'm not superhuman. We'll be fine for a few hours, a day or so before people start properly searching for you and realizing you've gone missing. I'm getting whatever rest I can before it happens."

He swung his legs over the side of the bed, keeping the covers over his lap. Checking the clock, he cursed. He'd been asleep for possibly two hours. It was more than he often got while on assignment, but he'd become used to having more since he'd retired. His problem was that as soon as he was awake, that was it. He was awake. Now, he had to deal with Jesse on two hours of sleep because there was no way he'd be able to sleep again. Especially with not having heard him creep across the hallway.

"Sorry. I'll go." Jesse's shoulders lowered, and he indicated over his shoulder.

The defeat in Jesse's posture shouldn't have bothered George, but he found himself shaking his head. "Hot chocolate would be nice." His voice was more of a growl, and when he stared at Jesse, he saw him shiver. "Get some clothes on. The nights can be cold near water."

Jesse opened his mouth, snapped it shut and nodded, escaping the room. George rubbed a hand over his face, yawned and stretched his neck, hearing several clicks. He rested his elbows on his knees and stared at his hands. Things were not going as he'd expected them to.

He pulled on his khaki pants and his "When nothing is going right, go left" T-shirt. The idea had come to him when his father had been in one of his moods and had been a middle finger to him when George was a teenager. He liked the idea of having something for himself, although most of the time, the T-shirts were hidden beneath a shirt or something else.

Sliding the gun into his waistband, George strode to the kitchen, where Jesse was warming milk on the stove. The guy wore loose pajama bottoms and those crazy unicorn slippers. George frowned.

"What are you doing?"

"Warming the milk." He glanced over his shoulder with a small smile. "I've always made hot chocolate with milk instead of water." His gaze dropped, and his smile grew. "Nice shirt."

George's cheeks heated, and he whirled away, grabbing mugs from the cupboard. He wasn't used to people seeing his quirk, and he'd forgotten to put his shirt over the top. Fetching a spoon, he added some hot chocolate powder to the mugs before placing them closer to Jesse.

"Thanks."

George leaned back against the table and crossed his arms over his chest, watching Jesse's sure movements and the play of the muscles in his back. As he found his gaze lowering, he averted his eyes and cleared his throat. Jesse poured a little of the milk into the cups and mixed it around before adding more. George had never seen hot chocolate made that way before, but he only ever bought it from a coffee shop and never watched them make it. He rarely made it himself, and when he did, he used hot water.

Holding a mug out for George, Jesse sipped his and hummed as he sat on the sofa, tucking his legs beneath him and resting the mug on his knee.

George followed suit and sank into the surprisingly soft cushions, sitting sideways to face Jesse. "Why couldn't you sleep?" He took a sip of his drink, eyebrows raising when he tasted the creamy texture.

Jesse's mouth quirked. "It's nice, huh." He sighed. "I don't sleep much. Haven't since I was a kid. Too much to do so little time."

George noticed the pained smile and narrowed his gaze, wondering if Jesse was using the time to try and win George over to his side. He'd play along. "What do you mean?"

Jesse huffed a breath. "You know my history."

"I know some of it."

Jesse shook his head. "You know what, if you want me to spill my secrets, here goes. I had a normal childhood until I was thirteen. My brother, Beau, was diagnosed with cancer when he was nine. No one knew when it had started growing, but he received treatment and was managing. By the time he turned fourteen, the treatments were no longer working." Jesse took a sip of his drink. "Our parents began researching other treatment avenues, trying to find something that might help. They found an experimental trial, and Beau agreed to it. Unfortunately, it cost money, and Mum and Dad re-mortgaged their house and did some fundraising to get the fee."

"Did it help?"

Jesse shook his head and swallowed hard. "When it didn't work, they found another place, then another after. Each time, Beau agreed, but I could see he was fading."

George wanted to reach forward and comfort Jesse, but he could see it wouldn't be welcomed.

"Beau died from toxicity when he was seventeen."

"Toxicity?"

"The side effects from all the drugs he was being pumped full of." Jesse snorted. "If our parents had left him… Anyway, all those treatments had left them with a huge debt they were unable to pay off."

"If you're against the experimental treatments, why are you funding them?"

Jesse's eyes widened. "Oh, no! I'm not against the treatments, but I want them to be thoroughly researched and provided carefully, not using people like guinea pigs, which were the ones my parents chose. They were clutching at straws because most places wouldn't take Beau because of how far along his disease was."

"You fund the experiments?" George was trying to figure out what part Jesse played.

"I give the money to a charity that pays for children to have properly researched treatments. I don't fund the actual experiments. And I only support the ones that have experiments that have passed certain tests first. I won't allow another child to be used as a guinea pig."

George couldn't detect any lies in Jesse's voice. It appeared this part of the story was true. "Why did you decide to start stealing?"

Jesse chuckled. "I don't think of it as stealing. I'm taking back what rightfully belongs to someone else."

"Semantics."

"Regardless, I came across an advert for someone who was searching for an heirloom and was interested in what happened to it. I began researching out of curiosity. The more I investigated it, the more convoluted the story seemed to be. I couldn't stop myself, and I finally found it with a family three hundred miles away. From what I figured out, one of the grandparents had been working for the family when they were younger and, when they were fired, took the figurine with them as a 'bonus' for their time there." Jesse grinned. "I called the family up and said I'd found it. When I retrieved the item after showing my evidence to the grandson, he gave the figurine back without complaint. When I took it to the family, they paid me for my service. It opened a whole new world for me."

"But Robin Hood? Really?" George raised his eyebrows. "Talk about blowing your own trumpet."

Jesse waved a finger in George's direction. "Ah, ah, ah. It wasn't me. Within certain areas of the internet, as your company probably knows, some places aren't easily found. The company I used to work for has a whole network there. People began calling me Robin Hood. To begin with, I laughed and ignored it, but the more I thought about it, the more I thought I could use it as my calling card. Hence the statue and my nickname."

George finished his drink, lowering his brows. He was usually good at hearing lies, but everything out his Jesse's mouth seemed to be the truth. Unless he was a fantastic actor, Jesse seemed to be the Robin Hood everyone had deemed him. He refused to change his stance on the guy. At least until he had proof.

"Time for you to try and get some sleep. I don't want you dead on your feet if we need to run."

He tried to sound firm but didn't think he succeeded when Jesse smiled at him. Taking Jesse's cup from him, he pushed him toward the hallway.

"Night."

George didn't reply, his thoughts going a mile a minute while he washed the cups, leaving them on the draining board to dry. He strode to the front window and stared into the inky night sky. All he could see was the ripples of the lake when the moonlight hit it. Nothing else stirred. He knew better than to wish for something to occupy him, but knowing Jesse was a wall away was difficult.

In the early hours of that morning, with nothing but the silence as a witness, George admitted he was attracted to Jesse, and despite what Ian said, he wasn't the best man for this job. Jesse's hazel eyes had lost the usual playfulness when he'd spoken about his brother and parents, but it had returned when talking about "Robin." Several waves of his hair curled around his ears, more so when he pushed it back, which he seemed to do unconsciously. His body was toned and athletic with smooth, pale skin, which George bet sported freckles somewhere. He refused to acknowledge he wanted to find out where they were. The man he was protecting barely reached George's nose, but his personality reached way higher.

Jesse was a conundrum, which George had no business trying to understand except where it related to work. As he sat on the couch and kept watch during the night, he reminded himself of the fact several times.

HE HEARD Jesse rousing as the clock ticked toward eight o'clock. George had not slept, but he would feel more alert once he'd had a shower. Wandering into the kitchen, he grabbed the bacon and sausages from the fridge and began cooking them. While they were sizzling away, he sliced some bread and popped it into the toaster when he heard Jesse go into the bathroom. When he didn't hear the shower turn on, he relaxed, knowing he'd have enough water for a shower.

Continuing with breakfast, he plated everything and set it on the table as Jesse emerged from the hallway, dressed in black jeans and a plain white T-shirt that fit him nicely, along with those rainbow unicorn slippers.

"Oh, thanks. I'll make breakfast tomorrow. It's fair as you seem to be cooking all the time."

"It's fine."

George dug into his food, sipping at his coffee in between mouthfuls. By the time he'd finished, Jesse was halfway through his. His phone rang when he put the plate in the sink, and he smiled when he saw who it was.

"Hey, stranger."

"Wash! My man! How're things?"

"Good, thanks. I've not heard from you for a while. What are you up to now?"

Will Kendal, aka Sykes, for how much he looked and sounded like the guy from the film Oliver, had been one of George's teammates—although George was a Corpsman, he had also been a SEAL. Sykes was an explosives expert and had left the Navy a few months after George due to family reasons. Will had been the teammate George was closest to during their time.

"Ah, nothing much. Finding my feet, but I have a few job opportunities lined up. Mainly in security."

"That's great news!"

"How are things with Trident?"

George pushed off the counter and strode toward the hallway, putting some distance between him and Jesse. "Things are going well. I'm learning the ropes, but they're a good fit, I think."

"Been doing anything interesting lately?"

George chuckled. "Nah. Doing grunt work until I've proved myself. Nothing unusual there, right?"

He couldn't tell anyone about the op he was currently undertaking. It was part of his confidentiality clause, and rightly so.

"Where do you usually hang out? I need a night out, man!"

Will's exuberance bounded through the phone, and George closed his eyes, imagining they were back in the Navy and shooting the shit. "I'm out of town at the minute, but as soon as I get back, we'll go out."

"Where are you at? You never leave Tampa."

"Are you wanting a shower—" Jesse stood in the doorway to his room and stopped wide-eyed.

George rested his finger against his lips, requesting Jesse to keep quiet.

"Who's that? Are you seeing someone, Wash?"

He mouthed a curse, and Jesse cringed. George narrowed his gaze on Jesse. "Yeah. It's new. He wanted to get out of Tampa for a few days, just him and me."

"Uh-huh. Alone, huh? Well, good for you. What's his name?"

"His name?" George's gaze ran down Jesse's body. "Jay."

"I'm happy for you, man. You deserve it after all the shit you got dealt from your father."

"Yeah, well. It's my life now, though he tries to intervene at times."

"I can imagine. Anyway, I have to go. I wanted to touch base. When you get back, give me a call. We'll go out, yeah?"

"Definitely. See you soon, Sykes."

"Back atcha, Wash."

They disconnected, and George slipped the phone into his pocket.

"I'm sorry. I thought you'd finished."

George shook his head. "I'm going for a shower." He now had a boyfriend, according to Will.

5

JESSE

Jesse squirmed when the bathroom door closed with a significant thump. He had honestly thought the call had finished; otherwise, he would've stayed away. Now, he'd pushed George into telling someone they were in a relationship. It wasn't the end of the world because they could easily "break up" before George saw the person again, but it was not fair on George having to lie.

He wandered down the hallway to his bedroom, grabbing his laptop and notebook and sat down on the sofa, getting comfortable. Once he was logged in, he realized he didn't have a way to use the internet. If he'd been told they were going to be in the middle of nowhere, he would've brought a book.

He put the laptop aside and made another coffee for each of them. The shower had shut off, and George would appear at some point. Placing both mugs on the coffee table, he sighed. He didn't know what his options were for using the laptop and wasn't sure if George would be forthcoming after Jesse had been so stupid.

Leaning back and staring at the ceiling, he ran through

the things he wanted to check up on. More information on Robert Baker would be nice, but he didn't want to trip any wires by using his name. It would be good if he could contact Rio. His old boss had links to many areas of the web, including the dark web. He'd need to run it past George first.

"Do you want a coffee?"

George's voice made him jump. "Fuck! I didn't hear you." The man merely raised his eyebrows. "I've just made one. Yours is here."

"Oh, thanks."

"No problem."

George wandered over and took a seat in the armchair adjacent to the sofa, and Jesse tried not to feel sad about him being further away. When George sat back, Jesse read his T-shirt.

"'I'm not rude. I just say what everyone else is thinking.' Nice." Jesse grinned and met George's gaze, noticing his cheeks darkening.

George ignored his words and waved toward the laptop. "What are you doing?"

"I had planned to do some research, but I wasn't sure about the internet connection."

"The connection is strong. You shouldn't have any problems, but you need to stay off sites you would normally go to. Use websites you wouldn't usually view."

"No speaking to my friends?"

"No."

"Or playing my usual games?"

"No."

"What about porn?"

George choked on the drink he'd taken. "What?" He coughed.

"It's a legitimate question. Can I watch porn? It's one of

my usual websites, and you said I couldn't go onto my usual sites."

"I'm sure it would...be fine." George wiped his mouth with the back of his hand.

"What about the saved videos on the porn site? Is it classed as a usual site? Because some of those videos are the only ones I can get off to."

He watched George close his eyes and breathe deeply. When he opened them, he froze at the heat blazing in them. "I would recommend staying away from those."

Jesse had no idea what George was talking about, distracted as he was by being caught in George's full focus. "Huh?"

"Find something new to beat off to."

Jesse blinked rapidly to clear the cobwebs, then cleared his throat, his cheeks heating. "Right." He tried to wipe his mind of the images of George and him wrapped together in the covers of his bed and focused on their conversation. "Basically, I need to forget my bookmarked pages and go somewhere else is what you're saying?"

"Definitely."

"It makes life a little more difficult."

"What were you going to research?"

"The next job I have lined up. Someone wants me to find a jewelry box that has been missing since 1987."

"Jesus! How the hell can you find something from thirty years ago?"

George leaned forward as if interested in his process. Jesse wasn't fooled, but he pretended he was.

"It's not as difficult as some people think, although it will be more so because I can't use my usual sources. The first thing I do is a general search for the item and see what shows up. Sometimes, a news article about a recent acquisition or a museum piece will show up and give me a lead. It can't be much different than what you do."

Jesse curled his legs underneath him, cradling his cup, which grew colder by the minute. He watched several emotions pass over George's face and didn't think he would reply.

"I suppose it is."

Any further conversation they might have had was interrupted by George's phone again.

"Boss-man. Okay." George pulled the phone from his ear and pressed a button. "You're on speaker."

"Good morning, both of you. I wanted to check in with you to make sure everything is going well. I know it was a bit short notice to get you out of where you were staying, but I hope the cabin is suitable."

"It's fine. I'm grateful to you for helping me out." Jesse knew when to be sarcastic, and this wasn't it.

"We were beginning to brainstorm about doing some research ourselves, but we need to be careful." George leaned forward, focusing on Jesse.

"Without a doubt. Try not to bring any attention to yourselves on the internet, don't go triggering any warning flags by using words that might link to Baker. We have no idea who he might have on his side."

"Agreed."

"Egghead is working this end to find everything he can, but it's a struggle. He's had to contact several of his sources to help him out. That should tell you how deep this goes."

Ian's voice was gruff and no-nonsense. Jesse wouldn't want to cross him.

"I'm sure you'll keep me up to date on whatever is found."

"Of course. In the meantime, relax a little, Nipper. We've had no chatter to say anyone is searching for either of you."

After the conversation with Ian finished, George set up his laptop next to Jesse, and they chatted amicably while they did some research. Jesse had no idea what George was checking out, but Jesse did the bare minimum he could do without tripping any wires. He doubted anyone knew how he did his research, but he wanted to be careful, just the same.

He yawned for the fiftieth time and closed his laptop, rubbing his eyes. "I'm beat. I'm going to bed."

"You know where I am if you need anything."

Jesse glanced at George, and for a long moment, neither of them dropped their gaze. When Jesse's knees trembled, he pulled away, turning his back on George and shuffling down the hallway. The door closed behind him with a soft snick, and he rested back, leaning his head against the wood. He couldn't have anything to do with George, no matter what his body said. George would only want a fling, and while it would scratch an itch, Jesse knew he couldn't do it.

His past relationships had shown he was unable to keep his heart out of the picture when it came to men. Of the three relationships he'd had since he'd known he was gay, all three had ended because the other guy hadn't loved Jesse as much as Jesse had loved them. They were sorry, but he was a little clingy and needy.

Jesse rolled his eyes and pushed away from the door. He didn't need anybody, but he also didn't need to tempt his heart with things it couldn't have.

~

SEVERAL HOURS LATER, Jesse woke with a start. His breath came in gasps, and his body was slick with sweat. He sat upright, rubbing his hands hard over his face and through his hair to calm him down. It had been a long time since he'd had that nightmare, but he understood where it was coming from.

Swinging his legs over the edge of the bed, he leaned his elbows on his knees and blew out a long breath. When he was steadier, he stood and ambled toward the door, needing a drink. Not wanting to wake George, he was careful with his movements and tiptoed to the kitchen, running the tap for a short time before filling a glass. After draining the glass, he rested it against his forehead, cooling his temperature.

"You okay?"

Jesse jumped, the glass falling from his hand and smashing on the floor. It was only his built-in instincts that stopped him from moving away and, potentially, stepping in the glass.

"Shit! Sorry. Stay where you are. I'll get the dustpan and brush." George slipped out of the kitchen. The cupboard in the hallway opened and closed, and he was back, complete with shoes. He knelt and swept away the evidence.

"Sorry. I was in a world of my own and thought you were asleep."

"I was, but I heard you and wanted to make sure you were okay?" George peered up from where he was crouched and raised an eyebrow.

Jesse sighed. "Yeah. Had a bad dream. I'm fine."

George worked his way closer until he told Jesse to lift one foot at a time to clear away around him. Once he was done, George disappeared, then came back with Jesse's slippers.

"They won't stop any shards from getting to you, but they will help."

The kindness had Jesse closing his eyes to stop his tears. He didn't deserve it. "Thanks."

"Go sit in the living room. I'll make us some hot chocolate."

"No, it's okay. Go back to bed. I'll head that way myself now."

Jesse pivoted but was stopped by a warm hand on his forearm. He peeked over his shoulder.

"I have some experience. Hot chocolate will help."

Jesse tried to get a read on George, but it was impossible. He inclined his head and drifted to the sofa, bundling himself into the corner with a throw around him, surprisingly cold after the sweat had gone from his body. Staring at the blank TV, he was comforted by the sounds coming from the kitchen: the boil of the kettle, the clink of the cups and spoon, the pouring of the water. He had no idea if George was making it with milk or water, but he didn't care.

George appeared beside him, carrying two mugs. He lifted one side of his mouth. "I know you make yours with milk, but I wasn't sure how to do it. This is my version."

The way George avoided his gaze had Jesse's heart missing a beat. It was such a shy response; it surprised him.

"I'm sure it's great. Thank you."

Jesse took the proffered mug and cradled it in his hands, bringing it close to his mouth and blowing across the top.

George went back to the kitchen and returned with a small bag. "You can't have hot chocolate without marshmallows."

Jesse snorted when he saw the large sugar treats, and when George dropped one gently into his mug, he grinned. "Perfect."

George didn't say anything. He sat on the opposite corner of the sofa and brought his knee up until he was facing Jesse. "What happened?"

He knew exactly what George was asking, but he couldn't talk about it. He shook his head.

"Was it about your brother?"

Jesse flicked his gaze over, seeing no sympathy or

annoyance, just a bland expression that allowed Jesse time to think.

Staring at the melting marshmallow, he went back into the dream. "We were in the waiting room at the hospital, Beau and I." He nudged at the lump with his fingertip. "A doctor came in asking Beau to come with him, and he stood to follow, but the doctor grew horns. Beau tried to run back to me, and I gripped his hands, but he was being pulled away. Our hands slipped, and he tumbled into the doctor's arms. They disappeared."

He took a shaky breath, trying to calm the shivers now wracking his body. The cup was removed from his hands, and an arm came around his shoulders, pulling him close. He dropped his head to George's shoulder and let the tears fall silently. George murmured to him and rubbed a hand up and down his biceps.

Time ceased to exist while he sat there being comforted by a large alpha male who could easily break every bone in his body. He needed to pull away, but he couldn't find the energy.

"Come on, Jesse. Let's get you back to bed."

He was pulled upright, the throw falling from his shoulders. George rested a hand on Jesse's lower back as they trailed down the hallway and stopped outside Jesse's room. The hand dropped, and George stepped back. Without conscious intent, Jesse grabbed his T-shirt and stopped his retreat.

Their gazes locked. Jesse's nerves fizzled, and his hand trembled while his breathing increased. The tension between them was palpable.

"Stay," he whispered.

A stretch of time passed while they stared at each other—Jesse had no idea how long—and he saw the moment George's restraint snapped and had time to brace himself.

Their mouths clashed, and George clamped his hands on either side of Jesse's face as their tongues tangled. Jesse wrapped his arms around George's neck and tried to climb him. George hooked his hands beneath Jesse's thighs and pressed him against the wall or door or wherever they were, and Jesse's legs circled George's waist, locking his ankles at his lower back.

Jesse's cock pressed between their bodies, and he rocked his hips to gain friction against George's stomach. They were both wearing sweatpants, and Jesse had no T-shirt; his dick was hardly confined. He dragged his mouth away from George's and groaned, dropping his head back while George nipped and sucked along the column of his neck.

Fluttering his eyelids open, he glanced at where they were —right next to his open door.

"Bed," he rasped, bringing his mouth back to George's. "Bed, please!"

He knew this was a bad idea, but he was loathed to stop it. The release was sorely needed.

George lifted his head and stared at Jesse, panting. There was some internal fight going on, but Jesse hoped he won. George clenched his jaw and took Jesse's weight, stepping into the darkness of his room. There were no sounds other than their harsh breathing, and Jesse lowered his head to George's mouth, licking at his lips.

Their kiss became passionate once more, and his thoughts drifted away. All he could do was feel: a soft pressure against his back, a solid warmth at his front, heated kisses, fumbling hands. He was lost within the fog of arousal.

"Yes!"

His voice was a hoarse shout when George's hand wrapped around both their cocks. Jesse couldn't help but drop his head back onto the mattress and arch his back at the delicious friction George's hand gave him, and the gentle but insistent nudge of the head of George's dick against his own was overwhelming.

George braced himself on one hand, rising above Jesse, eyes glinting in the limited light and tightened his hand around them. The slick noise of their cocks being forced through George's fierce grip heightened Jesse's senses. He was so close.

Jesse embedded his fingernails into George's shoulders when Jesse's climax closed in on him.

"Fuck, George!"

"That's it. Come for me."

The words were grated out, and the sound tingled along Jesse's spine. Unable to stop the orgasm barreling through him, he panted and moaned as it destroyed his mind. Distantly, he heard a grunting sound and a warmth across his stomach. He was too blissed out.

He floated on the edge of sleep, knowing there was something he needed to do but unable to remember what. The heat to his front was replaced by cold air, and he tried to grumble about it, but he was too tired. Something wet brushed along his stomach and chest, then something dry. Hands lifted him, and he ineffectually pushed at the firm bands in an effort to be left alone, but he was quickly cocooned in warmth once more.

6

GEORGE

He closed the bedroom door and silently stalked across the hallway to his room. Trailing through the darkness, he dropped onto the bed and stared at the shadowed floor, his eyes adjusting slowly.

The high he had been feeling minutes ago had already left, and he regretted what they had done. No, regretted wasn't the right word. He wished it had been under different circumstances—mainly, it could have been a hookup situation where he wouldn't have to peer into the man's eyes again afterward. That wouldn't happen here.

George sighed and laid back, shifting his feet to the bed and plumping the pillow beneath his head. It had been a bad choice, and he would pay for it in the morning.

Several hours later, he rubbed his gritty eyes and wished he'd been able to sleep more than a handful of hours. He'd tossed and turned all night, trying to figure out the best way to circumvent the strained tension that was undoubtedly going to be there when Jesse woke.

After a shower and getting dressed, George strode to the kitchen and started the expensive-looking coffee pot—a startling find when he'd only expected to have a kettle. At least, until he remembered whoever owned the cabin must be military with all the small hiding places George had found when he searched the place. He knew plenty of places to grab a gun or two if he needed them.

As the coffee began to gurgle, he did his rounds of checking their surroundings and ensuring no changes had been made while he'd been…indisposed. Finding nothing of consequence, he filled a mug with coffee, adding a splash of milk, and aimed for the front window. The trees around the perimeter were good at keeping people away, especially with the expanse of land between those trees and the cabin vast enough, George would be able to see any approach, but they could also hide people.

He had one arm across his waist and the elbow of the other resting on the first while he sipped his drink and stared. Pushing away the unsettled feeling, he reached for the binoculars he'd left, lifting them to his eyes. The trees became larger, and he took the time to scan the full length, checking for any changes in them. Satisfied despite the niggling in the back of his head, he twisted and came face to face with Jesse.

Luckily, he'd heard the guy opening his bedroom door, but he hadn't expected him to be standing directly behind him. His military training stopped him from jumping.

"Good morning."

Jesse's voice was rough from sleep, his hair mussed, but at least he wore more clothes than he had in the middle of the night.

"Morning." George stepped around him, swallowing hard to stop from reaching for him. He drained his coffee, refilled his mug and sat in an armchair, dragging his laptop closer.

There was silence until Jesse tucked himself into the

corner of the sofa, holding his mug close. "It's going to be like this, is it?"

George's eyes remained glued on his screen, although his focus was wholly on the man who had been in his arms less than twelve hours ago. "Like what?"

Jesse sighed and stood. "Never mind."

George lifted his gaze to Jesse's retreating back, and his heart pounded painfully. He hated the dejected slump of his shoulders and wanted nothing more than to make everything better, but George had nothing to give him. He needed to give everything to Trident to ensure he would stay as part of the team. He refused to give his father any more ammunition against him.

At a reasonable hour, he checked in with Ian and found they had no more information than before. He sat back, wishing there was something he could do other than sit there and wait. His lips pressed together, and he stared at the window.

The longer he stared, the more something niggled at him. There was something he was missing, and he needed to get Jesse out of his head to think properly. Problem was, Jesse's leaving the room wasn't sitting well with him.

Blowing out a breath toward the ceiling, George stood and put the laptop on the table, striding down the hallway until he reached Jesse's closed door. He knocked.

"What?"

George's mouth twitched at the snarky question, and he opened the door without comment. Jesse sat with his back against the headboard, laptop resting on his partially bent legs, hair mussed from where he'd obviously run his hands through it several times.

"What?"

"I'm sorry. I didn't mean to be..." George couldn't think

of a decent enough word to use. He shrugged instead, hoping his meaning got across.

"Ignorant. Pig-headed. Selfish. Bitter. Irritated. Moody… should I go on?"

Jesse's face was impassive, but the hurt in his eyes was clear to see. George shouldn't be getting distracted by a pouting boy, but he couldn't stop himself from feeling like an ogre for upsetting him. He rubbed a hand over his face and rested the other on his hip.

"I get the idea." He moved his jaw from side to side. "We don't have long until the deadline Baker has given you is over. I've spoken to Ian, but they haven't found anything yet. Egghead is waiting to hear back from his contacts."

"What is the plan if they don't hear anything?"

George knew Baker would be searching for Jesse when that happened if he wasn't already. "We're well-hidden here. We should be fine for the time being." He stared at the floor, trying to figure out their next move.

Jesse cocked his head. "You don't seem sure."

George usually had a good poker face, but for some reason, when it came to this man, Jesse saw through everything. He crossed his arms over his chest, deciding to be honest, which was a new thing for him when it came to those he protected.

"I feel like I've missed something somewhere. I can't explain it, but it's bugging me."

Jesse sat forward, pushing his laptop aside and crossed his legs. "Talk me through it."

"Through what?"

"What's bugging you."

George flung his hands out, palms to the ceiling. "I can't! That's the problem. I don't know what it is."

"Okay. Talk through the case. Give me your thoughts, feelings, whatever. Just talk. My mother used to tell me that before everything happened with Beau. Talk it through, work through it. The answer will come. It doesn't always work." Jesse shrugged a shoulder, his focus dropping to his hands, which were playing with a pen.

"I need coffee for this."

George rubbed at his mouth as he retraced his steps but diverted to the kitchen. Making up a new pot of coffee, he stared at it while it brewed, his hands curved around the edges of the counter. He supposed it wouldn't hurt to go through everything with Jesse. He wanted to be able to go back to the easy way things were before they'd…last night. There were too many things bouncing around in his skull, and he needed order to process everything.

He poured two mugs of coffee and exited the kitchen to find Jesse sat in his usual spot on the sofa.

"I thought it would be better to talk out here."

His words were soft, but the underlying meaning was clear. He handed him a mug and sat in an armchair, staring at his drink. The brew was hot and bitter but a welcomed reprieve from Jesse's stare.

"I don't know what to say."

"As I said, talk."

George sighed, taking a sip of his coffee. "Well, Baker is a bad guy. Surely, he has enough people on his payroll that he would be able to find you without much effort?"

"Yeah, but what does it matter?"

"I'm not worried about him finding you here. Ian said this place was far enough off the radar anyway, but the team has found no evidence of anybody sniffing around your old apartment. If Baker has so many sources, surely someone would have been observing where you were staying. Even if it was to ask around about you. You weren't exactly hiding where you were living, which by the way, was a bit stupid."

"Hey, I resent that. I thought it was a good idea to hide in plain sight, and staying somewhere like student housing, especially with how young I look, seemed like a good idea."

"It would have been a good idea if you hadn't stayed close by. If you had chosen somewhere a little further afield, it would have worked out a lot better. We would have found you, but it would have given you a head start at least." George rubbed the back of his neck and cleared his throat.

"All right. I bow to your expertise."

"We don't have a lot to go on with Baker. Can you give us any more information about how you found the vase and how you knew it was with Baker?"

Jesse tucked his legs underneath him on the sofa and brought the cup to his mouth. George didn't think he would say anything.

"I'm not telling you where it is. I can easily explain to you how I found it, but I won't be able to do it without showing you on my laptop, which is something we can't do at the minute."

"Why won't you let us have the location of the vase?"

"Because you don't need to know. Having the vase won't give you any more information about Baker."

George jumped to his feet, turning away from Jesse and running his hands through his hair repeatedly. He paced back and forth in front of the coffee table, trying to figure out what was going on. In some ways, Jesse didn't appear hiding anything except the location. At least as far as the team could tell. His main concern was Jesse keeping a secret at all. George shook his head, grabbed his drink and stalked to the front door.

The gentle breeze coming off the lake was cool but refreshing as it cornered the cabin. George sat on the top step, his feet resting two steps below while he stared across the vast expanse of land toward the trees. He hadn't brought his binoculars out with him; therefore, he was unable to check their surroundings, but he had done it not long ago and didn't expect much to have changed.

Lifting the mug to his mouth, he took a small sip. The glint of the sun sparkled off the lake in the corner of his eye, and he glanced in that direction to see what it was. It took him barely five seconds before he realized the sparkle hadn't come from the lake. He didn't react, waiting a few more minutes, pretending to drink his coffee, despite the potential danger of being a sitting target. He stood, stretching his arms above his head and leaning to each side before going inside as if nothing was amiss.

The moment the front door closed behind him, he stood by the window, lifting the binoculars to his eyes. It wasn't easy to see through the sheer fabric, but he refused to move it aside and give away his position.

"What's wrong?"

Jesse came to stand next to him, close enough George could feel the heat of his breath on his biceps.

"We need to get out of here."

"What do you mean? Why?"

"I'm not sure, Jesse. My instincts are telling me we're not safe here despite what I said earlier."

George studied the length of the trees, starting from the lake and spanning the whole length to the other side of the property. He couldn't see a damn thing, but his nerves were tingling.

"Right, we're going out the back door. I'm convinced there's someone out there. We need to keep the house between us and the tree line." George stalked to the coffee table, grabbed his phone, hitting a button, and shoved it into a plastic bag in his pocket before grabbing Jesse's arm and pulling him toward the back of the cabin. They shoved their feet into their shoes quickly.

"This is going to be cold, I'm afraid."

"What is?"

George didn't say anything else, opening the rear door and dragging Jesse behind him. The breeze from the lake was cooler from this side of the cabin. Neither of them was wearing more than T-shirts, and George knew they should have stopped for better clothes. He couldn't guarantee they had the time.

"I'm sorry about this."

George spared a glance at Jesse, who appeared confused until George continued their path toward the lake. He began to pull away from George's hold.

"No! No way am I going in there. It'll be freezing, George!"

"We have to. It's something they wouldn't expect us to do, whoever they are. Even if they have military training, no one would expect me to take you into the lake. They'd expect me to edge around it. And besides, it's the height of summer; the water won't be as cold as in the winter."

Jesse stopped pulling away, but his steps were hesitant.

"We're going to wade in until it's up to our necks, and we'll use some of the floating plants to hide us while we make our way across to the other side. We're not talking front crawl, either. This is going to be fucking slow and tedious, Jesse. I promise you, as soon as we get to those trees on the other side, I'll sort out getting you warmer."

"We're in the middle of fucking nowhere, George. Where the hell can we get warm?"

"Trust me."

George faced him and held his shoulders, the gentle lap of the water loud in the silence as they stared at each other. Jesse sighed and closed his eyes.

"I don't know why I trust you so much."

"I'm glad you do because I'm going to get you out of this alive." George paused. "You can swim, right?"

Jesse quirked the corner of his mouth. "Now you're asking, huh? Shouldn't it have been a question you asked before we got our toes wet?"

George shook his head, fighting his smile. There was something about this guy. He ruffled Jesse's hair and stepped into the water. It took his breath away, and *he* was used to working in different temperatures of water. He had no idea how it would feel to Jesse. Well, he didn't until Jesse's muffled cursing began. He needed to get Jesse safely across the lake as soon as possible. Jesse wouldn't be able to survive in this water for as long as George could. Despite what George said, the water was colder than he would've liked.

They bobbed down to their necks, and George grabbed several clumps of plant life to hide their movements. Choosing larger ones that rose above the surface gave them the chance to keep their heads above water for longer, but he also chose some clumps to give it a better three-dimensional appearance.

"Here we go. Hold onto me if you need to, and try not to make any fast or big movements when we move. No splashing either. If you feel yourself sinking under, go under, and I will help you back up. Understand?"

"Yes, but I don't want to do this."

"I know. I'm sorry."

"If you miss military training so much, you could go back in. You don't have to make this an Olympic event."

Jesse's grumbling lightened the mood a bit, and George snorted as they slowly stepped through the water toward what probably seemed to Jesse like an impossible destination.

They didn't speak much, although George provided positive comments through chattering teeth. Jesse's lips tinged blue, and George knew he was struggling, but he carried on without complaint. George didn't think it would last long once they got to the opposite bank, but he'd take what he could get.

He had no idea how long it had taken for them to reach the bank on the opposite side of the lake, but there had been no shots fired or any shouts to indicate they'd been seen. For George, it was a bonus. It meant they might get out of the water in one piece.

Either that, or George had been wrong, and there was no one in the trees.

"We n-need to Army crawl o-out of the water, k-keeping as l-low as possible. Just f-follow me." George's teeth were rattling so much, he could barely talk. Numbness was invading his limbs, but he refused to stop.

They kept low to the ground when they exited the water, the breeze triggering a fresh round of shivering. He could see Jesse struggling to pull himself along the ground and slid closer, grabbing under one arm to help maneuver him faster toward the blanket of trees on this side. It seemed insurmountable to him, but to Jesse…George couldn't imagine. It reminded George of his initial training when he thought he would fail and end up on the wrong end of his father's temper.

Finally, they made the tree line, and George pulled Jesse behind a tree, sitting him upright with a tree to his back. George dragged himself to a seated position close to him and lifted the hem of Jesse's T-shirt. Hands ineffectually pushed at his, trying to stop him.

"Wh-what a-are y-you d-doing-g?"

"The c-clothes will make us c-colder. Need to s-strip."

He had no idea whether Jesse understood or not, but the man stopped pushing him away. George managed to get themselves down to their underwear and drifted closer. Pulling out his phone, he checked for any messages. Ian had sent an address and instructions to follow. He'd also stated there was a stash of clothes on that side of the lake but further afield than they were at present.

Wrapping his arms around the smaller man, George decided to try and warm themselves first, then go searching for the clothes. It shouldn't take too long, and he would be able to shield Jesse from some of the breezes.

He tucked Jesse in as close as he could, rubbing his limbs and murmuring nonsense. This wasn't how he expected his day to pan out.

7

JESSE

Jesse had never been so cold. He was surprised he could feel anything with how numb his limbs felt. Height of summer, his ass. He could barely get his brain to work, let alone his fingers or toes. He had no idea how George was functioning. The man chatted to him despite the words coming out disjointed and stuttered. George had barely explained anything about why they needed to go into the water in the first place, but Jesse knew better than to complain. He trusted George. Even though they had barely known each other a few days, he found himself believing in him, trusting him.

He needed to find out the reason for their impromptu swim, but at that moment, he was more concerned with getting warm. When George began taking his clothes off, Jesse's brain couldn't understand what he was trying to do. Something in the back of his head had him remembering about body heat, but he couldn't grasp what. And he didn't care. He let George do what George needed to do. It was how he found himself wrapped half-naked around George as their skin temperature began to rise once more.

"How are you feeling?"

"I can barely feel my fingers and toes, but the rest of me is becoming a little warmer."

Jesse's life had never been normal, but this, even for him, was a stretch. He had no idea what the plan was, and he said as much to George.

"Ian messaged to say there were some clothes stored around here, but we have a little bit of a trek first. I thought it better if we warmed up a bit, then we wouldn't be dragging along the distance and potentially giving away our location."

"I won't say no to new clothes or at minimum dry ones." He couldn't believe how close he sat to George. He had no idea how long they'd been sitting with their arms around each other, but George warmed a lot quicker than Jesse was, or at least that was how it seemed.

"Do you think you can manage to walk a bit?"

Jesse wiggled his toes and his fingers, brushing them against George's skin accidentally. Feeling was returning in the tingling sensation that usually happened when one had been out in the cold.

"Yeah, I think I can, but it depends how my legs hold me up when I stand. No guarantees."

George huffed a laugh, the heat whispering across the top of Jesse's head.

"Let me get up first, and I'll make sure I catch you if your knees buckle. I can also help to pull you up."

Jesse half-heartedly pulled away from George's heat, allowing the man to pull their freezing wet shoes on before standing, using the tree to brace him. He could see George's fingers clenching against the tree trunk and his legs wobbling, but he remained upright. Jesse wasn't too sure whether he would be the same.

"Come on. Let's give this a try."

George rested his hip against the trunk and reached

down for Jesse's hands. Jesse tried to get his feet underneath him to help with the momentum, but it wasn't easy. His legs didn't want to cooperate. In the end, George yanked him upright, pulling him in close and wrapping his arms around Jesse's body once more. Jesse's knees grew stronger every second he stood, and eventually, he was able to take his own weight. He didn't pull away from George straight away. He wasn't looking a gift horse in the mouth.

"Okay, let's take some baby steps now. One foot in front of the other. Slowly."

They both held onto the tree trunk when they separated. Jesse's feet were freezing, but at least he could feel them, which was better than he had before.

It was slow going, but he did what George said: one foot in front of the other. George threaded his fingers through Jesse's, which startled him.

"We can help each other."

Jesse didn't think George needed any help, but he wasn't gonna deny the pleasure of having George's hand in his. As they stumbled, they used the tree trunks to push themselves forward and keep themselves balanced. Their steps became surer and more confident the further they went, helping to warm their bodies despite the cool air being blown through the branches.

"Ian said there was some sort of box around here somewhere."

"Did he not give you any coordinates?"

"Yes, but they're not an exact science. We need to search around a specific area to find them."

"What's the plan once we're dressed?"

George squeezed Jesse's hand and glanced over at him with a little smile. "We have a bit of a hike, unfortunately, but once we get where Ian is sending us, we will have a car."

"What if we don't?"

"We will. The team has not let us down yet."

"I'm not used to working alongside someone. All my jobs have been me on my own. It's weird having to think about other people."

"And it's strange for me to think about working alone." George grinned across at him. "I don't think I've ever been on a mission where I'm the single person having to do something. There's always been at least one other person alongside me."

"I'm not sure it would work when I'm trying to get into buildings as quietly as I can and get out again without being seen." Jesse chuckled, surprised he was able to find the humor with how the day was playing out.

"You'd be surprised how easy it is to get a team of five or ten people into a building quietly."

Jesse withheld his laugh this time.

"Right, we're in the right area. Now, we need to find the box."

"How big is this box? I mean, are we searching for shoebox size or suitcase size?"

"It will be the size of a large suitcase." George didn't let go of his hand as he began examining their surroundings. "I can't see anything. Let's move a bit further away, and we can stop and have another check. It's not going to be easy to find because that's the whole idea after all."

"It needs to have some sort of tracker on it that can be beeped onto your phone. You'll know exactly where it is instead of fumbling around in the semi-darkness."

"I will take it to the boss. It's something to consider."

Jesse saw something out of the corner of his eye, and he squinted in the distance, tugging on George's hand to pull him to a stop.

"What's that over there?" He pointed to a big tree trunk, far bigger than the rest. He wasn't sure if it was his eyes playing in the dusk light and with the shadows of the trees, but it appeared like a box of some sort.

"I think that might be it. Come on."

They trudged toward the item, which took the shape of a metal box the closer they came.

"This is it." George knelt in front of the box, brushing off dead leaves, bugs, and god knows what else before pressing his thumb to the lock. When nothing happened, George cursed. He pressed a button on his phone and lifted it to his ear.

"Egghead, I'm at the box, but it won't open." George listened for a moment, his eyes fixed on the box in front of him. Jesse wrapped his arms around himself, trying to stop the cold from invading again. Now that they'd stopped moving, he shivered.

George shifted from side to side, checking around the exterior of the box, talking to whoever this Egghead was. While he was occupied, Jesse inspected their surroundings but was unable to see anything except trees. He could hardly see the lake from where they were either. When night fell, it would certainly be spooky.

"There doesn't seem to be any keypad that I can see."

Jesse glanced at the box to see if he could see something George couldn't, though he doubted it. From where he stood, he could see something tucked at the back and nudged George's shoulder to get his attention. When George barely glanced at him, Jesse crouched down, pointing at what he could see.

"I think we found it. Not sure if it's gonna work, but we can give it a try. What's the code?"

Jesse watched George press numbers. This wasn't a four-digit pin code; this was a full-blown ten or more numbers to make sure it would take someone a long time to figure it out. It made Jesse wonder what exactly was in the box. When

George had finished entering the numbers, they waited. Several seconds passed by with no click or any other kind of sound to indicate the box had opened.

"I punched the number in, but it's not done anything."

Jesse heard mumbling on the other end of the phone, but he couldn't hear the words. George leaned back, wedging the phone between his shoulder and ear, releasing his hand to use both to open the clasp at the front of the box.

"Wait! What happens if we try to open it, but it's not unlocked?"

The question sounded silly to his own ears, but George seemed to understand what he was trying to say. He didn't repeat the question into the phone; Egghead must have acknowledged his words.

"There are no explosives, according to the team. I'm willing to trust him."

That received some more noise from the other end of the phone, but George chuckled lightly. He went for the clasp, undoing it with a quiet snick, and lifted the lid. At first, nothing happened, the lid didn't come away from the box, and Jesse was ready to say the code they entered was incorrect. George, however, wiggled and pulled and knocked the lid until it sprung open by itself.

George said a few more words and hung up the phone, resting it beside the box. He began to rummage through the contents, passing some clothes over to Jesse. Jesse pulled off his sodden shoes but left his socks on for the time being. He also left on his underwear but pulled the thick dry trousers up his legs, jumping into them. They were cool themselves, but he knew they would soon warm up with his body heat. He tugged the T-shirt over his head, the hemline dropping to halfway down his thighs, and pulled the hoodie over his head. The same thing happened with the sleeves, falling way past the ends of his hands. He didn't care. He knew he'd be warm in no time. He began to put his shoes back on when George told him to wait. George passed over some boots.

"I don't know if these are your size but give him a try first before you put back on your old ones."

Jesse put them on while George dressed himself. The boots fit him well, surprisingly. He watched George pull on his old shoes, the ones that were soggy and cold and raised his eyebrows.

"They don't have my size." George curved his mouth.

When they were both sufficiently dressed, George returned to his kneeling position in front of the box. He picked a couple of things from the bottom of the box and shoved them into one of the many pockets of his khaki trousers. The final thing he picked up was a gun.

Jesse took a step back. He wasn't scared of guns, but he hadn't been expecting it.

"I left mine in the cabin, sorry. I need to have one in case we come across anything. Or anyone."

"No, it's fine. I know guns are a daily occurrence for you and your team. Surprisingly, I rarely come across them, and I certainly don't need to have one myself. Not that I could shoot it if I did have one."

"It would never hurt to have shooting practice, even if you never owned a gun yourself."

"It's something to consider." Jesse smirked. "What's the plan from now?"

"As I said, we have a bit of a trek. Ian said to head for the shopping mall."

"A shopping mall? Where the hell is a shopping mall in the middle of nowhere?"

"Hence the trek." George pulled out his phone and pressed a few buttons, concentrating on the screen. Jesse thought about how far they were likely to have to roam to get to this mystery shopping mall and what they would do when they got there.

"I have directions, and it's saying it's about twenty miles in that direction." George pointed to Jesse's right.

"I guess we're going hiking." Jesse sighed. He was already exhausted from their impromptu swim and from being so cold. All he wanted to do was lay down and go to sleep, but if George thought they were in danger, it wasn't a good idea.

"Lead the way."

Instead of taking the lead, George paced beside Jesse, threading his fingers through his as they had done on their first stroll through the trees. For a short while, neither of them said a word. Their companions were the rustle of the trees and the occasional animal sound made all the spookier by rambling through a shadowed forest.

Jesse had no idea how long they'd trudged along for. What he did know was he was becoming stiff, and he wasn't sure how much longer he could stand.

"George, I don't want to sound like a seven-year-old going on holiday, but how long till we get there?"

George chuckled and checked his phone. "I'm afraid we have roughly another four hours of walking."

Jesse groaned, pulling George to a stop. "I can't. I seriously can't."

George glanced around him and nodded. "All right. Let's go."

He pulled Jesse along despite his protests until they reached a sheltered area, surrounded by a close-knit clump of tree trunks.

"This will give us some protection while you rest up. I'll keep watch."

George sat, patting the ground beside him. Jesse dropped unceremoniously next to him and dropped his head back against the trunk, closing his eyes.

"I'm sorry." Jesse rolled his head toward George.

"Don't worry about it. Get some rest. Sleep for a bit if you can." George gave him a tight smile and transferred his gaze to their surroundings.

Jesse closed his eyes again, the tingling in his feet and legs advertising how much walking he'd done already. He would have blisters upon blisters on his feet by the time they made it to the shopping mall.

"What made you think we needed to run?"

George remained silent, and Jesse lifted one eyelid to gaze at him. Initially, George surveyed the area, then he stared down at his hands. "I thought I saw something in the trees."

Jesse lifted his head and peered at him. "You think?"

George pursed his lips. "I could've been wrong."

The words were quiet, barely heard above the wind in the trees. He had never expected to see a vulnerability to George, not about this anyway. Shuffling around to face George, Jesse rested his head on his shoulder and slid his arms through George's closest one.

"Nah, if you think you did, you did. They obviously don't see how cool you are, sniffing out their hiding place."

"I didn't exactly sniff them out."

Those words held a bit of humor, which was what Jesse had hoped for. If George lost faith in his instincts, they were both dead.

Jesse snuggled in closer, breathing deeply of George's scent.

8

GEORGE

George wanted nothing more than to keep going, but he knew, despite Jesse's lifestyle, he didn't have the training George did. It wasn't fair to keep him marching on when he couldn't. An hour's rest would do him some good.

He had sent a message to Ian explaining the situation and that they were going to be running behind schedule. Ian sent back an affirmative, but it rankled because he had to go slower than he wanted to. As far as he was concerned, the larger the distance between them and whoever was in the trees, the better.

When Jesse's head fell off his shoulder for probably the tenth time, George carefully extricated his arm and maneuvered Jessie to a lying position, using George's thigh as a pillow. He tried to keep his hands away from the man but found his fingers caressing his hair several times. It was as if he couldn't stop touching him.

Despite the night falling around them, bringing with it shadowy hiding places, he didn't feel overwhelmed. If it had been any other time or place, he would have been happy to be stuck there with Jesse.

Jesse mumbled in his sleep and fidgeted, moving his head into a slightly different position. George's breath hitched when Jesse's ear rested over his cock. Once Jesse had settled again, George carefully maneuvered him away and breathed a sigh of relief. He'd lost track of how many times this had happened over the past few minutes, and every time, it took his breath away.

Jesse certainly hadn't been the sarcastic, uptight guy George had been expecting when they first heard about him. He'd done well for himself. It was a matter of time before he chose the wrong mark, and things went wrong. George's only reassurance was that they were there to help him.

After checking his watch one last time, he knew they needed to get going. He'd given Jesse an hour of sleep, and although it wouldn't help with his aching muscles, he hoped Jesse would feel a bit more refreshed. George had grabbed the backpack that had been in the box and filled it with several bottles of water. Grabbing one now, he clicked it open and closed the lid again, resting it next to him.

"Jesse. Jesse, it's time to wake up."

Jessie grumbled and groused, using his hands to rub against his face as he slowly woke. He shifted his head again, resting it higher against George's crotch. George inhaled and held the breath for a beat, letting it out slowly through his teeth.

"Jesse." He tried again. "Jesse. Come on. We've got a distance to go."

George rested one hand on the back of Jesse's head, encouraging him not to move any closer. It was bad enough where Jesse was at that moment, and George couldn't hide his reaction. He rested his other hand on Jesse's shoulder, shaking him gently, repeating his name, hoping to get some reaction from him.

"A little bit longer, please."

"We don't have any longer. Time to get up."

George firmed his voice, raising it a little, so Jesse knew he meant business. Jesse yawned, hiding his mouth behind a hand, and rubbed against his eyes again, this time blinking them open and groaning.

"What did you wake me up for?"

George shook his shoulder again. "Are you with me, Jesse? Come on, you need to wake up now."

"What?"

Jesse pulled himself to sitting, gazing around them, and his shoulders drooped.

"Sorry, it wasn't a dream." George felt a little sorry for him.

"I guess this means we've got some more walking to do."

"You guessed right. How are your legs and feet doing?"

The man groaned when he stretched out his legs, uncurling them from their bent position.

"Ouch. This is not going to be pleasant."

"Do you think you can make it?"

Jesse stared at him and quirked his mouth. "I can make it. It's going to hurt like hell."

George stood, his own body betraying him, and he cursed, having been in the same position for so long. He stretched his arms above his head, his T-shirt and hoodie rising, allowing the cool breeze to pebble his skin. He caught Jesse's gaze focused on his exposed skin and inwardly smiled. He dropped into a crouch, then rose to his tiptoes, repeating the action several times to get the blood pumping once more. He held out both hands to Jesse, tugging him to his feet and wrapping his arms around him when he stumbled. Jesse rested his cheek against George's chest, and George could do nothing more than drop his lips to the top of his head.

They stayed that way for a moment, and George reluctantly pulled back. He kept his hands on Jesse's upper arms, hoping Jesse would be able to put one foot in front of the other like he said he would. He helped Jesse do the stretches George had completed, and George could see the tension and pain on Jesse's face, but not a whimper left his mouth.

George reached down, slipping the backpack onto his back and offering Jesse the opened bottle of water. Jesse greedily drank some, closed the lid and gave it back. George tucked it into the side pocket of the backpack and held out his hand. Jesse stared at his face and his hand repeatedly before giving a small smile and threading his fingers through George's.

They began their new journey with at least four hours stretching in front of them, but they stepped one foot in front of the other. George tried to keep up the conversation, giving a mix of funny anecdotes and stories from when he was in the Navy and a few small stories from when he was a child. There weren't many of them to share, and most of them had gotten him into trouble with his father.

"When did you decide to join the military?"

George blew out a breath and stared resolutely in front of him. "I joined the Navy at eighteen." He ignored Jesse's actual question, not wanting to get into why he joined the Navy. "I retired over six months ago and joined Trident four months ago."

"What did you do in the Navy?"

"I was a corpsman and a Navy SEAL."

"What's a corpsman?"

"I deal with all the medical things." George snorted.

"What made you decide to retire?"

George was quiet for a moment, trying to figure out the best way to explain his reasoning for not wanting to stay under his father's control more than the years he'd already given him. It wasn't anyone's business but his own, although his father had changed that by turning up at Trident.

"I wanted to try something different."

They continued trudging—stumbling in Jesse's case—along the uneven forest floor. George noticed intermittent flashes of light coming from the distance. From what he could gather, they appeared to be car headlights, and if his eyes weren't deceiving him, it meant they were close. He checked his watch. They had been wandering for over three hours.

"How are you doing there?"

Jesse had been leaning on him more and more the further they went, which was understandable considering.

"I've been better, but I'm managing."

"You're doing amazingly." And George wasn't just saying that. He'd honestly thought Jesse wouldn't manage the whole twenty miles, but it showed how strong he was inside.

"Well, can you see those tiny flashes of light up ahead of us?" Jesse nodded. "I have a feeling it's the start of the main road we need to follow that will take us directly to the shopping mall."

"We're nearly there?"

"Well...not quite. We probably have about an hour to go."

Jesse was silent, but George could feel this tension riding him. "Yeah, okay. I've come this far; I can keep going. The one thing I will say is I cannot stop now. And by that, I mean I physically cannot stop because if I stop or pause, I will not be able to move again."

George understood exactly what he was getting at. When you've been walking or running or jogging or doing anything for any length of time, it was easier to push through and continue than it was to stop and rest and carry on afterward. He had no idea how Jesse had made it this far, but he'd done a damn good job.

"Duly noted. I will keep you going no matter what happens."

"I wouldn't mind another drink of water."

George disentangled himself from Jesse despite Jesse's protests and grabbed the final bottle from the backpack, slipping the bag on his back again, and held out the bottle to Jesse. "Sip it. It's the last one we have."

Jesse tried to undo the lid but didn't have the strength. George took it back, undid it and held it out once more.

"Thanks."

Jesse drank a few sips and gave it back to George. He held out his hand for Jesse to take hold of. Jesse gave him a small smile, held George's hand and wrapped his free hand around George's bicep, resting his head on his shoulder.

"Don't go falling asleep on me, will you?"

Jesse snorted. "I don't think it will be possible in all honesty. But I will take it under advisement."

George chuckled. It had seemed they had created an in-joke between them.

Several minutes later, Jesse said, "Oh, this is bad."

George snapped his gaze to Jesse's. "What's wrong?" His voice sharp.

"I need to pee."

The expression on Jesse's face had George rolling his lips inward to stop the laugh from escaping. Some of his humor must have escaped because he received a fist in the ribs from Jesse.

"It's not funny!"

"Sorry. I know it's not. At least there are plenty of trees." Those words gained another half-hearted punch to his stomach.

"My issue isn't with where to go. It's the fact that I will have to stop moving so I can go."

George could see the dilemma. "How about you do your business, and I will help you get going again after?"

"You may have to drag me."

"We'll deal with it whatever happens."

George pulled him to a stop and gestured at the trees around them. "Which tree do you want?"

"Any of them. Although it might be better to choose a slim one to hold onto it."

George helped him to a nearby tree and rested him against it. "I'll be directly behind you, but I'll face away. Make sure you tell me if you're falling. I'll catch you before you hit the ground."

"That's generous of you." Jesse was quiet. George didn't hear the tell-tale sound of liquid hitting the forest floor.

"Are you okay?

Jesse cleared his throat. "This is super embarrassing. My legs are wobbling so much I can't let go of the tree to unfasten my trousers."

"Okay, I'm going to turn around, but I will hold you under your arms to help you remain upright, but I will look away while you do your business."

"Okay." The response was quiet, ashamed even.

George did what he said, sliding his arms under Jesse's and holding him across his chest. He rotated his head to the side as if to stare over his shoulder to give Jesse his privacy or as much of it as he could get considering their positions. He heard Jesse's zipper and felt the relaxing of his body, followed by the unique sound of pouring liquid.

When Jesse was finally finished, he rested back against George's chest and blew out a breath. "Bet you didn't wake up this morning expecting to be helping me go to the bathroom, did you?

George snorted. "I can honestly say it's never been on any kind of list I have."

Jesse's laughter filled the night, and George grinned. He had never felt this overwhelming light-heartedness before and assumed it came from the man he held in his arms. Shaking his head, he held Jesse tighter.

"How are your legs doing?"

Jesse hummed. "They're complaining, and my feet are burning, but if you can help get me started, I think I will be able to step under my own steam again."

"All right. Let's give it a go."

George transferred his hold, one arm braced around Jesse's back and the other under his arm. It gave George the ability to take Jesse's weight should his legs fail him. They stepped in tandem, Jesse's legs faltering for several steps before they grew stronger once more. George gentled his hold until Jesse was once more plodding along beside him.

He found he didn't like Jesse trailing next to him independently after having him holding onto George for the past several hours. It was a stupid thought, and he brushed it aside, focusing on their next step in the plan.

"It's definitely a road up ahead. I can hear the engines. Ian left instructions to enter the twenty-four-hour shopping mall and find our way to the reception area or customer service desk…whatever it's called. From there, we need to ask if there is an envelope for Douglas Sharp."

"Who's Douglas Sharp?"

"An alter-ego." George gave him a small smile.

"You don't seem like a Douglas."

"Good thing I'm not."

They both chuckled.

"What's in the envelope?"

George sighed. "If all goes to plan, keys to a car and some money. We desperately need some new clothes, especially jackets."

As if his words conjured up the weather itself, spots of rain dripped through the leaf canopy above them.

"You and your big mouth! You had to jinx it, didn't you?" Jesse sighed heavily and wrapped his arms around his waist.

"At least, it—"

Jesse's hand covered his mouth. "No! Don't say anything. You've made it rain, don't make it worse. No!" He held the finger of his other hand up to George's face, waving it at him.

"Okay," he mumbled.

Jesse removed his hand, slower than George expected, brushing his fingers against George's lips in the process. Their eyes locked, and both slowed their steps until George stopped. He cupped Jesse's jaw, smoothing both thumbs across his cheeks.

"There is something here, between us, but we can't do anything now. When things have died down a bit…"

Jesse licked his lips, and George groaned, dropping his head to fasten their mouths together. He refused to get side-tracked despite the taste of Jesse bursting onto his tongue, so he kept the kiss quick, licking into Jesse's mouth and pulling away. He rested their foreheads together and closed his eyes for a five-second beat.

"Let's go."

He grabbed hold of Jesse's hand once more and tugged Jesse along behind him until he managed to shuffle to his own rhythm next to him.

"That wasn't fair," Jesse grumbled. "Giving me that and taking it away again. It was mean."

George grinned and squeezed Jesse's hand. "I could've not given it to you at all."

"Fuck you."

The words were said without any kind of heat or remorse, a tentative attempt at being cross with George, no doubt.

His phone vibrated in his pocket when they reached where the forest petered out, and a road began. He pulled it out and answered immediately.

"How are things going?" Devon asked.

"We've reached the edge of the forest. I can see the shopping mall in the distance." He glanced around him. "We're going to be extremely visible as soon as we step out of the trees. There are hardly any buildings except the mall. Just a wide expanse of concrete and road."

"Yeah, we did see it on the satellite pictures. There's nothing you can do about it, unfortunately. You'll have to risk it. There's nowhere else you can get to without another huge hike."

George blew out a breath and studied their surroundings. "For all we know, whoever was in trees could be waiting for us out there."

"That's true, Nipper."

Devon didn't give him any platitudes, and George was grateful. As much as he was concerned, he also knew they had no other choice. He glanced at Jesse, seeing the strain around his eyes and mouth while he leaned against a tree.

"I'll call again once we have the car. It should be within the hour."

"Talk to you soon."

Devon hung up, and George shoved the phone back into his pocket, pivoting to Jesse.

"I heard. What's your plan?"

George clenched his jaw, trying to figure out the best way of getting to their destination, but there was nothing that would help them. If their watcher drove down this way searching for them, they would be found immediately. Not many people would want to wander as far as they did, wearing what they were.

"We go for it. I suggest we pretend to be a couple and

stroll along the road instead of rushing. If we go too fast, it's likely to bring more attention to us."

"Whereas if we are lovers, we could've been for a jaunt in the forest."

George's lips twitched. "A jaunt?"

"Shut up."

"How are your legs and feet doing?"

"Don't ask no questions, and I won't tell you no lies." Jesse grimaced.

"Understood."

Jesse pushed off the tree and held out his hand. "Come on, lover. Let's get canoodling."

George laughed this time. "Canoodling? Where are you getting these words from?"

"I happen to be a fan of Jane Austen and other older books. Their words might be fancy, but often, they're right on the money."

They stepped onto the road, George wrapping his arm around Jesse's shoulders and Jesse's arm around George's waist. This had not been his plan, but he was adaptable, if nothing else.

9

JESSE

They wandered down the road, wrapped up in each other, and Jesse would've been happy to stay there indefinitely. Unfortunately, they had a job to do, or in his case, he had to follow George's instructions.

Jesse could see the mall rising from the ground in the way large shopping malls with hundreds of shops inside can do. He had never been a fan of shopping and always avoided these types of places like the plague. The one time he had ever willingly gone to one was when a small antique shop had been nestled amongst the clothing shops and shoe shops, and…he shuddered.

"Are you okay?"

George glanced down at him, and Jesse pursed his lips. "I'm thinking about how I'm going to get you back for making me enter one of my most hated places on the planet."

George's forehead furrowed. "What do you mean?"

"Shopping malls? They are torture devices. I'm sure of it."

A short laugh escaped his companion. "I'll be by your side the whole time. Nothing big, bad and scary in there will hurt you. I promise."

Jesse ducked his head, his cheeks flushing from his words. When he'd first met George, he'd been concerned for his safety. The man had been so angry and disbelieving of Jesse's plight, and when he'd been told George would be his protector, he'd been dubious. Not because George couldn't protect him, but he would *want* to protect him? Jesse knew George would do what he was told, but he also knew accidents happened. He'd been expecting to eat a bullet at some point—not that he would tell George that.

He couldn't pinpoint when things had changed. Their shared passion the previous day had helped release some tension, but it had been before that point when George's edges had softened toward him.

The previous night had been amazing. He knew other guys would've preferred to have had a dick in their ass, but what he and George shared had been perfect. Don't get him wrong, he loved cock as much as the next person, but sometimes, he felt closer to someone when he'd been less sexual with them.

"Would you say what we did last night was sex? Or was it playing around?" As soon as the words were out of his mouth, he covered it with his hand and squeezed his eyes shut. "I said that out loud, didn't I?"

George was quiet, then he cleared his throat. "You did. A random topic of conversation, but I'll go with it. Um, I'd say it was sex. Why?"

There was no going back from the conversation now that it had started. "Well, I know some people who say only penetration is sex, but I think any act that has a mutual sexual connotation is sex. It's weird how people's opinions vary so widely on something like this. It's as if by saying some acts aren't sex, they can get away with saying they haven't had sex. Does that make sense? Sorry, I'm rambling."

Jesse glanced into the distance, trying not to pull away

when the whole point of being tangled together was to make them appear like they were in a relationship.

"I agree with what you're saying. Some people like to have excuses for their behavior, and when something is not clearly defined, it's easy to muddy the waters." George sighed. "I don't regret it if that's what you're worried about."

How had he known? "I don't either. For the record."

He peered up at George from under his eyelashes, a slight curve to his lips. George huffed a laugh and pressed a kiss to Jesse's temple. What Jesse would give for more kisses and touches.

"We're almost there. How are your feet?"

"Don't talk about them because they're fine when I'm not focusing on them."

"Sorry, mouth zipped."

Jesse beamed at him. "You are nothing like I imagined you to be."

"You either." George focused on something behind Jesse, then back to him again.

"What is it?"

George leaned down and nuzzled against Jesse's ear. "There's a single car parked away from all the others. It has someone in it, but I can't see anything else. If I was alone, I'd go check it out, but let's get going. It will be easy to see if someone follows us. I'm probably paranoid."

"Hey, don't. I trust you, George. If you say there's danger, there's danger."

George stared at him for a second and dropped a kiss on his lips. "Thanks. Remember that when I tell you to do something later."

They disentangled their arms but held hands, weaving through the parked cars, and approached the entrance. George raised their hands and twirled Jesse around before stopping and standing in front of him. He cupped Jesse's face.

"Pretend I'm saying sweet nonsense to you while I check out our surroundings."

Jesse stared into his eyes for the second it took George to glance away, and even then, he studied every part of his face. His lips were moving as if talking, and his face was right in front of Jesse's, but his eyes were examining their surroundings. All Jesse could do was hold onto George's wrists and try to breathe normally.

George was larger than life, and he gained all of Jesse's focus when he was near despite Jesse wishing he didn't. Their...relationship, or whatever they were, was doomed from the start. Jesse lived in the UK, and George lived in the US. There was no way Jesse could afford to fly over the Atlantic every month to visit, and he doubted George would be able to get time off as often.

He blinked rapidly at the direction of his thoughts. Why was he thinking about this? It wasn't like they were going to live happily ever after. Jesse had broken too many promises over the years; he refused to do the same to George.

"Are you sure you're okay?"

George's thumbs were smoothing over Jesse's cheeks, and Jesse forced a smile. "Yeah. Everything all right around us?"

"Yeah. We're going to head straight for the desk, grab what has been left for us, then we need to get some clothes, another backpack and some medical supplies."

They drifted through the automatic doors hand in hand. "Why medical supplies?"

"You're going to need some things to help with the blisters on your feet and your aching muscles. Plus, Tylenol. And food and drink."

"Do you remember me telling you I detested shopping malls?"

George grinned, his face becoming younger and more handsome. "We'll be done faster than you know." He glanced around and dragged Jesse over to a board, showing where the different shops and services were. "Here we go." He pointed to their destination. "Come on. Last burst of energy, Jesse. I promise you can rest in the car."

Jesse grumbled but followed along beside George. When they approached the pristine white customer service desk, a harried-looking man stood with a phone to his ear. Jesse tuned out the man's words and rested against George until he spoke.

"Hi. We were told you had a package for us. Douglas Sharp."

The man trudged over to the back of the desk, flicking through a box until he lifted a large, brown envelope from it and brought it to them.

"Thank you."

The man nodded and effectively dismissed them by turning his back. George tensed, and Jesse braced for a tongue-lashing, but he blew out a breath and marched away, tugging Jesse along behind him. They entered a public bathroom, and George pushed him into a stall, locking the door behind them.

"What are we doing?"

George tore open the envelope. "I need to check what's in here before we go any further."

Jesse leaned against the partition, his energy levels nearing depletion, but he refused to cave when they were so close to the end. He rested his head to the side and closed his eyes, jerking when he stumbled.

"It's okay. I've got you."

George pulled him against his chest and wrapped an arm around him, the keys he held jangling in the quiet restroom. Jesse could feel himself falling asleep; he raised his head.

"If we don't move, I'll be asleep."

"All right. Let's go. We don't need to get any clothes,

there's a suitcase full of clothes in the car, thanks to Devon. We need food and extra medical supplies. I'm positive they'll have a first aid kit, but we need some special ointment for your feet."

George unlocked the cubicle and led Jesse out, going straight out of the main door into the increasingly busy mall. Jesse grabbed his hand and held tight as George wound their way to the pharmacy and a small shop that sold sandwiches and snack items. Within half an hour, they were exiting the mall into the bright morning sun. The hustle and bustle and noise of the mall died down as soon as the doors closed behind them, and Jesse was finally able to breathe.

"The car is this way."

"How do you know exactly where it is?"

"It was in the note."

George's focus never wavered from their surroundings for the whole journey to the car, which had been parked near several others. Jesse had expected it to be at the far end of the parking lot, but when he'd asked George, he'd been told it would have stood out more being alone. Jesse had never thought about that.

When George stopped next to a sleek, black Dodge Challenger, Jesse perked up.

"This is ours?"

George narrowed his eyes at Jesse. "Yes, why?"

"Oh my god! You got a Dodge Challenger! This car is fucking awesome." Jesse shuffled around it, skimming his fingers over the outside.

"I guess you like cars?"

"Awesome cars, yes."

George snorted. "Get in the back seat." At Jesse's raised eyebrows, he explained, "I want you to take your shoes off. I can put the ointment on your feet before we leave. You can lay on the back with your shoes off while I drive us out of here."

Jesse had no idea what to say. He'd expected them to need to get out of the area as soon as possible. George indicated again for him to get in after he opened the door and slid the front seat forward. While George deposited the bags on the passenger seat, Jesse sat against the furthest side of the car and tried to remove the boots, hissing at the stinging sensation.

"Here, let me do it."

George crouched and carefully slid off the boot, repeating the action with the second and dropping it with the other in the footwell. He reached for Jesse's socks, peeling them off slowly to the sounds of Jesse's whimpering. Jesse could see the blood seeping through the fabric and didn't want to see the mess of his feet.

Once the socks were off, he blew out a breath. The cool air was refreshing on his feet.

"This ointment is going to hurt as much as walking did, I'm afraid. Take these, and the pain will ease soon."

George handed him two pills and a bottle of water. Jesse obediently took them, finishing half the water before refastening the lid.

"Ready?"

"What would you do if I say no?"

George's mouth twitched, the only indication he was going to move, and Jesse yelped when the ointment stung the open sores on his skin. He bit his bottom lip when George gently applied the cream to the areas it needed to be. Once he was done, George wrapped his feet in dressings and stood back.

"There. That should keep them from getting infected while we travel. Scoot backward and rest your back against the door. You should be able to rest your legs along the back seat."

George helped him to maneuver, so he didn't need to use his feet. When he was settled, he rested his head back against the window and sighed.

"Thank you, George."

"You're welcome." He pushed the front seat back into its usual position and slipped into the driver's seat. "Are you ready?"

"As I'll ever be."

The roar of the engine was loud in the early morning, but Jesse grinned. The vibrations beneath him soothed him in a way he hadn't expected. He watched the mall disappear through the back window. Closing his eyes, he inhaled like he hadn't been able to for the last eight or so hours.

"Jesse. Jesse. You need to eat. Come on, wake up."

The insistent shaking, prodding and words pulled Jesse from a dreamless sleep, and he damn near growled at the person until George's grinning face came into focus.

"What—?" He cleared his throat and fidgeted, wincing when his body screamed blue murder at him. "Ow, ow, ow! What the hell? Where—?" He glanced out of the window, seeing several houses of varying colors and a few cars, surrounded by intermittent trees and not much else.

George chuckled beside him. "Yeah, you're going to be feeling what you went through last night and this morning. Here, drink this and take these. You'll feel a bit better soon."

Jesse pulled himself reluctantly to an upright position from where he'd been slouched, biting his lip against the pain in his muscles and from his feet. He took the pills and water, draining the entire bottle.

"Where are we?"

"About two hours north of Tampa."

Jesse frowned. "I thought we were going back?"

George shook his head. "There's no guarantee it's safe." His jaw firmed, and his eyes blazed. "We can't go back to Tampa yet. The team is researching. They found more information on Baker. Let's get into the house, and I'll tell you everything I've found out since you were sleeping."

"I don't think I'm going to be able to stand." He grimaced.

"I'll carry you into the house. No one around here will think it's anything more than we're newlyweds or something."

The words sent a slight thrill through Jesse's body. The thought of belonging to this man was…out of reach. Jesse shook his head and concentrated on listening to George's instructions. By the time he had his arms around George's neck and was held securely, he was sweating and panting, completely depleted of energy once more.

Jesse opened the front door when George asked him to, and he was deposited on the couch. "Didn't you need to sweep the house before we came in?"

"I did before I woke you. Anyway, I wasn't given an address to get to. Egghead was my sat-nav." George glanced at Jesse and chuckled, obviously seeing Jesse's confusion. "To remove any chance of someone seeing an address he sent, we took precautions. He told me what road to get on and when to turn. Only he knew where we were going until we got here. It's unlikely someone would have been able to get into the house before we arrived."

"Sneaky. I like it."

George laughed again. "I'm sure you do. I'm going to grab the stuff from the car."

Jesse watched him leave and studied the room. It appeared to be well cared for without a speck of dust, meaning someone either cleaned it recently or lived in it. He took stock of his body, twitching his limbs to find out which ones hurt the most. A bath later might soothe his muscles.

George entered again, carrying several bags and a suitcase. "Are you hungry?"

He would've said no if his stomach hadn't chosen that moment to grumble. "A little."

George put the suitcase by the front door. "We have the snacks we bought, but the house has been stocked as well. There's plenty to choose from. What would you like?"

"Anything. The only thing I don't eat is fish."

"Okay. Rest up for a few minutes, and I'll bring you something."

"I can—"

"Stay where you are. You can't be on those feet yet."

Jesse slumped back against the cushions and nodded. "All right." He twiddled his fingers and cataloged everything in the room. None of it appeared to be valuable in a historical way, although he could tell some items were expensive.

"Here you go."

A tray appeared with two sandwiches and some fruit. George rested the tray on Jesse's legs and took one of the sandwiches, sitting down next to him and taking a huge bite. Jesse watched his Adam's apple bob when he swallowed, chasing it down with the water he'd also brought.

"Eat. I'll tell you what we've found out." George set his empty plate on the coffee table and leaned back again. "Baker began his business in a similar vein to you. He used to be an antique dealer, funnily enough. He'd had his own business around fifteen years ago, then it closed, and Baker disappeared. Egghead managed to find what he'd been doing. He'd created a new business of stealing artifacts and selling them at a profit or sometimes auctioning them. It doesn't stop there. Artifacts are not the only thing he's stealing and selling. People, organs, cars, it doesn't matter, what someone wants, Baker gets it. From what we can figure out, it is because he wanted to continue with the extravagant lifestyle he has become accustomed to."

Jesse frowned. "He's a selfish asshole."

George nodded. "He has a lot of people who do his dirty work."

"It goes with what I saw at the mansion."

"I want to ask you about that. Can you give us as much information as possible about your research into the man and the building? What you found out, what you saw, anything. We want to nail this fucker."

10

GEORGE

George wished he didn't have to ask Jesse to remember all the details now, especially since he was so tired, but they were running out of time. Jesse's forty-eight-hour deadline drifted closer—they had around twelve hours left—and although George knew they weren't giving up the vase, they had no idea what would happen once the time was up.

While Jesse ate his other sandwich, George called Brody and put him on speaker to allow him and the rest of the team involved to be able to hear what Jesse said. It took Jesse a while to get everything out and answer the questions they had. Finally, they finished and said goodbye.

"I hate hiding. All I want is to get the job done, get the artifact sent to its rightful owner and go home. I'm not sure I like America at the moment." Jesse pouted, and George tried to ignore how cute it was.

"I can understand, but you can't go anywhere until this is sorted, one way or another."

"What does it matter if I get caught? Can't I send the item off like I normally do and let them catch me? What's the worst that will happen? I get arrested?"

George couldn't speak. His heart stopped for a second before starting at a rapid pace. The image of what could happen to Jesse should those people find him was startlingly vivid. Why couldn't Jesse understand when they'd explained to him what Baker did for a living?

He glowered at Jesse, whose eyes widened. "The worst? You'll die. The best? You'll disappear, and no one will find you. Which would you prefer? You know what Baker does to make his money. Why would you consider subjecting yourself to something like that for a vase?"

Jesse stared at him as if the possibilities had finally registered with him. "The threat wasn't just smoke, was it? He'll kill me?"

George raised his eyebrows. "Yes, Jesse. This is your life we're talking about. Why do you think we're all doing this? Baker needs to be stopped, and it needs to happen before he finds you."

Jesse stayed silent, staring at the tea George had given him.

"Come on. Time for some rest. You're dead on your feet." He tried for some levity, but Jesse rolled his eyes.

George carried him to a bedroom, helping him to get into bed and covered him as if he was tucking in a child—or lover. He closed the door behind him and stayed leaning against it while he thought about everything they had been through so far.

If their research was anything to go by, Baker would not be leaving anything to chance. Therefore, they were to expect the unexpected. Same with missions.

George rubbed a hand over his face, wandered to the kitchen, grabbed a bottle of water, and sat on the couch. The team had sent several people to check out the cabin but had seen nothing to indicate someone had been there. If the people after them were any good, that wasn't a definitive answer. They could've covered their tracks well. Nobody had said George was wrong, and no one had made it sound like he was, but he had the feeling he'd been too cautious. He didn't like being uncertain.

He stood, checking all the doors and windows to ensure they were locked. It was mid-afternoon, but he'd had no sleep the previous night and needed to catch up. He laid out on the couch and let sleep wash over him.

His phone woke him, and he automatically reached for it, answering before he'd checked the display.

"Wash! I'm setting up a barbecue get-together for some of our old team members. Are you interested?"

Sykes's excited babble had George wincing. He cleared his throat. "Hey, man. Uh, yeah, sure. Let me know when and where it is, and if I can be there, I will." George sat upright, rubbing a hand over his face.

"You sound like you've just woken up, man! It's the middle of the afternoon. What've you been up…Never mind." He boomed out a laugh. "Your new boyfriend must be keeping you up at night. What was his name again? Jason? Joss?"

George caught himself before he said the wrong name, narrowing his eyes as his brain cleared more and more. "Jay. And yes, we were up late. You know how new relationships are. Can't get enough of each other." He laughed, though he stood abruptly, palming his gun. His instincts were going crazy.

"Yeah, I remember it well. I need to visit a club. I've not been for a while."

George stepped to the front window, moving it aside gently to peer out. "You need to get yourself some, Sykes. You know how your brain doesn't work properly unless you've been laid. How many missions did we do to figure that shit out?" Something was wrong.

He proceeded toward the back of the house, repeating the surveillance of the back area. He couldn't see anything.

"God, don't remind me. I should've had my ass handed to me so many times." Sykes laughed.

A beep came through his phone, and he pulled it away from his ear.

BRODY: Get the fuck out of there!

George jogged to Jesse's room, trying not to make any noise when he opened the door. He shook Jesse awake, holding his free hand over his mouth and putting a finger in front of his mouth. "Hey, Sykes. Hit me up with the details of the barbecue, yeah. I'll bring Jay with me if we're still going strong."

"Sure, man. Is he waking up? I better let you go. Have a good one."

George closed his eyes and shook his head, not wanting to believe it. "You too." He hung up the phone. "We have to go. Now!"

"What? We've just got here!"

"Maybe, but I fucked up."

George lifted Jesse to a standing position. Luckily, he was dressed from earlier apart from his shoes. "We need to run. You won't make it like this. Get on my back and wrap your arms and legs around me." He cupped Jesse's jaw. "I'm sorry."

"What's going on?"

"No time. Come on, get on." His phone beeped again.

BRODY: Move it, asshole! Throw this phone. There's
a burner in the box by the back door.

George clenched his jaw and gained his balance as Jesse climbed on his back. When he was clinging to him, George kept his hands free, one for his gun, the other for opening doors. They reached the back door, and he dropped his phone, rummaging in the metal box by the back door for the phone Brody had said was there. He switched it on, tucked it into his pocket and unlocked the back door quietly.

He cracked the door enough to check for unwanted visitors before they exposed themselves. "If anything happens to me, you run. You got me?" George twisted his head to one side to watch Jesse's face. "You run through the pain, as fast and as far as you can. Ian or Devon will find you. Do you understand me?"

Jesse nodded, fear etched onto his face. George swallowed hard and directed his attention to their surroundings. He couldn't see anyone, but it didn't mean anything. There were enough trees around to cover anyone who might be there for them. George carefully exited, eyes scanning their surroundings.

A splinter of wood flew from several inches beside them, and George ducked and ran, cursing as much as Jesse was. They were sitting ducks in the expanse of land before they could use the trees for cover, so he did all he could to avoid being predictable about where he ran and using some sheds and smaller buildings for cover.

He felt a spike of fire in his leg and knew he'd been hit. The shots were silent, although the tufts of grass flying into the air showed the shooter was firing at them. He couldn't be sure, but it appeared as if the shooter was toying with them. He increased his speed, not wanting Jesse more exposed than he already was, and finally reached the tree line. The ordeal wasn't over because he had no idea how many people were there for them. They could be waiting for them within the trees, but George carried on running, aiming for the destination Brody had told him about when they'd spoken earlier.

It was around a mile away. George wasn't sure if he'd be able to run the whole distance while he carried Jesse on his back, but he refused to put him down. They'd be slower, and he also didn't want him to hurt any more than he already was.

Sweat poured off him while he raced through the trees, eventually exiting into the bright daylight once more. He ran, his legs burning with exertion, his lungs screaming at him, sweat pouring off him. He needed to get Jesse to safety and to remove himself from his protection detail. He couldn't be relied upon to keep him safe when he was the one who'd advertised where Jesse was hiding. He'd never forgive himself if something happened to him.

The destination came into view, and a car was waiting at the curb. He saw Jake, Nick and Boomer inside and aimed straight for it. Boomer flung the back door open, and George spun around so Jesse could get into the car.

"Watch his feet. He won't be able to put pressure on them unless there's no other choice; one of you will have to carry him." He could barely get his words out with how fast he was breathing.

He slammed the door shut on Jesse's protests and pivoted to face the way they had run, hand clenching around the gun by his side. A car door opened, and Jake exited before the car sped off.

"What are you doing?"

"Having your back." Jake was carrying a black bag George knew held his sniper rifle.

George spun around. "You need to look after Jesse!"

"There are plenty of people keeping an eye out for Jesse; you don't need to worry about it."

He probably had a lot to worry about regarding his job when this was all over, but for now, he needed to find the shooter.

"Tell me about him." Jake's words were not unexpected, and George sighed, jogging back the way he'd come, although with a slight limp. "Hold up, you're hurt."

"Forget about it for now. Will Kendal, aka Sykes, joined my team a few months after I did, and we hit it off. We were friends right from the start, went through everything together. I was partnered with him on several missions. No marks on his record that I'm aware of; nothing happened while I was on the team with him, no fingers pointed at him for anything. There is nothing I can think of to make him turn on me."

Frustration poured off him. He couldn't believe a man he'd come to think of as his best friend could do this to him. What price had been high enough for Sykes to willingly give up his friend? George could barely contain his anger.

"Talk me through the two conversations."

George did, relaying everything they had said, and about Jesse giving himself away during the first one, and how George had covered it up.

"He must've used your phone to find where you were. It was the same phone you had then, isn't it?"

"The same number but a different phone."

"He must've triangulated your position. Stop beating yourself up about it. Shit happens. You can't be in control of how other people will react to any given situation." They reached the trees, and Jake passed him an earpiece. "He's probably hightailed it by now, but I'll come in from the back and see if we can't figure out what's going on."

George nodded, preferring to defer to Jake despite this being his operation. He didn't deserve to be in charge now. They split up, and George retraced his steps as fast as his injury allowed him. He could no longer feel it, so it couldn't be too bad. He'd survived worse.

"Coming in from behind now."

Jake's voice in his ear was a small comfort, especially when he'd planned on facing Sykes alone, but he needed to focus on the man who had betrayed him.

Raising his gun as he closed in on the house they'd been staying at, he stared into the shadows, checking for movement. He murmured his position to Jake and advanced. Seconds later, he was thrown backward, and pain flared through his right bicep.

"Fuck! I'm hit. He's still here, Reverend," he mumbled into the mic.

"Stay down. I'm coming in."

The split second before he'd fallen, he'd located Sykes's position. He stayed down, pretending to be unable to get up while shifting his gun to his opposite hand that rested against his stomach. There was one thing not many people knew: he was ambidextrous in everything. Sykes knew, but he hoped it was something he'd forgotten.

"I didn't want it to come to this, Wash." Sykes stepped closer. "I wished you hadn't been given the assignment." George didn't say a word. "All he needed to do was return the item, and this would've been shoved under the rug."

George laughed at that. "Who are you kidding, Sykes? You know he'd be taken out on the chance he'd do it again. He'd disappear from the face of the earth, and no one would be the wiser. You know the type of man your boss is."

"True."

"What happened to you, man?"

"Life happened. No one wanted me to work for them until I was approached by my boss. It was a good opportunity." He shrugged, standing several feet from George, pointing his gun.

George fired, barely moving the gun, hitting Sykes in the upper thigh and knocking him backward. The moment he was down, he scrambled for his rifle, but Jake was there to kick it away, stopping him with the end of his rifle.

"I don't think you need it." Jake didn't take his gaze off Sykes. "You doing okay, Wash?"

"Yeah." He had been shot at least three times from the burning coming from several parts of his body, but he was fine. He frowned at the nickname choice from Jake and was going to ask him about it when the sound of incoming people focused him, and he tried to rise, lifting his gun in their direction.

"All good. It's Boss-man and Devil Dog."

George dropped back to the ground as soon as he recognized their faces, not taking anything anyone said for granted anymore.

"Where's Jesse?"

"Hidden." Ian crouched beside him. "How are you holding up?"

"I've been worse." His arm was going numb, which was a good thing as far as he was concerned.

"Come on, stay with me, Nipper. That's an order." Ian slapped his face.

George blinked blearily. "Request to sleep, sir."

"Fuck it. Go to sleep, soldier."

"Boss-man, is that a good idea? We don't know the extent of his…"

He felt a pinprick, and everything went black.

11

JESSE

"Stop! Don't fucking leave him! He's hit!" Jesse tried to open the car door to get out, but the locks engaged. He shoved at the door with his shoulder. When it didn't work, he spun around to stare out the back window, watching George and another guy disappear. "Go back! He's going to get killed!"

Gentle hands grabbed his arms. "Calm down! He'll be fine. More guys are meeting up with them to help him out. He's not alone."

Jesse transferred his focus to the guy sitting next to him in the back of the car. At first glance, sturdy was the first word that popped into Jesse's head. He had dark brown hair, golden amber-colored eyes and took up more room than Jesse wanted him to.

"Who are you?" He didn't know these people. Despite George knowing them, Jesse struggled to trust anyone but George.

"I'm Boomer, and that there is Junior."

"Where are we going?"

"Another safe house until the rest of the team can join us."

"The previous safe houses weren't exactly safe." Jesse crossed his arms and stared out of the window, watching the passing scenery, although his mind was on George.

"It was…unexpected. And no one's fault." Junior snorted at Boomer's words. "*No one's* fault."

The repeated words with the added emphasis grabbed Jesse's attention. He glanced at Boomer, then at Junior through the rearview mirror. "Someone leaked it?"

Boomer shook his head. "No. Our team is tight. It was a mistake."

Jesse recalled George's words before they left the house. *I fucked up. I'm sorry.* "George was *not* at fault." His words were sharp, and Boomer raised his eyebrows.

"I never said he was."

"*You* might not have." Jesse glared at Junior. "What happened? I have a right to know."

Boomer held up a finger and dialed his phone. "We're two minutes out and coming in hot." He faced Jesse. "When we get secure, and the team has returned, we will go through it all with you. I can't tell you anything without the Boss-man's agreement, and he's out saving asses."

Jesse sighed. "This is fucked up. I should've left as soon as I got the damn vase."

"It wouldn't have been the end of it. The same way you've come across the pond to get the vase, they would've gone across the ocean to get you."

Junior's words, spoken in a monotone, matter-of-fact way, sent shivers down Jesse's spine, and he closed his eyes and prayed George would survive whatever was going down at the house. He could read between the lines of what these guys were saying. George was the reason for them being found, but Jesse couldn't understand why. George would never hurt anyone, of that he was sure.

He rubbed at his face, wishing for more sleep than he'd been given over the past couple of days. Had George slept at all in the last forty-eight hours?

The car sped up on a straight road, and Jesse was thrown against the door when it rounded a corner and sped toward a garage door. The metal rose as they approached, and Jesse braced his hands against the headrest in front of him, knowing exactly what would happen.

As expected, he was thrown forward as the car stopped. Both doors were opened, and the men exited. Jesse's door pulled open, and hands grabbed him, swinging him up into strong arms. Jesse automatically gripped Junior's shoulders, so he didn't fall. They hustled through a doorway and into a living room. Junior deposited Jesse on the couch and disappeared.

"Sorry about that. Junior hates it when things go wrong." Jesse raised his eyebrows. Boomer's eyes twinkled. "Would you like a drink?"

"Is this place any more secure than the last two?"

Boomer sat on the coffee table in front of Jesse. "Yes, it is. We eliminated the issue. It shouldn't come up again."

Jesse wondered what issue had been dealt with, but he assumed that was all the information he would be given until the boss arrived. "Who's the boss?"

Boomer grinned. "Boss-man is the nickname for Ian Sawyer. I believe you've already met him."

At the news, Jesse settled further. Ian was a good man; he could tell from when they'd met, even though it had only been once. "And he's out there with George?"

Boomer nodded, standing. "Drink?"

"Do you have coffee? I think I need the caffeine to keep me awake."

"Sure thing."

The curtains were closed, and there was nothing else for

Jesse to focus on apart from the contents of the room. It was bland by all accounts: white walls, wooden furniture, and brown fabric couches and curtains. There were pictures on the walls, showcasing landscapes pictures, but none identifiable about where it was. Jesse had no clue where they were. George hadn't told him an exact location when he'd asked.

"One coffee. I brought milk and creamer in case you use it." Boomer held out a mug, which Jesse gratefully took and cradled in his cold hands.

"Where are we? George never told me what the town was called."

"Gainesville. We're about two hours north of Tampa."

"Can you give me any information about what is happ—?"

"Boomer! Get your ass in here!"

A new voice interrupted his words, and Boomer jumped up and raced through a door to the left of Jesse. Jesse put his mug on the table and shifted to stand up.

"Get your ass back on the couch."

Jesse jumped and peered over his shoulder. Junior stood at the bottom of the stairs.

"Something's happening."

"Yeah, and you need to stay where you are until the Bossman says otherwise." He crossed his arms over his chest, his face resolute.

Jesse cursed and sat back, reaching for his mug again, but straining to hear what was being said in the other room.

"—typical. The damn medical member of the team is the one that's fucking unconscious. They're on their way."

Jesse's heart raced, knowing someone was injured because of him. He wished he had never taken the damn job. This had become much more than he'd expected. Putting his cup down again, he raked his fingers through his hair. The specific words that had been spoken registered abruptly.

"Fuck! George is hurt?" He glanced at Junior, witnessing the tightening of his features but receiving a slight incline of his head.

He stirred, ready to stand, and Junior stepped forward. "Ass down. If you don't keep your ass on the couch, I will make you. George specifically said you weren't to walk unless necessary. This is not necessary."

Jesse slumped back down when Boomer and another guy raced from the room and to the garage entrance. He could do nothing but watch and wait. The noise of a car screeching to a stop was evident before lots of voices shouting and calling. Seconds later, a swarm of guys entered the room, carrying George between them. Jesse's heart stopped at the sight of all the blood.

"You may want to keep him close to the guy. Seems he's going to disobey George's orders unless he's within sight of the man."

"We'll get him situated in a bedroom. Junior, carry Jesse into the room. Boomer, Egghead, get to checking our tails. Polo and Reverend have taken our acquisition to a different location."

Ian's orders were immediately obeyed, and the man disappeared with Devon up the stairs.

"Come on." Junior appeared at his side, bent down and lifted Jesse into his arms with ease.

Despite his gruffness, Junior held him gently and trailed down the hallway without bumping him. When they entered a room, George was already on the bed, and Ian and Devon were stripping him. Junior deposited him in one of the armchairs near the head of the bed. "Stay there so you're not in the way."

"Is he okay?" He leaned his elbows on his knees and hissed when his feet pressed on the floor.

"He'll be fine. He's been shot, but they're all superficial." Devon's voice was matter-of-fact.

"ALL! How many times was he shot?"

Ian glanced at him. "Three."

"Fuck!" They continued tending to George as they answered Jesse's questions. "Where?"

"Once in his calf, one in the upper arm and one that skimmed his hip."

"Can I do anything?"

Ian shook his head, then narrowed his eyes at him. "Let's get the chair closer on his good side, and you can talk to him. See if you can bring him around."

Ian and Devon cleaned George's wounds while Junior lifted Jesse—armchair and all—next to George's head. The moment he was down, Jesse reached for him, resting his hand against his head and stroking his forehead with his thumb. His other hand wrapped around George's and squeezed.

"Hey, George. I need you to wake up. Come on. No more sleeping for you. If I have to stay awake, you do, too; otherwise, it's not fair."

He had no idea what he was mumbling about for the most part. He ignored the other people in the room, focusing solely on George. When George's fingers twitched within his hand, he spoke more, resting his head on the pillow next to him.

"He's coming round."

"What the—? Ow, fuck." George's eyes fluttered open, a glazed look in them despite the glare he sent in Ian's direction.

"Nice of you to join us again."

"Fuck off. That hurts. What the hell did you do to me?"

Jesse glanced over at Ian, watching while he finished

putting the tape over the dressing pressed against George's side.

Devon snorted. "Nothing you wouldn't want us to. I've been told it's like doing a jigsaw."

George's forehead furrowed, and Jesse refrained from rubbing away the tension, not wanting to make him jump.

"What do you mean a jigsaw? What happened?" George's eyes widened, and he tried to rise. "Jesse!"

"Jesse is right next to you." Ian attempted to withhold his grin, but he failed. "Medical people are the worst patients."

Jesse's words dried up the minute George focused on him. He forced a smile, but he wasn't sure he was successful. George tried to move the opposite hand to what Jesse held but groaned instead, closing his eyes as sweat beaded across his upper lip. Jesse squeezed his hand again. "I'm here. Don't worry. Everything's fine."

Peering at him again, George asked, "You're not injured?"

Jesse shook his head. "You helped me."

George closed his eyes again. "No, I didn't. I put you in danger."

Jesse frowned over at Ian and Devon, both of whom had stoic expressions on their faces. "What do you mean?"

"You should move him to another house. He can't be safe when I'm here." George aimed his words at Ian.

"He's safe. The issue was resolved when you left your phone at the house."

"You don't know for sure."

"Yes, we do. There were no trackers on you at all. We checked. There is nothing that can find you."

"What's going on?"

Ian sighed. "We couldn't figure out how you were found at the cabin. It wasn't until George received a second call from Will Kendal that he figured out why the man had called him twice in as many days when he hadn't heard from him in months."

George rolled his head to stare at Jesse. "He'd been using it as a diversion to figure out what we were doing. When he heard you on the other end of the phone, he knew I was protecting you. He must've tracked my phone to find where we were. He'd been at the cabin, and he was the shooter at the house."

"He called you again. It's why you woke me, isn't it?"

George nodded and grimaced. "Yeah. I figured it was too much of a coincidence to have him contact me twice, especially when he asked about you."

"Did you get him?"

"He's being held at a different location." Ian stepped closer, tugging a sheet over the remnants of George's clothes. "You need rest. There are enough of us here to keep Jesse safe, and you need to heal."

"No, we need to—"

"It's an order if it needs to be."

Jesse rolled his lips in, withholding a smile at George being bossed around. He'd have to remember that for the future. He could easily say he'd set Ian on him.

"Rest up. I'll send some food and drinks up shortly."

Ian and Devon left the room, pulling the door closed behind them. Jesse wasn't sure what to do, but there was one thing he had to say.

"Thank you."

George stared at him, eyes wide. "What for? Nearly getting you killed?"

"You saved my life. If you hadn't put the clues together, we'd be in that house and probably dead. Both of us."

"It's because of me he was there at all."

"And as soon as you realized it, you got us out of there."

"We're going to have to agree to disagree about this." He

stared at the ceiling. "They should be getting you far away from me."

Jesse rested his head on the pillow next to him once more. "You can't get rid of me."

George's eyes closed, and he rolled his head toward him again, their lips coming close. Jesse could feel his breath wafting over him. "How are your feet?"

"Sore. I've been carried everywhere so far. Junior lifted the chair with me in it to bring me closer to the bed. I feel like an invalid."

George chuckled. "Ouch. Don't make me laugh."

"Sorry, not sorry."

They were quiet while Jesse mapped the lines and features of George's face. A knock sounded, and the door opened to Junior with a tray of food and drink, his face appearing younger now that he wasn't scowling.

"Nipper. Glad to see you're awake. I've brought your new best friend—Vicodine." He grinned, setting the tray on a small table and bringing it next to Jesse.

George smirked. "Hopefully not for too long."

"All being well, you'll be rocking and rolling again in a few days."

"What's for lunch?"

"Soup. Eat up, and you can have the pills after. You know the drill."

George nodded. "Thanks."

Junior circled to the other side of the bed and slid an arm around his back and under his legs. "This will hurt."

"Don't I kno—fuck!"

Junior sat him upright, and George closed his eyes, his jaw clenching.

"Couldn't you have been a bit more gentle, you big oaf?" Jesse glared at the man he was beginning to think was an asshole.

Junior grinned again, and Jesse hated that expression on him. "It would've made it hurt for longer if I had. Enjoy." He left them, closing the door again.

"He's such an asshole. Are you okay?" Jesse wiped the sweat from George's forehead.

"I'm good." His voice was hoarse, and Jesse wasn't sure he believed him, but he'd give him his delusions.

"Let me know when your stomach has settled, and we'll try you with some soup."

"You don't need to feed me."

Jesse quirked an eyebrow. "You're going to manage it yourself, are you?" George remained silent, staring at the soup, then pouted and clenched his jaw. "It won't be for long. It's the least I can do for you."

"Fine." Jesse raised his eyebrows. "Thanks."

"I won't tell anyone. Promise."

George's mouth twitched, which had been what Jesse had wanted. They were far too serious for his liking. He grabbed the soup and spoon and held it close. Laying a napkin over George's chest, he blew on the soup, cooling it, and held it in front of George's mouth. George hesitated for a second before opening. They continued in the same vein until half of the soup was gone, and George declined any more. Jesse put it on the table and picked up the pills and a bottle of water.

"Open up." Jesse smirked.

George rolled his eyes but acquiesced. Jesse dropped the pills into his mouth and held out the bottle. George took it with his good hand and swallowed all of it.

"Now, you eat."

George stared at Jesse, and he felt his face flush hot. There was the stern, caring man he had fallen for. Jesse's heart jumped, and his breath stuttered. He refused to believe he had fallen in love with this man. It was an impossible situation to be in, and he couldn't promise George anything. All his promises soured to shit.

He rested back in the chair and ate his soup, keeping his gaze on the bowl instead of on George, although he could sense George's eyes on him. When he finished the soup, he couldn't avoid the man any longer.

"Took you long enough. What's got you inside your head?"

The words were spoken the minute Jesse met George's gaze. His cheeks heated, and he, again, cursed his pale skin.

"Just thinking about what's going to happen next."

"I call bullshit, but if you want to do it, fine." George sighed. "I have no idea, to be honest. We need to have a sit down with Ian and see what he wants to do. Baker has ignored the forty-eight hours he'd supposedly given you." George yawned. "We need to figure out what he's likely to do next."

"We can do that later. For now, you need sleep."

George stared at him for a beat. "Only if you sleep, too."

"I'll shout Junior and—"

"No." George patted the side of the bed. "Here."

Jesse bit his lip, heat flowing through him when George's eyes darkened. "Okay."

George slowly slid down the bed, wincing and groaning with each movement, but eventually, he lay prone once more. "Come on. Be careful of your feet."

Jesse stood, withholding a wince as best he could, and slid onto the bed. He scooted closer on his side. George lifted his arm, and Jesse rested his head on his good shoulder. He carefully slipped his arm over George's waist.

They were silent while they got settled. Jesse would've loved to know what George was thinking at that moment. His own thoughts were messed up, but as soon as George's lips pressed against the top of his head, he relaxed. Thoughts could wait.

He didn't think he'd be able to sleep, but he was happy to hear the soft, slow exhales from George. If nothing else, George was resting, and if his being there with him helped him to do it, he would.

1 2

GEORGE

George woke to a contentment he had not felt in…ever. He blinked open his eyes and let them adjust to the different light. Someone had come in and put a lamp on at some point while he'd been sleeping. A sleepy sigh wafted across his neck, and he glanced down at a fast asleep Jesse cuddled up to his side with his legs wrapped around his. Luckily, his feet were missing his injured calf, although he wouldn't have complained if they had been pressing against it, causing him undue pain and suffering. He'd have to be dying before he repositioned Jesse.

He slowly flexed the fingers of his injured arm, wincing when the tightness around his injury pinched. The tape pulled against all three injuries. George rolled his eyes at himself; he couldn't believe he'd managed to get shot three times. It was something he was sure his teammates would not let him live down any time soon. His mouth curved when he imagined the jokes he'd no doubt receive.

Jesse snuggled closer in his sleep—not that he could get much nearer than he already was. George nuzzled his nose into the curls on top of his head and inhaled deeply. He hadn't expected to feel anything for Jesse, especially with how their first meeting went, but he was beginning to believe he needed to stop expecting things in his life to go how he wanted them to.

Life as a bachelor had always been on his agenda. He wouldn't knowingly invite anyone to deal with his father.

Damn. His father would be expecting to hear how things were going. Had Ian heard from him? He didn't want to ask and find out his father had been annoying. The man was a dog with a bone and would do anything to ensure George lived up to his name. Disappointment would be the first thing that was vocalized when he found out what had happened to George. He doubted his father would ask how he was healing. His mother would have, but only after his father had finished his rant.

"You think too loud."

Jesse's voice rasped through the quiet, silencing his troublesome thoughts. "I apologize." He cleared his throat, the hoarseness apparent in his voice. "Did you sleep well?"

"As long as when I move, I haven't left a wet patch on your T-shirt, I slept well, especially as I wasn't expecting to."

"Ah, the morning-after drool party. Yeah, I understand."

Jesse snorted and wriggled, pressing his knee closer to George's groin. He grimaced, trying not to let his cock react to the action, especially when he felt Jesse's erection resting against his hip.

"I feel like I could sleep for another week."

"We both probably could if time allowed. How are your feet feeling?"

"Sore, but more manageable than yesterday. I'm going to get some more cream and bandages to clean them up again. Hopefully, I can put pressure on them a little today."

"Don't push yourself too hard. We have time to let them heal, so I'm told. Otherwise, I wouldn't be laid up in this bed. If I have my way, I'll be at least sitting on the couch today."

"What time is it anyway?" Jesse yawned, covering his mouth with his hand and scrunching his nose and eyes like a newborn baby about to cry.

"No idea. If I were to guess by the amount of light coming through the sides of the curtains, I'd say five or six in the morning."

"We've been asleep that long?" Jesse's eyes flashed open. "Wow, we did need it."

"I've put you through a lot over the past few days." George sighed, staring at the ceiling.

Jesse cupped his jaw and pulled his face to him. "You've kept me safe these past few days." The softly spoken words threaded through the quiet, and George closed the distance, a chaste meeting of their lips.

There was a gentle knock on the door, and George cleared his throat. "Yeah."

Jesse tried to move, but George firmed his arms around him, keeping him where he was.

Devon entered, carrying a tray with what smelled like toast and coffee. George's stomach grumbled, and Jesse snorted, burying his laughter in George's chest.

"Good morning to you, too." Devon shook his head, smiling. "I heard voices, and I thought you'd be hungry because you slept through dinner."

"Thanks."

Jesse sat upright, and George let him go this time, immediately missing his warmth. He tried to sit up himself and hissed through his teeth. Devon and Jesse flanked him, helping him to rise.

"This is going to get old." George closed his eyes when a wave of dizziness hit him.

"You'll be fighting fit in a couple of days. Be patient."

George narrowed his eyes at him. "Like you would be?"

Devon chuckled. "Point taken. At least try. We're safe here for now."

"You need to get back to Kristen, don't you?"

Devon nodded. "Yeah, but she's safe while we deal with Kendal."

The reminder of who was the cause of his injuries and putting Jesse's life in danger had his hunger receding.

"Has he said anything?" He stood, using Devon as a crutch to gain his balance, and braced his legs to take his full weight. His calf and hip screamed at him, but his shoulder wasn't too bad if he kept it in one position; he'd need a sling soon, but the more he could be without it, the better.

"No. He says he wants to see you."

Reading Devon's expression gave George his opinion about the idea, but George would do whatever was needed to ensure Jesse's safety.

"Let's eat, then we'll be down. Do you have some spare clothes for us?"

Devon indicated the chest where two piles of clothes were stacked. They must have been put there while they were sleeping. He glanced at Jesse. What did he think of them being seen wrapped around each other while they slept? If his darkening cheeks were any indication, he was embarrassed.

Devon hid a smile behind his hand, and George glared at him. "We retrieved your things from the cabin as well."

Jesse's head rose. "Everything?"

Devon nodded. "Everything that was there, anyway. We don't know if anyone had been in there before the team arrived, but nothing appeared to have been disturbed. There was no evidence of the cabin having been searched."

George frowned. "Why wouldn't it have been searched if

they were after the vase? Surely, the first thing to do would be to check whether Jesse was carrying it with him."

Devon shrugged. "Unless they were meticulous and put things back neatly as if they had all the time in the world, it wasn't searched." He peered at George. "Is it something Kendal would be capable of?"

George shook his head. "He was always untidy. It drove the team nuts. I suppose he could have changed, but you know as well as I do, things like this don't usually change."

"Yeah. It was a long shot. Another question we can ask him."

George sighed again. "We'll be down in a little while."

Devon nodded and left the room. He would have to ask Jesse to help him get dressed because he hadn't thought past the idea of dismissing Devon.

"Eat. We'll juggle the clothing dilemma afterward."

Jesse grinned at him, and George shuffled to the small table surrounded by two chairs Jesse was already sitting at. He gingerly lowered into the seat, positioning himself as best he could. A plate of toast appeared before him, and a mug of coffee was pushed forward. He winked at Jesse and grabbed the coffee, groaning when the first sip touched his tongue. The first cup of coffee in the morning was the best thing in the world as far as George was concerned.

When his eyes opened, his gaze stopped on the flushed skin covering Jesse's face and neck and the clenched fists on the table. "What?"

Jesse blinked repeatedly and cleared his throat. "Nothing." His voice was raspy.

George's mouth twitched. "See or hear something you like?"

"Nope." The shredded napkin told another story, but George wouldn't push.

They finished breakfast in companionable silence until

Jesse stood. "Come on, big guy. Let's figure out how to get you out of those rags."

George glanced down his body, understanding what he meant by the flaps of fabric that had been cut away from his body to reach his injuries. Bracing himself on the table with his good hand, he rose, wincing a little as his skin pulled and stung.

"I think the best way to do this would be for you to stand holding onto the chair, then I can pull your trousers off and replace them with the new ones without you having to move too much."

The idea of Jesse being on his knees in front of him had his dick reacting, and he closed his eyes, trying to think about something else before he made a fool of himself.

Jesse's muted laughter had George peering at him. "What?"

"There's no way you'll get that to go down until you're dressed and ready to face your teammates."

The reminder of what he would face helped to calm his libido. Without replying, he stood where Jesse had told him to and gripped the back of the chair. Jesse drifted closer, his mouth lifting at the corner and sank to his knees. George stared resolutely at the wall opposite him while Jesse's hands unfastened his belt and pants, lowering them with care over the dressing covering his hip. He lifted one foot at a time to slide them off, his injured calf burning with the extra weight despite it being for mere seconds. George's briefs were barely staying on, the waistband the only part that hadn't been cut away.

"I think these are done for. I'll cut the band to make it easier." Jesse reached for the scissors that had been left on the dresser and dropped back to his knees.

The cold metal against his skin and so close to his erection should've cooled his arousal, but in fact, it sent him higher, his breathing loud in the quiet room. He would have to wait for several minutes after this before he could face his colleagues. The snip of the scissors jerked him back to the present, and George jumped when Jesse's hand grabbed the fabric and tugged it down his legs.

George firmed his jaw and breathed deeply. He tried to ignore that he was naked from the waist down with Jesse in a position George would love to have taken advantage of had he been in better condition.

Jesse tapped each of his feet and slid the loose fabric up his legs and over his dressings before resting it against his waist. Dropping his gaze to his pants, he saw sweats, which were the easiest thing to wear when he would need access to each of the bullet sites for dressing changes.

"Thanks."

"No problem. Now for the hard part."

"Cut this one off. I'll talk you through how to get a T-shirt over a gunshot wound."

Jesse bit his lip, expertly wielding the scissors once more. When the T-shirt fell away, George tugged the lip from between Jesse's teeth. "What have I told you about that?"

Jesse swiped his tongue over his lips and the tip of George's finger. Their gazes connected. George had no idea what they were, but he didn't care to define it. He lowered his head, licking into Jesse's mouth immediately and receiving a groan in return. Unable to stop himself, he cupped the back of Jesse's head and tasted every inch of the inside of his mouth. When he tried to wrap his free arm around Jesse's back, he pulled away with a curse.

"Sorry. Fuck, that hurt."

"You need to get it in a sling to stop moving it." Jesse reached up and swiped at George's bottom lip.

He hated to admit it, but it was exactly what he needed, but he didn't like the idea of being restricted. Jesse reached for the T-shirt, and George talked him through how to get it over his arm and head without putting too much pressure on the wound. Once it was done, he was sweating and sat on the chair by the table while Jesse put some socks on him, then got himself dressed.

George's new favorite thing in the world to watch.

When they were both presentable, Jesse picked up the tray of breakfast plates, and they descended the stairs slowly, George unwilling to admit how much he leaned on the banister. They went to the kitchen, where the sounds of conversation seemed to be coming from.

"Ah, here they are. Glad to see you up and about. How are you feeling?" Ian came forward and rested his hand on George's good shoulder, squeezing gently.

"Good. Could do with more coffee." He quirked his mouth.

"Couldn't we all? Sit."

George sat at the large, ten-seat wooden table, and Jesse dropped beside him. Ian brought over two mugs filled with coffee and placed them in front of each of them. Jesse wrapped his hand around the mug but didn't drink.

"Do you have hot chocolate, by any chance?" George's request brought several raised eyebrows, but Ian didn't bat an eyelash and returned to the kettle and grabbed a new mug. George pulled the cup from Jesse's hand and pushed it across the table toward Junior, who accepted it with a grin.

Jesse accepted the new cup with a smile and ducked his head. George didn't care what anyone else thought; he wanted Jesse happy.

And wasn't that a shock?

George frowned at the top of the table. What was it about the guy that threw every one of George's preconceived notions out the window?

His family had never been bothered about his sexual

orientation, but he never made it common knowledge when he was in the military. When he'd retired, he hadn't changed that. He didn't see the point in making waves when he didn't have a relationship to think about. Now, Jesse had him twisted into knots. His mind told him to stop getting involved any deeper because he wasn't worth Jesse's time. If his parents couldn't see any good in him, what would a potential boyfriend see?

"George?"

He raised his head, staring across the table at Ian's raised eyebrows. "Sorry?"

"Everything okay?"

He nodded and sipped his coffee. "Sure. What's the plan?"

"Kendal is not giving up anything. He wants to talk to you and you alone. It's up to you. You don't have to. I know how difficult this must be."

George shook his head. "I'll see him. If the asshole could turn on someone who was his closest friend, there's no telling what he's capable of."

He glanced at Jesse, finding his face pale in the bright overhead lights.

"All right. I'll take you over there after lunch. First, let's get your arm in a sling." Devon appeared at his side, and the sling took seconds to secure, but the relief was instantaneous. He blew out the first full breath he'd taken in days. Jesse had more people to protect him now. George could relax a little.

Devon held out some pills to him, and he washed them down with his coffee. "Now you're set for a bit; let's head to Brody. There's a lot we all need to catch up on."

"Do you want me to go back upstairs or something?"

Jesse's voice wavered, but Ian beat George to an answer. "No, we need your intel as well."

Two hours later, after receiving a bucketload of

information from Brody and his contacts, George was ready to beat Sykes within an inch of his life when he found out exactly what type of man Baker was. How could the person George had known put their lot in with a guy like Baker? It was worse than the selling of artifacts and people. Much worse. He had business in a lot of places most people only see in horror films. Jesse's face paled more and more during the information session they'd had until George pretended to be tired. Jesse jumped up to help him back to the room and curled around him when they laid down. George would visit with Sykes later, once he'd calmed down.

He had no words he could give Jesse to make what he'd heard any easier to bear, except they would find him and take him down. George promised that much. When Jesse's silent tears soaked into his T-shirt, he feigned ignorance and silently promised retribution.

13

JESSE

The nausea in Jesse's stomach rolled and pitched when he'd listened to the team explain exactly what and who Robert Baker was. A monster would be too kind a name to call him. Not only did the man steal and sell artifacts, but he stole babies and children and sold them as adoptions to anyone willing to pay the price, no questions asked.

In some ways, he wished he hadn't become embroiled in the business, but on the other hand, he was glad it was finally being brought to the team's attention.

They had been in contact with someone called Carter, who had been able to provide some more information for them. All in all, Robert Baker was the worst of the worst.

As he laid entwined with George again, he tried to work through his options. If he gave the location of the vase, it wouldn't stop the team from trying to take Baker down. There was no point in giving the vase back and asking for the slate to be wiped clean. Too many bullets had been fired for that to happen.

"You're thinking hard over there." George's sleepy voice was warm and comforting.

Jesse closed his eyes and nuzzled his cheek against George's chest. "I've been trying to figure out what to do."

"About?"

"The vase."

George's chest rose and fell several times before he spoke, "I would double-check with Ian or Devon, but I think you'd be fine sending it to its owner. This has gone far beyond the vase now."

"That was my conclusion, too." Jesse pursed his lips and sighed. "It's in a luggage storage facility near the airport."

Silence claimed the room until George pressed a kiss to his head. "Thank you for telling me."

Jesse shrugged a shoulder. "It seems pointless keeping it a secret now. And besides, someone else should know, in case…"

George's arm tightened around him, and his breathing hitched. "Nothing will happen to you."

"I don't want anyone else to get hurt because of my decisions. It's bad enough you have been. Nobody should pay with their health or their lives." He sniffed. "I need to find a different job. I can't do this anymore."

"Look at me." Jesse didn't want to. "Don't make me move my injured arm to lift your chin, Jesse." He rolled his eyes, but his mouth twitched as he raised his head. "There are other ways to make money for those people you help, like fundraisers and stuff. I'm sure we can figure out something. I do, however, think you need some protection. At least, for a short while after this blows over."

Jesse snorted. "And paying someone to do it would take money away from the people who needed it. No, thanks. I'll be fine on my own."

"You need someone to keep you safe. Someone like Ian or Devon who will do whatever it takes to keep you from harm." George's voice cracked, but he cleared it, possibly trying to hide the sound.

"You mean as you did?"

It was Jesse's turn to get George to meet his gaze this time, but he could move his arm. He cupped George's cheek, pulling him to face him.

"I put you in danger."

"And saved my life."

"If it wasn't for me—"

"I'd be dead."

George inhaled through his teeth, his eyes closing, the lines deepening on his forehead. "It's not an image I want to consider right now."

"It's the truth." Jesse smoothed his thumb across George's cheek. "I won't deny you played a part in us being found, but you were also instrumental in getting us out of there. Twice. You work with an amazing team. You wouldn't be here with them if you weren't as good as they are."

When George opened his eyes, they glistened with unshed tears. Jesse couldn't take him appearing so defeated, and fastened their lips together, trying to show George exactly what he thought of him. He gentled the kiss after several long moments and snuggled as close as he could get.

It would hurt when he had to leave this man.

JESSE GRUMBLED when George said he had to sit with the team again, but not because it was tedious. When George sat upright for any length of time, it seemed to drain his energy, and he spent the next couple of hours sleeping. George needed the rest, that was a given, but his team kept requesting George's presence when he could've probably been given the highlights later. Jesse was certain they were only doing it because George had told them to keep him in the loop, but Jesse wished they would let him rest instead.

George's movements had eased some in the day they'd been cooped up, but Jesse knew they wouldn't be staying for much longer. Whenever George slept, Jesse retreated to the same room because he was uncomfortable around the other team members. It wasn't that he thought they would harm him, but tension rode the room when he was in it, even after he'd told them where the vase was.

Ian had agreed the item didn't need to be returned and could either stay safely hidden or sent on its way as soon as Jesse was free and clear of the trouble hounding him.

George exhaled heavily and shifted on the bed, and Jesse's mouth curled at the stress-free expression on his face. It wasn't often Jesse saw him so vulnerable, and the idea George was comfortable to do so around Jesse softened him somewhat.

A gentle knock came, and Devon's head came around the door. "Sorry. I wasn't sure whether you wanted to know, but your parents have called your cell phone. They didn't leave a message, but that's twice in the last hour. We think it would be okay to speak to them, although we'd like to listen in if you'd agree to it. As a precaution."

Jesse's heart jumped, and he frowned as he rose to sit. He hadn't spoken to his parents in several weeks, but it was unusual for them to call him. It was usually him calling them.

"What's wrong?"

George's scratchy voice had Jesse jerking his head around to stare at him. "What do you mean?"

"Do they not usually call you?" George winced when he sat upright, rubbing a hand over his eyes before he met Jesse's gaze again. "You frowned. Is it unusual for them to call?"

"No…" His voice sounded unsure, and both men picked up on it instantly.

"I think you should call them." Despite the measured hesitation, Devon's tone brooked no argument, and he left.

Jesse nodded, staring at the floor. Were they caught in the crossfire of what Jesse had inadvertently started?

"Jesse?" He blinked across at George. "Let's not borrow trouble. We'll see what they say first. If you're all right with us listening in, we might be able to pick up on clues."

Jesse nodded, wringing his hands. "What if I've hurt them without realizing?"

George rested his hands over Jesse's. "We'll figure it out. No matter what."

"How did they know my parents called? You left my mobile behind when we first left."

"Brody diverted the calls and messages to another phone to stop it from being traced."

"Ah, okay."

Swallowing hard, Jesse stood, helping George until he found his balance. "God, I hate being like this."

The cute grumble made George more human in Jesse's eyes, but he held back on voicing it, knowing he'd earn one of George's scowls if he did. They made their way down the stairs and to the room that had been commandeered as the meeting slash computer room. The one and only time Jesse had seen Brody out of the room was when he'd run out of coffee, and a scowling hulk of a man had stomped into the kitchen, filled his mug and left again.

Jesse entered the room behind George and settled himself in the seat he usually took, furthest away from the computers.

"Jesse." Ian beckoned him over, and Jesse glanced at George first, then drifted over to the man. "If you could sit here for me, we'll put the phone on speaker as soon as you're ready." Ian squeezed his shoulder. "I'm sorry for the intrusion, but they may know something. Treat this call as if it's a normal one but lift your hand if you notice anything unusual. We can go back over it at the end and talk it through. Does that sound okay?"

"It's fine." His voice cracked, and he cleared his throat, taking the seat Ian indicated. He was immediately aware of George sitting beside him, and he glanced to the side. "I'm ready." He wasn't, but there was no point in delaying it further.

A ringing tone peeled through the room, and he winced. A hand rested over his, and he forced a smile for George.

"Is that you, Jesse?"

"Yeah. How are you, Mum?"

"How do you think I am, Jesse? You've not called us for weeks, and I've had to resort to calling you. How long would you have gone without speaking to your parents?" His mother sniffed, and Jesse closed his eyes.

"Sorry, Mum. I've been busy with work. You know how time flies when I get engrossed in what I'm doing." It wasn't a lie.

"But you *promised* you'd keep in touch. Especially being as far away as you are now. Where did you say you were?"

Jesse blinked and lifted his hand. "I'm visiting a friend as well as working, remember? I'll be home soon, and I'll take you to the restaurant you like."

"When are you coming home?" His mother's voice had the bite it usually had when she spoke to him, but there was something else behind it...a tremor of sorts. He lifted his hand again.

"I'm not sure yet. I'll let you know as soon as I've finished here."

"You need to come home, Jesse. Your father wants to talk to you."

There was a rustle, and his father's voice came across loud and clear. "You're upsetting your mother, son. You need to come home. Stop messing around wherever you are and come back. You have responsibilities here. There was no need to go flying halfway around the world to work. You could do it from here."

Tears trickled down his cheeks, and he blinked them away as he raised his hand once more. "Once I've finished here, I'll make sure to stick closer to home."

"Not good enough, son. Get your backside home. You're needed here."

Jesse clenched his jaw. Whenever he spoke to his father, it always ended up with an argument between them, but he didn't want to do it in front of these people.

"Be natural. No one will care if you fight back," George's whisper was soft in his ear and warm against his skin.

"You know I'm not, Dad." Jesse let his anger rise but knew he had to keep his wits to stop him from saying something that would give anything away.

"Not what?"

"Needed there. I never have been."

"Of course, you're needed. How can your friend catch up with you if you're not here?"

"Friend?"

"Yes, friend. Your friend from college dropped by this morning, saying he'd like to get in touch after not seeing you for so long. People are relying on you, young man. You need to stop messing around and get back to doing what you should be doing."

"And what's that, Dad? Being at your beck and call and being ignored the rest of the time?" Jesse huffed a laugh. "You know what, whatever. Which friend was it?"

"Oliver Hamilton." His hand shot up.

"Do you have a number for him? I can call him and explain the situation."

"No, I don't, and anyway, it doesn't matter because we offered for him to stay here until you can get back."

Jesse's heart pounded. His eyes widened, and he stared at George. George motioned for him to continue but placed an arm around his shoulder.

"Okay, great. That was good of you." He glanced at Ian and mouthed, "Do I talk to the guy now?" Ian shook his head. Jesse focused back on his father. "I can't talk to him right this minute because I'm actually in the middle of something, but I'll talk to him later."

"I can't believe you don't have two minutes to say hello to an old friend. We didn't bring you up to be so dismissive."

"You didn't bring me up at all," he murmured, closing his eyes again.

Despite their differences, he wouldn't want any harm to come to his parents.

"What was that?"

"Nothing, Dad. I have to go."

"I'll tell Oliver you'll call in a couple of hours."

"Okay. Tell Mum I said goodbye."

The phone went quiet, and Jesse knew his father had hung up without a goodbye from himself. Nothing unusual in that respect.

Jesse bowed his head. George's warm hand cupped his nape, and it settled him. Taking a deep breath, he threw a smile in George's direction and focused on Ian. "Sorry. You didn't need to hear my drama."

"Don't apologize for them." Ian's words were sharp, and Jesse jerked. "Sorry." Ian blew out a breath. "People who don't worship their kids don't deserve them."

"They weren't always like this." He didn't know why he was trying to defend them.

Silence filled the room for several seconds before George cleared his throat. "You indicated several things in the conversation. Can you explain them?"

"I flagged the areas so we could re-listen to them," Brody explained. "This was the first."

He listened. "Yeah. Mum has never asked where I was. She never cared enough to know. And I know the next one. I flagged it because Mum's voice didn't sound right. She's never had a tremble in her voice. She'd prefer not to speak instead of being caught as being anything less than perfect. Even in her grief." The last words came out quietly.

They listened when his father spoke. "I never told them where I was going. How would he know I flew halfway around the world?" The next flag. "I went to school with Samuel Hamilton, not Oliver."

George grew still. "I think the 'Oliver' was a message to me."

Jesse frowned at him. "Why?"

George stood, pacing the small area. "Will Kendal is named Sykes after the film *Oliver*. He either orchestrated this before we caught him, or it's a message from the top."

Ian crossed his arms over his chest. "It could be either. I think it's time we had a proper chat with Kendal."

"I agree."

"Let's grab some lunch first, and we'll take a ride over." Ian dropped his arms and strode for the door.

George trailed over to Jesse and crouched in front of him, wincing when he did. "Are you okay?"

"Get up! You'll hurt yourself!" Jesse stood, almost knocking George over. He cringed when George hissed and stood gingerly.

"I would've said I'd be fine, but damn, you're like an eager puppy when you're riled."

A snort sounded from behind George, and Jesse threw a narrow-eyed glare at Brody.

George cupped his jaw. "Are you okay?"

"Not really. I hate the idea that they're in danger because of me."

"Come on. We need food." George rested his hand on the back of Jesse's neck again, and they followed the others to the kitchen, where the conversation was loud and inviting.

Jesse had never had many friends, and there was only Linc who was in his life now—and Rio, he supposed. His parents wouldn't know any different as distant as they had been since Beau had gotten sick, more so when he died.

A plate slid in front of him, containing a sandwich, an apple and a yogurt. He glanced up at Junior, who winked and sat opposite him, devouring his sandwich as if he had not eaten for days. He couldn't eat much, but he managed a few bites of the sandwich and the yogurt. Anything else would come straight back up.

There had to be something he could do to get everyone out of the mess he'd created.

14

GEORGE

Facing Sykes was the last thing George wanted to do, but he knew it needed to happen. Sykes had been held for two days now, and the more information they got, the better they'd be able to protect Jesse. The problem was, he wasn't sure he would be able to stop from breaking his hand on the guy he'd thought was his friend.

"You need to make sure you don't go hurting yourself, Nipper. We need you fighting fit for this, and if Kendal gets you worked up, you won't be able to do it because you'll have beaten the crap out of him." Devon drove them toward the house they were keeping Sykes at.

George set his jaw. "I know. I can't guarantee it, but I'll try my best."

"I know you will." George raised his eyebrows at him. "You have something—or should I say someone—who means more to you than revenge."

His face flushed with heat, and he stared out of the window instead of replying. Yes, Jesse meant something more to him. More than friends. More than friends with benefits. More than…most everything else in his life. His heart raced. When had it happened? Their attraction had been there sizzling under the surface, and they had let it take over once or twice, but when had it become more to George?

"Don't overthink it, Nipper." Ian's voice held a bite of humor.

"Fuck off."

They chuckled but said no more, which George was grateful about because he needed time to work through it himself. What would his parents say? "Have you heard anything else from my father?"

"No, but I have been selective with the calls I answer at the moment, as have the rest of the team."

"Why?"

"You're not the only one who has 'friends' who could crawl out of the woodwork. We're all taking precautions."

The weight of his words hit George like a tank. He'd been so immersed in his and Jesse's life, he hadn't considered what it meant for the rest of the team. "Sorry."

"Don't you dare be sorry for something out of your control. It's as much my fault as it is yours, and that's next to nothing. I could've chosen anyone to protect Jesse, and it could've caused the same situation. Maybe not with Kendal, but with a different 'ghost.' If anything, I believe Kendal didn't go in as hard as he could've because it was you."

"What do you mean?"

"You said so yourself, it seemed like he was toying with you when he was shooting, and you also mentioned he'd said he wished it wasn't you who had been protecting Jesse. He obviously feels something."

If that was the case, he shouldn't have done anything. As far as George was concerned, Sykes had left their friendship deep in the lake at the cabin.

They exited the car in an area heavily surrounded by

trees, and George was concerned about the places people could hide in.

"We can hide as well as anyone else can." Devon clapped him on his good shoulder.

"Will you take the sling off me, please?" George faced him.

"I don't think it's a good—"

"I will *not* show up with my arm in a sling showing weakness. If it helps, I will leave my hand in my pocket the whole time to give it some relief."

Devon glanced at Ian, who nodded, and with slow movements, slipped George's arm free of the sling. George winced at the action and was grateful when he did what he'd said he would and pushed his hand into the pocket of his jeans despite it pressing against his hip injury. He stepped around Devon and strode for the house, both men following him.

"Afternoon, Boss-man. Devil Dog. Wash." Jake nodded at George, whose eyebrows rose at hearing his original nickname instead of his new one.

"How has he been?" Ian asked.

"Quiet. He'll drink but won't eat."

"He's not eaten?" George was surprised because Sykes had always had a huge appetite.

"No, nothing."

It wasn't unusual for them to have to go without food for a short length of time when they were in the military, but to do so now… What was Sykes up to? Was he trying to make George feel sorry for him?

"Anything I need to know before I go in there?" George wanted this over and done with. Jesse was being protected by Nick and Brody, but he wasn't happy to be away from him.

"The only time he talks is to ask to speak with you."

"Why have *you* not tried talking to him?" His question was aimed at Ian, who was the best interrogator around.

"I thought he might be more likely to talk to you. I can tell by observing him he could withstand a lot. If I can avoid it—for my own sanity—I will."

Jake led the way to the basement of the house, and when George descended, his spine tingled. The stone walls appeared as ominous as they would in a horror movie, and there were no windows, only two small bulbs. If he had been in a laughing mood, he would've chuckled at the memories of the interrogation training he'd done years prior. Each of them had taken turns being the hostage and chained in a similarly fashioned room.

Sykes lay on a bare mattress, his wrists shackled above his head with a chain long enough for him to pull himself to sitting, which he did when George's feet hit the cement floor.

"Wash." Sykes's voice was hoarse. "I didn't think you would come."

"You don't have anything important to tell me; otherwise, you would've told them." He thumbed over his shoulder.

"I never said it was either important or unimportant. I said I wanted to talk to you."

"Talk. I don't have all day."

The chains rattled while Sykes got as comfortable as he was likely to be able to. "You're one difficult man to take down."

George snorted. "You didn't want me dead, Sykes." He saw the slight widening of the man's eyes, confirming Ian's belief.

"I do my job."

"Which is?"

"Whatever needs to be done."

George shook his head. "You've gone down in my estimations. You could've come to me, and I would've helped you find work."

Sykes glanced behind George, then refocused on him. "I

was passed over by Trident. I wasn't going to add it to the list of things that made you better than me."

George withheld his flinch. "Better than you? What are you talking about?"

"The descendant of a long line of military people. You got so much special treatment because of who your father is."

"It was *not* my fault, Sykes."

Sykes snorted and coughed. "Maybe not, but it made your career easier than most."

It was George's turn to laugh. "Or harder than most. You have an idea of what I went through. Am going through." He fisted his hand. "What does Robert Baker want?"

He needed to move the conversation in the direction they wanted instead of wallow over their past. Why Sykes believed George had an easy life, he didn't know. It wasn't like he hadn't laid his whole life out in front of Sykes before.

"Mr. Flint."

George clenched his jaw. "Why?"

"Initially, it was to return his missing artifact. Now, he wants recompense."

His blood ran cold at the words said so matter-of-factly in his best friend's voice. "In what way?"

Sykes curled one side of his mouth. "The only way he'll deem it acceptable."

"Stop talking in riddles, Sykes!" George could sense his temper fraying, and he inhaled.

"Mr. Flint will be auctioned off, which is why no harm will ever come to him. At least before he's sold. After that, there's no guarantee."

George stared at him, nostrils flaring. What had happened to his friend? If this was how he'd always been, why hadn't George seen it? Had he been friends with a psychopath all this time?

"What does it matter to Baker? If the artifact was returned, why would he not let it go?"

Sykes chuckled. "Baker has to do what he's told as much as the rest of us. You didn't think Baker ran the show, did you?" He smirked. "Many people are embroiled in this *state of affairs*."

George frowned at the emphasis he put on the words. "What did Baker hope to gain from getting Trident involved?"

"A quicker result and a new ally."

"A new ally?"

"A tangled web we weave is not just a figure of speech when it comes to this business. It's impossible not to have contacts everywhere if you want to sweep things under the rug, so to speak."

George hesitated. "Why are you willing to give us information?"

"I know I've chosen the wrong side, Wash. I can't change it, but I can change what happens from here. I won't be around much longer; I need to give you as much as I can."

"Why won't you be around much longer?"

"One of three results will be the outcome of this…prison. One, I will be found and freed by Baker's people, then he will kill me because he knows I'll have told you everything. Two, you or your men kill me for what I've put you and a whole heap of others through."

When Sykes didn't continue, George prodded him. "And three?"

"Three, I will die because my own body is failing me."

"What?"

"I have a brain tumor. I've been living with it for years, but the treatments are expensive. It was the reason for aligning with Baker in the first place. He offered enough money to wash away the issues I had. In the beginning, I didn't know what he did, but the more I worked for him, the deeper I sank until there was no way I could get out."

George swayed, and a chair appeared behind him. He sat, wincing, and rubbed a hand over his face. "You should have told me!" He couldn't believe the reason for Sykes's defection was something so close to the heart of the man he was willing to hand over to Baker.

"What's done is done."

"Do you know what Jesse does with the items he retrieves?"

Sykes shook his head. "It wasn't for me to know the reason. I needed to end it."

George blanched. "Jesse gets paid by people to retrieve stolen artifacts. The money he makes goes to charities that help medical expenses for those who are dealing with cancer." His voice was strained, the words barely audible.

He watched the information wash over Sykes, his eyes widening when he understood. George stood, clearing his throat. "I have to get back."

"Baker won't stop, Wash. He has too many people."

George glanced over his shoulder. "You give Trident every single piece of information you have before your time is over, and we'll take him down."

He climbed the stairs, his limp slowing him, and strode to the exit, gulping in the fresh air. Dropping to the steps at the front of the house, he winced again, having forgotten about his wounds. He stared into the trees, the memories of his and Sykes's past rushing past his eyes. His best friend was dying, and there was no cure. He needed information.

He needed Jesse.

George aimed straight for the bedroom when he returned to the house, racing up the stairs despite the pain it caused him. He had to check that Jesse was all right. Bursting through the door, he received a yell and a curse from Jesse.

"What the hell, George?" Jesse stood with his hand over his chest. "I think I've been scared enough lately. Jesus."

George said nothing but stalked over to him and wrapped his good arm around him, his injured one resting against Jesse's hip. He hadn't put the sling back on yet, but he would. He needed to feel Jesse, alive and well, in his arms first.

Jesse's arms came around him, tentatively caressing his back, and George closed his eyes. "What's wrong?"

He inhaled deeply, the clean scent of Jesse advertising he'd had a shower. His arms tightened for a moment, then he released him, dropping a kiss to his head before stepping back.

"We need to go downstairs. I'll go through everything Sykes said with them all. I have some thoughts I need to talk through with all of you."

Jesse frowned and smoothed George's forehead with his thumb. "Something's upset you."

"It's…" He shook his head. "Come on."

He marched to the door, but Jesse's words stopped him. "Is there anything I can do?"

George swallowed, staying facing the door and pressing his hand against it as he lowered his head. "No, but thank you."

He descended the stairs at a slower speed than earlier, his eyes focused on the floor in front of him. He couldn't believe Sykes was dying. After everything they had been through in the years they spent in the Navy, and it was his own body killing him. Slightly ironic.

"Nipper."

George blinked. "Hey, Nick. Everything okay?"

Nick crossed his arms over his chest, and his jaw twitched. "I'm sorry for giving you shit before. It was uncalled for."

George withheld his snort. Barely. "No problem."

"It was *my* problem, and I was an ass."

"Does that mean you're going to have a whole personality change?"

Nick raised his eyebrows and cracked a grin. "Not on your life. You have to put up with my assholeness."

"Joy," he deadpanned.

"Everyone is waiting. Is Jesse coming?"

"He's—"

"I'm here."

George watched Jesse circle the end of the stairs, and his mouth dried. There was something about the guy he couldn't ignore, and he was getting to the stage where he didn't want to ignore it.

"Get in here!" Devon whispered.

The three of them ran toward the room, stopping when Devon held out a palm and rested a finger against his mouth.

"—did you ask for us to work the case if you're going to ignore what we do?" Ian's voice was hard when he spoke.

"It's in everyone's best interests if you return the two people who belong to me, Mr. Sawyer."

George's blood heated at the words spoken in such a monotone voice; it could've been computerized if it wasn't for the audible breathing and sighing.

"It won't be possible, I'm afraid, Mr. Baker. We don't have anyone who belongs to you."

"You're playing a dangerous game, Lieutenant."

"Toying with people's lives is not a game. They have their own choices."

There was a pause. "I'm willing to give them both a choice. Return them to me, and no harm will come to them while they are within my home. If they don't wish to, their loved ones can pay their price."

Jesse gave a barely audible gasp, and his hand covered his mouth. George ignored the need to comfort him and concentrated on what was happening.

"I'm sure I can speak for them both when I say they need more assurances. Saying no harm will come to them while they are *within your home* is not enough. How long will they be within your home, Baker? And will they be safe outside of it?"

"You have twelve hours to make your decision."

The phone beeped.

"And you thought I was an asshole," Nick quipped.

Ian glared at him. "George, tell us your thoughts on your conversation with Kendal."

George sighed. "Well, I believe him for what it's worth. The thing I don't understand is his emphasis on 'state of affairs.' It was like it was a code for something, but nothing I can think of in our past points to it. If it was a code for me, I have no idea what it is."

"I've been thinking about it, too. What if it's the person who's behind it all?" Devon crossed his arms, bracing his feet. "Kendal might not know who it is, but he might have an idea about what their position is. He said a lot about it being swept under the rug."

"Brody, see what you can find out about the people Baker interacts with. Anyone who is in a chain of command or political alliances." Ian sighed. "Plan C...or whatever letter we're on now." He rubbed a hand over his face. "George, do you have a place no one knows about, not even your closest friends?"

George knew what Ian was asking, and one thing sprung to mind. "Yes. It's—"

"No." Ian held up his hand. "We don't need to know

where it is. Take Jesse and go. We'll give you supplies. You won't have to visit anywhere for a while." He glanced at his watch. "In two days, at thirteen hundred hours, we'll meet at the address Brody will text you. Not before, not after. Once you receive the text from Brody, throw your phone. He'll give you another burner, but none of us will have your number."

"What if you need—"

"Your concern is keeping Jesse safe as you have done. Do not contact us unless you have no other choice. The aim is for you to hide until this is over, which will be in two days, either way."

15

JESSE

The whole place burst into a wave of activity while they prepared for Jesse and George's departure. He found a bag on the bed, which contained the clothing he had taken with him to the cabin, and he silently thanked whichever of them had managed it. He stared out of the window while George was busy finalizing details with his team.

Jesse had no idea where they were going, but that was the plan. If no one knew where they were, no one would be able to tell anyone else. He blew out a breath and sank onto the bed. How long would they need to hide? Would he ever get back to his normal life?

He snorted and shook his head, tying his shoes. Life was never normal, to begin with.

A knock sounded. "Time to go!"

Jesse closed his eyes briefly, grabbed his bag and hurried to the front of the house.

"Jesse." Ian stepped closer. "I'm sorry things have gone this far, but you'll be safe with George."

"I know I will, but you have nothing to be sorry for. It's my fault this whole thing started."

Ian squeezed his shoulder. "Let's leave the fault at the feet of Baker, shall we?"

Jesse grinned. "Agreed."

"Take care."

He glanced over at George, who was talking to Junior, and climbed into another new car, stuffing his bag by his feet. As he watched the guys interact, his chest constricted at the thought of any harm coming to his parents or Linc. He didn't want anything to happen to them, but he couldn't see a way out of their situation. Trident appeared to be a great company, but could they stop whatever was coming their way?

The driver's door opened. "Do you have everything?" George climbed in.

"Yes. I don't have much as it is."

"We don't need much where we're going. The car is packed with food and drink and other things we may need. I think we're set."

Jesse watched the team enter the house, Ian pausing by the door to lift a hand to them before disappearing inside. He hoped everyone would be okay. "Are you sure you're all right to drive?"

"Yeah. My arm isn't hurting as much now."

The journey was over an hour, going further north. Despite the silence that reigned in the car, it was comfortable, which Jesse hadn't expected. He asked a few questions, and George answered, but he didn't feel the need to fill the silence with inane words. The scenery was bland one moment, breathtaking the next and everything in between. He'd never expected to see so much of Florida.

George pulled up outside a small, clean house with a well-maintained front garden, and Jesse raised his eyebrows at him.

"Who does this belong to?"

George's jaw clenched. "It's a family house that doesn't get used often."

"Seems like someone lives here. Are you sure we're not intruding?"

George shook his head. "It is maintained by people who are paid to keep it running."

Jesse kept his other thoughts to himself because George's expression screamed for him to stop asking questions. He licked his lips as he squinted at the place. "It's nice."

George climbed out of the car, and Jesse followed, bringing his bag with him. If Jesse hadn't been watching as closely as he was, he would've missed the straightening of George's spine and heavy exhale before he strode toward the front door. His forehead furrowed. Why did this place have such a hold over George?

He followed at a slower speed, not wanting to be in the way when George checked all the rooms to be sure no one was waiting for them. He hesitated on the porch, smiling at a similar swing seat to what had been at the cabin. Taking in his surroundings, he let out a breath. If it weren't so far from home, he could see himself living in a place like this. The houses around them were of similar construction, some as well-maintained as this one, some not, but all showed signs of living, whereas this house had an empty feeling to it. He wasn't sure why.

"All set."

George's voice made him jump, and he spun around, clutching his chest. "Jesus! I'm going to have to put a bell on you."

Jesse stepped across the threshold, not missing the twitch of George's mouth.

"I'll grab the bags from the car. You get yourself settled in. There are two bedrooms; take whichever one you want."

Before Jesse could say anything, George had left the

house, closing the door behind him. He stared for a moment, then roamed around, getting his bearings. Climbing the stairs, he found a huge bathroom and two large bedrooms. The front of the house was deceptive. He hadn't expected the place to be so big.

As soon as he stepped into a blue room filled with wooden furniture, he knew he wanted to sleep in it. Blue had always been soothing for him, especially in a bedroom. He dropped his bag to the bed and moseyed around, checking out photographs and trinkets that were on show. Some of them were expensive, from Jesse's knowledge. The photographs showed a tall, dark-haired man standing next to a smaller woman with long blonde hair, who had her arms wrapped around the man's waist while one of his arms held the woman. Who were they?

Shaking his head, he went to find George. No noises came from downstairs, but it didn't mean George wasn't there. After all, he was good at creeping around, but Jesse didn't want to miss anything. He needed to be a part of whatever they decide to do, whether they wanted him to be or not.

George was in the kitchen, putting away the food they'd been given. "It's close to dinner. We have chicken. How about grilled chicken with baked potatoes?"

"Sounds good. What can I do to help?"

"You can make a salad if you want. I hate chopping vegetables."

Jesse chuckled at another facet of George's personality being shown to him. "I don't mind either way." He grabbed a chopping board and knife and placed it on the center island where George was putting the salad ingredients. "I chose the blue room. Is that okay?"

George stilled for a second, then carried on, nodding. "Yeah, sure. It has an en-suite as well."

"Oh, I didn't see it."

They worked silently for several minutes, the same comfortable togetherness they'd had in the car. Did George feel the same? The question made him nervous for some reason.

"I'm switching on the light. It's getting darker."

Jesse watched the muscles bunch and release on George's body when he made his way over to the kitchen doorway. His shoulders were broad and tapered to a narrower waist, where Jesse saw the outline of a gun resting against George's back before he twisted around to come back to the island.

"Are you going to be carrying the gun around all the time?"

George's gaze flicked to his. "Yeah. I'm not taking any chances this time." He picked up another knife and grabbed the tomatoes. "We will be able to go out if we want to, but it's not advisable to go too far. Maybe…" He cleared his throat. "I could take you to the restaurant in town tomorrow."

Jesse stared at him, his mouth curling up until he beamed. "I would love that." He returned to chopping. "I didn't think we would be able to go anywhere."

"I doubt anyone would be able to link this place to me. We should be fine."

Jesse interpreted a wealth of information in that sentence. He wanted to ask more questions but didn't want to ruin their evening.

"We can sit back and relax for a bit until it's ready. Would you like a beer?"

"Water for me, thanks."

George handed him a frosted glass of cold water, and they wandered to the couch.

"What's our plan now?"

George sipped his water. "We stay here and wait it out for the next two days. We have plenty of information we can go through—Sykes gave us a lot more to go on—and see if we can figure anything out."

Jesse thumbed through the condensation on his glass, staring at it. "I'm sorry about Sykes—both aspects." He couldn't believe the coincidence of Sykes's medical health and Jesse's Robin Hood antics. He glanced up at George.

After a brief hesitation, George said, "Me too."

This time, the silence wasn't as comfortable, and Jesse filled it, "I never did call my parents back. They're going to be so pissed at me."

"They can get over it." The growled words made Jesse's heart fill. "They haven't treated you as they should have. It wasn't fair to you. I would've expected them to hover over you more after your brother died, not push you aside. It's not right."

Despite Jesse's heart racing at the passion and conviction in George's voice, he agreed, "Yeah, but they didn't." He shrugged. "Life goes on."

"How can you be so calm about it?"

"What else can I do? There is no changing anything. I'm living my life the best I can. How do your parents treat you?"

George blanched and stared at his lap. "My—"

The timer beeped from the kitchen, and George leaped up. "I'll finish dinner."

Jesse watched him leave the room and concentrated on the blank TV, the kitchen sounds reaching him. What could've caused that reaction in George? He wanted to finish their conversation and find out what George had been about to say, but he left the man alone. He'd try readdressing it at dinner.

Linc would kill him when Jesse finally got in touch with him again. After their last conversation, he didn't think Linc would let Jesse out of his sight for a while.

Jesse knew what information Sykes had given them, to

begin with—something about a different person telling Baker what to do. Who could it be? A crime lord or something similar would be his first guess, but it seemed too much like one of the plotlines in the books he read. Money appeared to be the only benefit of the operation Baker was running, at least for Baker himself. Was there something they were missing? Some other aspect they hadn't considered?

"Dinner's ready."

Jesse uncurled himself and inhaled the aroma of freshly cooked jacket potatoes. It had always been a favorite smell of his. He sat opposite George in front of a plate of steaming food.

"It smells divine. Thank you."

"You're welcome. Although you helped, remember."

Conversation flowed well throughout the meal, and Jesse dropped the subject about George's parents, not wanting to ruin the evening. They returned to the couch once the kitchen had been put back to rights.

"What information has Sykes given you?"

Instead of telling him, George reached for a folder from the bag he'd left in the living room. "It's all in there. We need to try and figure out who the person behind it all is."

Jesse took the folder, opening it to the first page. "What was he trying to say about the *state of affairs*? I remember you saying that didn't make sense to you?"

"To begin with, it didn't. Sykes doesn't know who's behind it. At least, I don't think he does." George's forehead creased. "I don't know him as well as I thought I did. He could be holding things back. Anyway, all he knows is it's someone higher up the chain of command. I don't know if he means the military or politics or anything else it could be."

"Well, state of affairs to me is kind of a play on words. Could it have something to do with 'affairs of the state' instead?"

George stared at him. "Do you think Sykes knows who it is?"

Jesse lifted a shoulder. "I don't know, but the wording seemed specific. It's as if it was something that had been said to him repeatedly. Not like brainwashed or anything, but if Sykes had been asking a question and Baker would reply that it was someone else's state of affairs."

George narrowed his eyes. "Maybe Baker was playing with him. Telling him things to make Sykes want to know more. Taunting him when Baker refused to let Sykes in on the secrets."

"It doesn't help us figure out who."

They spent a couple of hours going through all the different possibilities they could think of, writing everything down to go over again the following day. Jesse yawned and stood, stretching his arms above his head.

"I'm going to bed."

George licked his lips, and Jesse realized his T-shirt had lifted to reveal his abdomen. He tugged it down and flushed. "Yeah, I should try."

"How are your wounds doing? Do they need the dressings changing?"

"Nah, I think they'll be fine for now."

Jesse dragged his feet slowly up the stairs while George locked up and switched the lights off. He had reached the landing by the time George caught up.

"You're that tired?" George chuckled.

"It's been a long few days." Jesse pouted.

"That it has." They stopped outside George's room, which was closer to the front of the house than Jesse's room. "Night, Jesse. Get some rest." George reached out and cupped Jesse's cheek, rubbing his thumb gently against his skin.

When he pulled away, Jesse grabbed his hand, holding it

against his face and closing his eyes. "Will you sleep next to me again?"

"Sleep?" George's thumb whispered across Jesse's lips.

Jesse opened his eyes, staring at George. "After." His heart raced at his words.

"This is not a good idea, Jesse."

George focused on him so intently, Jesse wasn't sure he could take any rejection should it happen. He watched George's expression change several times before his eyes darkened, and he licked his lips.

"Fuck it."

George stepped closer, crowding Jesse against the wall. He stopped millimeters away from Jesse's lips. Jesse didn't wait and closed the distance, sealing their lips together. The moment their lips touched, sparks flew. George slid his hands around Jesse's back, and Jesse encircled George's neck with his arms. The kiss went from naught to sixty in seconds. George licked along Jesse's lips, requesting entry, and Jesse could do no more than open. George tasted faintly of the dinner they'd shared, but the thought flew from his mind when their tongues tangled. Jesse lifted on tiptoes, trying to reach higher, deeper, closer.

George took Jesse's weight by gripping his thighs and lifting him with a grunt. Jesse pulled away.

"Wait. You're injured."

George punctuated each of his words with a kiss, going down Jesse's neck. "I'm fine. Wrap your legs around me."

Jesse didn't want to hurt George anymore, so he carefully linked his ankles against George's lower back, hoping he wasn't pressing on George's hip. He clung to the man's neck, trying to keep as much weight off George's hips as possible. George pressed Jesse against the wall, sliding his good arm under his thighs and gripping his hair with his other.

Jesse nipped at George's lips, wanting more kisses.

"Bedroom."

George resumed kissing him, deepening it, and pressed his weight against Jesse, the heat of his body a furnace against him. Jesse felt George brace himself and step back, Jesse following. Jesse held tighter.

"You're going to hurt yourself, and then where will we be?"

George didn't reply, too intent on getting through the door. Not that Jesse minded. With short steps, despite his wounds, George crossed the large room, kneeling on the bed and following Jesse down until he was blanketed with George's body. Their kisses began again. Jesse skimmed his hands up and down George's spine, being mindful of his shoulder. He wanted nothing more than to feel them skin to skin. With George by his side, he would never be cold again.

George released Jesse's lips, nipping along his jaw and down his neck, licking along his collarbone. As George descended, Jesse gripped the hem of George's T-shirt. When it could go no further, George lifted carefully, taking the T-shirt off, and removed the gun from his jeans before bracing himself over Jesse once more. Jesse licked his lips, his hands smoothing down George's firm stomach, his fingertips dipping into every valley and following every mountain. His thumbs flicked across George's nipples. George's breath hitched, and he lowered his mouth, claiming Jesse's nubs for himself. The change in temperature and the firm lashings of his tongue had Jesse whimpering with need and thrusting his hips, hoping to gain some friction.

As his arousal rose, Jesse's fingers gripped George's back harder, his nails digging deeper. After worshipping each of Jesse's nubs, George licked and kissed down his stomach. When he reached the waistband of the jeans, he swirled his tongue around Jesse's belly button while his hands made quick work of the button and zipper.

George stepped back, dragging the fabric with him, exposing Jesse. Or at least, more exposed than he was. Jesse's heart raced when George threw the jeans to the floor and crawled up the bed to resume their kissing. Jesse slid his hands down George's back and, avoiding his hip, dipped underneath the waistband and grabbed a handful of his ass. George thrust forward, the friction Jesse needed—not enough but helpful all the same.

With George's tongue inside his mouth, Jesse could barely think. His legs were spread, cradling George's hips. He circled his hips, sliding from side to side, hoping to bring George as close as Jesse was. George growled, the sound vibrating through his chest and into Jesse's. Jesse pulled away.

"George, please." Jesse's hand free reached for George's button, unfastening and unzipping before reaching in and wrapping his hand around the stiff shaft. It felt hot in his hand, and while he stroked, George's breath left his body, and he stilled, braced above Jesse, mouth open, eyes closed while Jesse swiped his thumb over the head of his cock.

"Fuck, Jesse. That feels good." George canted his hips in time with Jesse's stroking, each slight movement rubbing George's jeans against Jesse's barely covered dick.

"Take them off. I don't want to hurt you." For a second, George didn't move. He blew out a breath and pulled himself away from Jesse. Cold air flowed over him from where George had been covering him, and he shivered. George removed his jeans and his underwear and kissed his way from Jesse's ankle to his thighs before grabbing the waistband of his briefs and pulling them off. George stopped and stared, and Jesse fought not to cover himself. He wasn't used to people staring at him, especially when he was naked. It was slightly unnerving. George stepped away, and Jesse reached a hand forward, lifting himself to his elbow.

"Wait. Where...?"

He watched George stalk to his bag on the dresser and rummage through, returning with a tube and several packets. George threw them on the bed, and Jesse let his breath go in a rush, his heart racing for a different reason. He'd thought George was leaving. Now, seeing the darkening of his eyes, the flush creeping onto his cheeks and neck, the heaving of his breath, Jesse knew George wasn't going anywhere.

GEORGE

George crawled back up Jesse's body until he reached his groin. The red shaft strained toward Jesse's stomach. A bead of precum pearled at the tip. George slid his hand under the cock and lifted it toward his mouth. He blew a stream of cool air across the head before lapping up the fluid.

Jesse's taste burst across his tongue, and he needed more. His hand encircled the shaft, holding it in a tight grip so George could suck the head and flutter his tongue against the bundle of nerves on the underside. Jesse's hands gripped the covers beneath him, his head thrown back, whimpers and groans escaping his mouth. They had never gone this far before. Frotting had been their only simultaneous release. This time, George wanted everything. He wanted to own every part of Jesse. With that thought, George took Jesse deep into his mouth, swallowing around him and hearing the cursing coming from the man below him.

He lifted off, smirking when Jesse's hips followed his retreat. "This is going to be quick."

Jesse blinked at him, and George wasn't sure he'd heard a

word. He grabbed the lube and pushed Jesse's legs apart, exposing his hole. The little red rosebud clenched as George stared. He squirted some lube onto his fingers and glanced up at Jesse, who met his gaze and gave a slight nod. George refocused on Jesse's entrance, watching his fingers massage the cold gel into the skin and pressing gently against the pucker. Jesse released a breath, and George's finger slipped further in, and when Jesse bore down, George slid past the tight ring of muscle.

He watched in fascination when Jesse took his fingers, stretching him wider until Jesse was incoherent. After several more minutes to ensure he wouldn't hurt him, George rolled a condom down his length and slicked it. He covered Jesse's body, cradling his head, and lightly nipped at his lips while his cock pressed against his entrance. Jesse gripped George's back, the slight bite of his nails sending goosebumps down his spine and pooling in his groin.

"Ready?"

Their eyes met.

"Always."

George reached down with his injured arm, holding his cock while he pressed forward, wanting nothing more than to drive hard. He refused to hurt Jesse. Inhaling shakily, he took his time, moving in and out until Jesse stretched, and he sank balls deep. He rested on his elbows, their foreheads pressed together as they shared the same air.

"You feel amazing. Please, George. Please, move. I need you."

George pressed a kiss to his lips and withdrew until his tip was there, then he sank deep once more. Jesse groaned.

"Again."

Jesse drew his legs up and braced his feet on the bed, giving George more space to move. George lifted onto his hands, withdrew and drove deep, over and over again. Sweat ran down his back and his face, dripping onto Jesse's skin. Jesse's hands roamed George's body, licking his nipples and sending sparks down his spine.

"Fuck, Jesse. I'm close already."

"Come in me. Give me everything."

George's hip screamed at him, but he refused to stop. Jesse grabbed the back of his knees and pulled them closer to his chest, exposing himself further. George gripped Jesse's hips and increased his speed, hammering into him.

"Yes! Oh, yes. Please! Keep going. I'm almost there."

George's breath heaved as he kept up the punishing speed. The tell-tale tingle of his orgasm began at the base of his spine, and he wrapped his hand around Jesse's cock. The muted moaning advertised how close Jesse was. George changed his angle, and Jesse flinched, a long, low moan tearing out of him and stripes of come covering his stomach and chest. Jesse's climax triggered his own, and he held Jesse tight against him while he released into the condom, lightheaded.

When his orgasm released him, he leaned his forehead on Jesse's chest, both breathing heavily into the quiet room.

"Fuck, George. You can do that again."

George chuckled. After several seconds—or minutes, he'd lost track of time—he lifted, grabbing the base of the condom and withdrawing. Pressing a kiss to Jesse's stomach and licking at the cooling come, George pulled off the sheath and staggered to the bathroom. He ran the hot tap for a moment, allowing the water to warm before wetting a cloth and wringing it out.

He stared at his reflection, the usual lines on his face not as apparent as they had been. He smiled. He wandered back to Jesse—he was in the same position as when he'd left—and wiped him down.

"Come on, Jesse. Time for bed."

He received a grumble and a half-hearted attempt to roll over before George shook his head and bodily rearranged Jesse to one side. He dragged the covers back, moving Jesse beneath them and tucking him in. George retrieved his gun from the bottom of the bed and placed it on the bedside table within reach. Climbing into bed, he pulled Jesse toward him. Jesse curled around him, their legs entwining, arms around each other, and for the first time in a long time, George relaxed.

～

THE LAST TWO days had felt like a sort of vacation for George. They had eaten together, planned together and fucked like rabbits. That morning, Jesse had begun shuffling a little more gingerly than before, and George winced.

"Sorry. I should have held back."

"Don't you dare be sorry." Jesse glared at him.

George raised his hands, palms forward. "Okay. I'm sorry that I'm sorry."

Jesse snorted. "What time are we leaving today?"

George sighed at the reminder and dropped his head to stare at the ceiling.

"We're leaving about nine. You have about an hour."

"Okay."

"I'm going to take you to lunch before we meet up with them."

"Where?"

"Somewhere in Tampa I like to go."

"Is it safe?"

"We'll be fine." At least, George hoped they would. He couldn't see any reason why they would be found so quickly when they got back to Tampa. They would have enough time for a quick lunch.

The journey went by quickly. Both asked questions, although George struggled to answer some of them, especially when they related to his parents. Jesse didn't push. It made George feel bad that he couldn't explain his relationship with them, but Jesse squeezed his hand and told him it was fine.

When they parked at a little diner on the outskirts of Tampa, Jessie's eyes lit up. It was a quirky, 1950s designed diner that cooked amazing food.

George checked their surroundings before climbing out of the car and holding his hand out for Jesse's. They strode toward the diner entrance, and all the while, George was aware of his surroundings. No one appeared out of place, and his instincts were telling him they were fine.

He chose the table close to the rear of the main room near the back exit—the staff exit, that was—and made sure he faced the front door, his back to the wall. Jesse sat opposite him and grabbed the menu, a large smile on his face.

"This place is fantastic. How often do you come here?"

"Once a month or so."

George let his gaze wander around the other customers, seeing if anything stood out to him.

"Do you think this was a bad idea?"

George glanced back at Jesse. "No. I'm being careful." He gave a half-smile. "And it's also instinct for me to study our surroundings like this. I can't help it."

Jesse chuckled. "I can imagine that being in places where you had to be super alert, it became second nature."

He scanned the menu. George already knew what he wanted. It was the same thing he had every time he came.

"I think I'm gonna go with the cheeseburger. Although my eyes might be bigger than my belly."

George laughed. "You might be right there. I'm getting the same, and they come with fries and sides, too."

The waitress came over and took their order, George ordering for them both and including two Coke's as well. When she left, George glanced around once more and focused on Jesse.

"What are your plans once this is all over?"

Jesse threaded his fingers together on top of the table, staring down at them, and his mouth curved down. "I don't know. I'll be going back to England for sure. It all depends on the outcome of this situation, I suppose."

"What do you mean?"

Jesse glanced up at him. "Well, if something happens to anyone back home, or to anyone here for that matter, I don't think I'd cope well."

George leaned forward and rested a hand on top of Jesse's, stopping his fidgeting. "Everyone is going to be fine." George couldn't promise, but he hated seeing Jesse so unsure. He needed to do something to put a smile back on his face.

Jesse tried for a smile, but it didn't work. "We'll have to see what happens, won't we?"

Jesse seemed about to ask something else when the waitress bought their drinks. George waited for Jesse to continue, but when he didn't, only taking a drink, George prompted him, "What were you going to say?"

Jesse shrugged. "It's...Things are different now. Never in my wildest dreams—or nightmares—did I expect this situation. It's made me view things a bit differently. This is not the best way to go about my job."

George agreed silently. "The investigation side of your job could be your calling." Jesse cocked his head. "What I mean is you do so much research to find these artifacts, why not continue doing it but instead of stealing the object back, hand everything over to the authorities?"

Jesse winced. "Some of how I get my information isn't exactly legal."

George smirked. "Maybe. But by providing the information, they might overlook the legality of it. And anyway, their side of the law might be able to find the same information in a different way. You're giving them an advantage."

Jesse raised his eyebrows. "It's an idea."

"You can also do it from anywhere. You wouldn't have to travel unless you wanted to. And there's also no getting your hands dirty."

Jesse laughed. "There is that. What are your plans once this is over?"

George blew out a breath. He took a drink, trying to bide his time because he didn't know the answer to that. Not the whole answer anyway. He'd hopefully be working for Trident as long as they didn't hold this case against him, but from his conversations with Ian and Devon, it seemed like they weren't upset with him despite it being his friend who was on the wrong side.

"In all honesty, I'm hoping to go back to the way it was before this happened."

The waitress interrupted them again, bringing their food. George laughed at Jesse's open-mouthed expression when he saw the burger.

"I have a feeling you're not going to eat all that."

"I think you may be right."

He started eating, and George followed suit, their conversation dwindling but not uncomfortable. As they came to the end of their meal, with Jesse having eaten slightly more than half of the burger, George checked his watch.

"We're supposed to meet them at thirteen hundred. It gives us half an hour. We have time to finish our drinks."

Ten minutes later, they exited the diner, Jesse arguing behind George because he'd paid for both meals.

"Jesse, I don't mind. It's the least I could do." He faced Jesse, using a finger to lift his chin. "You're worth a meal and much more."

George hadn't planned on touching Jesse after last night —or this morning—but when Jesse licked his lips, George was helpless against fusing their lips. It didn't last as long as he wanted it to, but it was probably a good thing since they had places to be.

"Come on. Let's end this."

George threaded their fingers and took Jesse in the direction of the parked car. When they were thirty feet away, he pressed the button to unlock it, watching the lights flash and hearing the beep. Within seconds, he was flat on his back on the ground, smoke and flames reaching for the sky from the car they'd been headed to.

"Jesse!" George glanced around him, finding Jesse lying several feet away, covered in dirt. He scrambled across to him, wounds old and new screaming at him while checking Jesse for injuries. "Jesse?" He tapped Jesse's cheek gently, not wanting to move him in case he'd injured himself more than George could see. "Jesse. Come on. Wake up for me. We have to get out of here."

Jesse groaned, lifting a hand gingerly to the back of his head. He flicked his eyes open, squinting against the sunlight. "What happened?"

George sighed. "The car blew. We need to get out of here and fast."

Jesse's eyes widened, and he sat upright, wincing once more.

"Come on. I'll help you. We need to head for the trees."

"But isn't that likely where someone is hiding?"

"It's unlikely someone stuck around after planting that. It's possible but unlikely."

George pulled Jesse's arm over his shoulder when he

noticed him limping. Someone shouted for them to come back but neither listened, and they carried on into the trees.

"If I never go into a forest again, I'll be happy." Jesse's grumbled words put a brief smile on George's face.

When they were several trees deep, George allowed Jesse to sit on the ground, resting back against a tree trunk. He pulled out his phone and dialed.

"What's wrong?" Ian's voice came through loud and clear.

"We stopped for lunch. I thought we'd be okay. The car blew up." George crouched, resting his elbows on his knees and rubbing against his eyes, thinking this might be the end of his career with Trident. "I'm sorry I keep fucking up."

"No, you don't. It's these assholes that are doing it, not you. Where are you?"

George gave their location and added he could hear sirens. "People are gonna be pointing at us and the direction we came."

"Are you able to keep going and get further away?"

George glanced at Jesse, who nodded. "We can, yes. Where should we go?"

Ian gave them directions, and George put the phone down.

"I'm sorry, Jesse."

"This is not your fault, George." The sirens came closer. "Let's get the hell out of here, and we can deal with everything else." Jesse cupped George's face and kissed him briefly before standing and tentatively putting weight on his ankle. When he breathed a sigh, George also felt relief. "I should be good to go."

Jesse stood with his hands on his hips, and George couldn't help but chuckle. "You have some serious backbone."

Jesse grinned. "Hey, this is like a spy movie. I'm living a fantasy, man."

They began the short trek to where Ian had requested

they meet them. When they finally reached the destination forty minutes later, they found Ian and the team waiting.

"Any news showing up about the car?" George stopped in front of Ian.

Ian's expression said it all.

George's stomach sank. "How many?"

"One dead, three injured." Jesse gasped behind him, and George reached for him, dragging him close. "They were waiting in a car right next to yours."

"Damn it." George clenched his jaw, wishing Baker was standing in front of him so he could beat the living shit out of him.

"There were never supposed to be any other people getting hurt."

George pressed his lips against Jesse's temple at the young man's words.

"We need to decide the next route to go." Ian stepped closer, resting a hand on Jesse's shoulder. "We have another safe house not too far from here. Let's head over there now and gather whatever information we can."

"No. This is a terrible idea. He'll be in danger." George clenched his fists, wanting nothing more than to punch a wall.

"It's not your decision, Nipper. It's Jesse's."

George glared at Ian, then transferred his gaze to Jesse, pleading with his eyes to say no to the idea his boss had come up with. The moment he met Jesse's gaze, he knew that wouldn't happen.

Jesse's forehead creased. "I'm sorry, George. I have to. It's not fair that other people are getting hurt because of me. If this is going to stop them, I'm happy to do it."

George stormed out of the room, marching through the whole house and exiting through the back door into the large garden. He wanted to scream and shout at the sky, but it wasn't him. He knew exactly why he was reacting this way, as did everybody else in the room, but he didn't want Jesse in danger. He couldn't help his reactions when it meant Jesse was going to be wandering into the lion's den. He sat on the grass, feeling the recent rain soaking through his pants, but he didn't care. He dropped his head into his hands, trying to find some other way to get the same result. Anything except signing Jesse's death sentence.

1 7

JESSE

Jesse closed his eyes the moment George slammed the door behind him. If there had been any other way, Jesse would have taken it, but there wasn't. Ian had set the plan out in minute detail, and although Baker couldn't be trusted to keep his word, they were going to assume the money Jesse could make Baker would be the enticement he needed to keep it.

Jesse knew the outcome could be his death, but he also knew this needed to stop, and if his death stopped it, he could deal with it. No matter the outcome, he would be happy.

"Jesse, are you sure about this?" Jesse nodded. Ian stared at him for several long moments before nodding in reply.

Jesse stayed there, letting them do what they needed to do and, only after they finished did he search George out. He found him in the garden, and despite the sun shining down on them, George appeared cold. Jesse's heart went out to him. He crouched in front of George, pulling his hands away from his face and lifting his chin.

"This is my choice, George. But I'd like you to be with me

as much as possible before I go." He stared into the bright blue eyes of the man who had come to mean a lot to him. The pain etched onto George's face was too much to bear. Jesse steeled himself for George's refusal, but instead, George stood, grabbing Jesse's hands and pulling him close.

"I'll be with you every step of the way." George's voice was hoarse, and if Jesse didn't know better, he would have said he'd been crying. But George wouldn't show emotion like that, even if he felt it.

George led the way back into the house and up the stairs to the room they had been using. They no longer pretended to have one room each. He wasn't going to waste any more time.

"We don't have time to do what I want to do, but I need to feel you around me. Kiss me, George."

The words had barely left his mouth before George granted his wish. This kiss was different from the others they'd shared. It started harsh and punishing, with Jesse taking everything George gave him. After a few seconds, George paused with their lips together and slowed them down, and Jesse was able to taste every part of him.

With every moment the soft kiss lasted, Jesse gave his heart more to George. He wished he could explain how he felt, but it wasn't fair to George, especially if something happened to Jesse.

George pulled away, resting their foreheads together. "This is not goodbye, Jesse."

Jesse refused to cry as much as he wanted to. He had never been a weepy person, but there was something about George that made him feel like it was safe to bring out his softer side instead of being the hard-ass he had built his reputation up to be.

"Shall we get ready?"

He needed to prepare himself mentally for what he was

likely to go through for however long he would be in Baker's possession.

"I have one request."

George stared at him when Jesse outlined his request, his expression closing and becoming harder the more Jesse spoke. George stepped back, and Jesse felt the loss immediately.

"All right, follow me."

They exited the room once more and strode back to the room where the team was working. George stepped over to Egghead, talking quietly. Egghead handed him several items, and they retreated to the room once more. George set up the items.

"Come and find me when you're done."

Jesse watched as George left, closing the door firmly behind him. He faced the video camera, pressed the record button on the remote he held and began to talk. There were several of these he needed to make, and they were running out of time.

Half an hour later, he found the team in the computer room, as they'd labeled it. He crossed his arms over his chest, standing strong.

"I'm ready."

~

HE WAS NOT READY.

He wandered toward the parking lot of the diner, knowing the police had cleared out. The team expected somebody to come back and see the result of the bomb. When they checked the news earlier, the man who had died had not been named, neither had those who were injured. It wouldn't be difficult to find out who they were if they had connections, but they were hoping Baker was either lazy or too full of himself to check.

Jesse had been briefed on what to expect, but the idea of being caught and dragged into a dark van was unappealing. Still, he did as per the plan and drifted toward the police tape now surrounding the blackened parking lot. He stopped at the edge of the tape, wrapping his arms around himself, the chill having nothing to do with the cool breeze.

Pretending to be caught was no doubt going to be as scary as being caught for real. Jesse kept wavering back and forth about why he'd agreed to this plan, but in the end, he knew it was the best option they had.

A few people were milling around the area, the diner not having closed completely. Jesse eyed every person who came and went, trying to figure out if one of them would be the one who took him away.

"You're a sitting duck waiting here."

The deep voice made Jesse jump, and he spun toward the speaker, finding another military-looking man with his hands in his pockets, appearing as if he didn't have a care in the world.

"Who are you?"

"It's irrelevant. It was a stupid idea to come back here. Don't you learn anything from the movies?" Jesse's heart pounded, knowing this guy was the one he'd be leaving with. "Now, if I was a betting man, I would say this was a trap; otherwise, you're a lot more stupid than we gave you credit for. In any case, we're going to take a walk, and when we get to our destination, which is not far, I am going to run a scanner over you for any hidden tracking devices."

Jesse couldn't find his voice, but he nodded.

"You can talk if you wish, and you can ask questions, but there's no guarantee I will answer them." The man tilted his head. "This way."

Jesse inhaled shakily, tightened his arms around himself and began following. He had many questions, but he didn't know where to start.

As if the man beside him was a mind reader, he began talking, "If our roles were reversed, my first question would be, 'Why is this happening to me?' My answer to you is that you crossed the wrong man. Next time you do research, dig a little deeper, take another layer off the onion before deciding on how you are going to proceed. Another question I may have asked is, 'Where are we going?' That one, unfortunately, I cannot answer except to say you will be meeting Baker in person soon."

Jesse's heart tripped, and his breathing increased while fear began to work its way through his body.

"Whether you're here as part of a trap or not, it's unlikely your life will ever be the same again."

They stopped behind a blacked-out car, the man opening the trunk and pulling out a device that looked like a handheld metal detector they used at airports.

"Spread your arms and legs for me, please." The man was polite; Jesse would give him that. He did as requested, standing like a starfish while the man scanned every inch of him. He found a tracking device in Jesse's belt and gave a tut. He continued scanning until every part of Jesse had been covered, including his hair. Once the man was satisfied, he opened the car door and told Jesse to get in. Surprisingly, it was the front passenger seat.

Jesse climbed in, and the man shut the door before rounding to the trunk, the thump of the scanner being put back and the bang of the trunk being closed the only things Jesse could hear until the man climbed in beside him.

"Okay. My name is Mark. Feel free to talk if you wish or keep silent if you don't. There are two requirements from here. You will be handcuffed with your hands behind your back, and you will be blindfolded from this point forward. As you saw from the outside, it is a blacked-out car; therefore, no one can see you. Do you understand?" Jesse nodded. "Turn to face the door, so I can put the handcuffs on."

Jesse did what was asked, the cold of the metal making him flinch and the quiet snick of the locks making this more real. He had no idea what to expect, although his mind came up with several terrible options for him. Once the handcuffs were in place, he tried to get comfortable on the seat.

"I know it isn't the most comfortable of positions. I do apologize, but it is the best option for us. Now the blindfold." The man pulled the black fabric over Jesse's head. It was like half a balaclava, but it stopped under his nose and left his mouth completely free. The sudden darkness was disconcerting, but he breathed deeply, trying to calm himself.

"I'm going to clip your seat belt closed now."

Jesse wasn't sure whether the man was trying to calm him by telling him what would happen next or whether it was worse, but Jesse said nothing. The seat belt tightened against him.

"This is going to be a quiet journey if you have nothing to say."

Jesse heard and felt the engine start and the car begin to move. He tried to keep track of the twists and turns the car made, but it was impossible. He lost track of how long they had been driving, and as far as Jesse was concerned, they could have been driving in circles for several hours and be on the same road when they finished. In the end, he tried not to worry about figuring out where they were.

The car slowed, then sped up again, and eventually pulled to a stop, the engine silencing.

"Are you ready to meet the man himself?"

Jesse closed his eyes, even though he couldn't see

anything. He had no idea if he would ever see anyone ever again.

"I'm going to climb out, and I will come around and help you out." The man—Mark—exited the car, slamming the door behind him. Seconds later, Jesse's door opened, and Mark leaned over him to unfasten the seat belt. "Swing your legs out first. Bring your head down a bit and lean forward, and I'll help you out."

He followed instructions and stepped forward, his legs unsteady. The car door slammed again, and the man took hold of his upper arm, talking him through when to lift his feet and what to be careful of.

"We have ten steps ahead of us. If you lift your foot now, it will take you to the first one."

Jesse did and counted to ten, carefully stepping forward after that to ensure he had been at the top of the stairs. It was difficult to take note of any scents or aromas around him because the material blocked a lot of it. There were no sounds apart from their footsteps on what seemed to be a wooden floor. Had he been taken to the mansion he'd robbed? There was no way of telling until he saw his surroundings.

He was pushed and pulled around corners, upstairs and along what seemed like corridors until they came to a stop. He heard a knock. Someone shouted, "Come in," and they entered a space that felt a lot smaller somehow. The floor became stone, a different sound under his footsteps when he was pulled further into the room.

"Ah, I see we have a visitor." The voice was instantly recognizable as the one that had been talking to Ian several days before. "Thank you, Mark. You may step back."

"Yes, sir."

The hand loosened from his upper arm, and for a second,

Jesse wanted it back. He wanted something or someone he knew, even if the man was a bad guy.

"You have been causing me a lot of problems, Mr. Flint. This could have been finished much earlier than this if you had listened to my instructions."

Jesse didn't know what to say. Seconds later, the fabric was ripped from his head, and he blinked in the glaring sunlight, trying to get his bearings. When his eyes adjusted, he acknowledged they were in a conservatory, which was surprising considering it laid Baker out as a target.

Something must have shown on his face because Baker laughed, and Jesse faced him.

"The joys of having so much money mean I get to enjoy the sunlight with windows that let the sun in and I can see out of, but nobody can see in." Baker smirked.

He stepped closer, and Jesse stood his ground, refusing to move away. Baker raised his eyebrows and crossed his arms over his chest, tilting his head to study Jesse. His gaze flicked behind him.

"You're certain."

"Yes, sir. I checked him when I first picked him up."

Baker nodded and scraped his lower teeth against his upper lip. "I think we should have a little talk, Mr. Flint, don't you?"

Jesse said nothing. Baker stared at him for a few moments and spun away, returning to the chair behind the desk.

"Where is my vase, Mr. Flint? Or should I say, Robin?"

"I can tell you exactly where the vase is." Jesse's voice was rough from lack of use from however long he had been in the car.

He took a chance and studied the room surrounding him. It was covered on three sides with full-length panes of glass and the fourth side with the wall connecting it to the main house. Despite it feeling smaller, it was a large space. It held a large desk behind which Baker sat, and when he glanced over his shoulder, he was shocked to find armchairs and sofas and several people sitting in them. His eyes widened, and his heart rate increased. They were all wearing suits, and Jesse was concerned his time was a lot shorter than they had anticipated.

When he faced Baker once more, Baker grinned. "Yes, Mr. Flint. I would like you to tell me exactly where the vase is, and after that, we have other business to discuss."

Jesse had to delay as much as humanly possible. He cleared his throat. "May I make a request?"

Baker raised his eyebrows once more. "You may ask, but whether I grant it is another question."

"May I please sit down? I injured my ankle in the blast, and it's twinging some."

Baker laughed heartily and waved a hand. "By all means, let's make you comfortable."

Mark brought a chair over, resting it behind Jesse and helping him to a seated position. His hands were still handcuffed behind him, which made it slightly more awkward, but at least he would be able to use the small wooden chair as a weapon, however briefly he might have it for.

"Anything else I might get for you to make you more *comfortable*?"

The inflection on the words made it known the Baker was humoring him. How he longed to punch him, but he bit the inside of his cheek to stop any words from flying.

"No, thank you."

"Right, please give us the location of the vase."

There was no point in not giving the information to Baker. He would no doubt retrieve it one way or another. "It's in locker 367 at the luggage storage facility next to the International Airport."

Baker waved a hand, and two men exited the room. Mark stepped closer to Baker. "As I mentioned earlier, you are the bane of my existence, Mr. Flint. You are a hard man to find or an easy man to find, but a hard man to stay found. I thought Sykes had done a great job of finding you at the cabin, but you disappeared until he found you again at the house. Unfortunately, it seems he is no longer reachable, and as you are sitting in front of me, it seems he failed."

He faced Mark and nodded.

"It will be done, sir."

Baker refocused on him. "In case you were wondering, that was the go-ahead to kill Sykes. As you seem to like Trident so much, let's hope no one protests."

Jesse's heart jumped, and his palms began to sweat. "I doubt anyone from Trident will be bothered with me now that I'm here."

"That's not what the tracking device in your belt said." Mark's words were for Baker's benefit. Jesse glared at the man.

Baker laughed. "I have eyes and ears everywhere, Mr. Flint. You can stop trying to make me believe anything you say. Despite you giving us the location of the vase, I will not be sending anybody to it without a little bit of research first. I am not stupid. I have been in this business for a long time." Baker rested his hands on top of the desk and linked his fingers together. "You, however, have had a good reputation until this point. I had heard of you before you stole from me. I was in awe of your ability to get in and out of a place without being detected. I will admit to being slightly concerned, but because you had stayed on your side of the Atlantic, I was happy to let it go. The moment you crossed the Atlantic was when you made your first mistake, Mr. Flint. You should have stayed home."

Jesse understood that feeling deep in his soul, but it was too late.

"I now have quite the conundrum." Baker stood, rounding the desk and resting back against it. "I'm not sure what to do with you. My initial plan had been to kill you. Then I changed to selling you because you're good-looking, Mr. Flint, and you will make me a lot of money." Baker pointed behind Jesse. "These men here are happy with what I have told them about you. They're interested in taking you off my hands. But I have not yet made up my mind. I'm considering the potential waste of your abilities, but I am also hesitant because I know, as per the story of Robin Hood, you prefer good over bad."

He had no idea what Baker was trying to get at, but his words were true. No matter what option Baker gave him, he would do whatever it took to do the right thing, and he would forever refuse to hurt anyone intentionally, be it from holding a gun and pulling the trigger to being thousands of miles away on the other end of a computer screen.

No matter what part of a plan he was involved with, if the result was to hurt an innocent person, he would not be part of it.

GEORGE

George couldn't meet anyone's gaze. The minute they left Jesse at the drop-off point, his heart pounded. He knew everyone was giving him a wide berth, but he didn't care. All he wanted was Jesse back where he belonged—with him. They hadn't gone far and watched him discreetly.

When a former military man approached Jesse, George had to restrain himself from going after him. He saw Jesse flinch. His hands tightened around the binoculars, and he clenched his jaw. He had no idea how he was going to get through this.

"He'll be fine."

Ian's confidence in Jesse matched George's own, but it wasn't Jesse he was worried about. It was what Baker was capable of. He knew the type of man he was and what his business dealings were, but they let Jesse go face to face with a monster.

"Tell me that again when he's home."

Ian squeezed his shoulder, and it took everything in George not to shrug it off. He didn't want to antagonize his boss, but this case might be the death of him. He watched with increasing fear as Jesse and the man strolled toward a car. The man, as anticipated, scanned Jesse for tracking devices, removing his belt when he found one. But when the man opened the door, and Jesse climbed in, George had to swallow hard against the lump in his throat. They would attempt to follow the car, but they knew it was futile. Hopefully, the second tracker would do its job.

They drove around, following the car for about half an hour before they lost it. Despite knowing they would, George was pissed.

"The tracker is working."

George hoped Egghead's reputation was as good as he had been told it was. Now, it was a case of waiting. This was the part George hated most. There was nothing about this plan he was happy about. If anything happened to Jesse, he didn't know what he would do.

They returned to the Trident compound because Egghead had better equipment there. It took them further away from Jesse, or at least the direction he had been traveling, but George tried to calm himself. His body ached from how much tension was running through every part of him.

They had a feeling they knew where Jesse would be taken, but there was no guarantee. Baker had a warehouse near the coast, which he had been seen using from time to time for unknown reasons. They assumed that was where Jesse would end up.

The first thing they did was go straight to the war room and find out where he was. Despite the man removing Jesse's belt, it hadn't been the only tracker on him. What had surprised George was that the man hadn't checked in as much detail as they expected him to, but this was where their plan could go wrong. If Jesse was searched again when he reached their destination, there was a chance the small device that had been inserted under Jesse's skin in his armpit would be found.

"I have him. They're at Baker's mansion." Egghead's forehead creased, and he glanced at Ian. "Why would he be so stupid to take Jesse to the one place we know about?"

"I think Baker is as cocky and self-assured as what we thought." Ian crossed his arms over his chest.

George gritted his teeth. "It doesn't make sense. Why would he do that? I think this is some sort of trap."

"We can't expect Baker to play by the rules, Nipper. Let's watch it from here and see what happens. The tracker is working. We know where he is."

George blew out a breath, trying not to scream at his boss. "Where is Sykes?" George might be able to get some answers from him.

"He's in one of the bunkrooms at the moment." Jake came to stand beside George.

"I'm going to have a word." George whirled around and strode out of the room.

"I'll come with you."

Jake's reply was muted because George was already down the corridor. They jogged toward the one person who might be able to give them more information.

He opened the door to the room where Sykes was being held without any preamble. If Sykes was shocked by the abrupt entrance, he didn't show it. He had been reclining on one of the bunks, but when George entered, he rose to a seated position. He wasn't handcuffed, and George was surprised Sykes was still there. He could have easily escaped.

"Why would Baker take Jesse to the mansion?"

Sykes frowned at him. "What do you mean?"

"Jesse has gone to Baker. We expected him to take him to the warehouse at the coast, but he's taken him to the mansion instead. Why would he do that?"

Sykes was quiet for a moment, his eyes on the floor. "It's probably because it's where he feels more comfortable. The mansion is a fortress. Despite Jesse managing to get in and out without detection, there are not many people who can."

"But it's right under everyone's nose."

Sykes shrugged. "It doesn't matter. He doesn't care. He has plenty of visitors coming to and going from the mansion. It doesn't make a difference to him."

"It doesn't make sense. Baker knows we're likely to go after Jesse."

"That's probably why they're at the mansion and nowhere else. Jesse was the one who got in, not you, not your team. Jesse. And Jesse is already there. However Jesse got in, he wouldn't be able to get in the same way. If he told you how he did it, it wouldn't make a difference."

"What's likely to happen to him?"

Sykes sighed. "In all honesty, there are a variety of options. I very much doubt he would kill him unless he was seen to be more of a problem than Baker had first thought. If I had to guess, and it would be a guess because I am not inside Baker's head despite what you might think, I would say he would be sold...and quickly."

George's heart raced, and he swallowed hard. He didn't want to think about what would happen to Jesse should he disappear and not be found.

"What would—"

The door opened, and Devon poked his head in. "You have a visitor." Devon stared directly at George.

"Who is it?"

Devon's eyes tightened. "Your father."

George rubbed a hand across his mouth and closed his eyes briefly. He could do without seeing his father, but he knew the man wouldn't leave if he knew George was in the building. He glanced back at Sykes.

"Please tell Jake everything you can think of that may help us." He stared at Sykes and said the words he never thought he would. "I beg you." Their gazes locked for several moments until Sykes gave a single nod.

He spun around and exited the room, following Devon to Ian's office. Devon paused outside before opening the door and squeezed George's shoulder.

"You have a new life here, Nipper. Remember that when he's talking down to you."

George watched Devon stalk off, then inhaled deeply and knocked. Ian's command to enter came swiftly, and he opened the door to see his father standing by the window with his back to the room. He closed the door behind him and stepped forward.

"Your father is interested in the progress on your case." Ian's expression was unreadable. George knew his father well, and he had undoubtedly upset his boss. "I've explained we are in the middle of it, and he wanted to speak to you."

George stared at his father's back, waiting for him to acknowledge his presence. Had they been alone, George would have waited until his father started the conversation. With Ian in the room and with George's temper fraying as it was, he couldn't.

He straightened his spine. "How may I help you, Father?"

His father glared over his shoulder at his son, and George hoped he wouldn't say anything else to upset his boss. He knew Ian wouldn't take anything out on him, but he didn't want to take the chance at losing the job.

"I hear you have yet to close the case. Why is it taking you so long?"

"We have come across a few issues that have stopped us from progressing as quickly as we had hoped."

"What is this we? This is your case, George. You shouldn't be relying on other people to do the work for you."

George opened his mouth, but Ian beat him to it.

"We're a team, Captain. We don't complete cases individually. I find they get completed quicker when more than one person is working on them at the same time."

"Be that as it may, surely George has begun to make progress?"

"With all due respect, Captain, it is not your concern how long it takes for us to do our job."

George watched the tennis match between his father and his boss and swallowed hard.

"He is my son, and therefore, I have the right to know if he's doing his duty."

George's temper heated because his father was not only saying George wasn't doing his job, he was also pointing toward Trident not doing their job. And that wasn't fair to Ian. Both men stared at each other for several moments until his father whirled to George.

"So, are you?"

George clenched his jaw. "Father, I cannot give you any details about the case. I will tell you that I am doing everything I can to work with the team to get it completed promptly."

"In other words, you have no idea what you're doing. I knew this had been a mistake."

"In other words, Father, I am doing my damn job. And if you weren't here interrupting me, I would have more time to do it. It is not up to you to find out whether I am doing my job. I am sure, should I begin to stop doing what I should be doing, Ian will be the first to tell me. And if it happens, I am sure you will also hear about it. But as of this moment in time, I am busy. *We* are busy. I will happily take you to your car, but it is time for you to leave."

His father stared at him, mouth gaping open, and George couldn't believe what had come out of his mouth. He gulped.

Ian, on the other hand, smiled at George as if he was a proud papa.

George breathed heavily while he awaited his father's answer. His father lifted his chin, stormed past George and threw open the door. He stared at Ian, knowing his eyes were wide open and sweat dripped down his forehead. Ian tilted his head toward the door, and George snapped his mouth shut and left the room, following in his father's wake. He would no doubt receive backlash from his speech, but he couldn't find it in him to care.

He caught up with his father when he exited the warehouse where the offices were situated. His father didn't stop as he stalked across the parking lot and unlocked his car. George didn't say a word, expecting his father's wrath.

Captain William Valmonte stopped and pivoted on his heel, his jaw tight, his stance straight, his fists clenched. George halted in front of him and waited. His father worked his jaw back and forth several times, clenching and unclenching his hands before shaking his head and climbing into the car without a word.

George's eyebrows rose. He'd expected to be chewed out, but for his father to leave without a word probably meant more harm than good. George felt the first tingles of pride at slipping his father's leash. As his father reversed, George stepped out of his way, and he watched him leave the compound without regret.

He put his hands on his hips and stared at the ground. He hadn't expected that to happen today of all days. He huffed a breath and strode back the way he came. There was plenty of work that needed doing and a conversation to finish with Sykes.

Poking his head into the war room, George asked Brody if there was any change to Jesse's location.

"No. Jesse is in the same place."

"Tell me the moment it changes." George left, quickly returning and adding, "Please."

Brody's laughter followed him down the corridor as he returned to the bunkroom Sykes was staying in. Jake was still in there, but he had sat down on one of the empty beds, and they seemed to be having an engaging conversation. He waited until they finished talking.

"Have you thought about anything that might be helpful?"

Sykes held his hands out, palms upward. "I don't have any more information other than what I've already given you, Jake and Marco. I can try and answer whatever questions you can think of, but I might be reiterating the same information again and again, which I'm happy to do."

George rubbed his hands over his face, wanting nothing more than to scream to the ceiling or punch something. They were missing something. He became still, an idea brimming in his mind, but he needed a sounding board.

"All right, thanks."

He left the room, jogging to the war room to see if Nick was there. When he asked to speak to him, Nick stared at him as if he was an alien. They wandered to an empty office, and George rested against the door, second-guessing his decision about who to talk to. He stared across the room at the man who had been the least welcoming of the team. Despite their differences, or possibly because of them, Nick would be the best choice to brainstorm the idea with.

"What?" Nick rested against the far wall with his arms crossed over his chest.

"I have an idea."

~

GEORGE CRAWLED THROUGH THE UNDERGROWTH, slowly making his way toward the hole Jesse had created when he first stole the artifact. He could hear and see guards pacing along the perimeter fence. When he reached the exact point Jesse had used, he waited. The cloudy night sky helped hide his presence by shielding the moon.

He checked his watch. Five minutes until he needed to get in. Five minutes until the plan either worked or blew up in his face.

His earpiece gave him the information the rest of the team relayed to them all.

"Are you sure about this, Nipper?"

Ian's concern was palpable, but George had no qualms about doing this. "Yes. If he can, I can."

"Jake has your back, but unless anything goes wrong, you won't know it. Good luck, Nipper."

"Understood."

He kept his eyes on the movements of the guards, double-checking the information he'd been given by Sykes. When everything seemed to be correct, he firmed his jaw and watched the time drew closer.

"Go."

George tightened his muscles to stop himself from moving. That signal was for the rest of the team, not him. He had thirty seconds. A guard rushed past him as they had anticipated, and when the time came, George went to work on the fence. He wasn't as small as Jesse, and therefore his entry point would need to be bigger, but it wouldn't matter. When he finally slithered through the opening, he pushed the fencing back into place, hoping it wouldn't be seen for several minutes.

As they had seen from the satellite photos, there weren't many places to hide. George kept low to the ground but ran across the expanse to the first bush he came across. He did this several times until he reached the edge of the mansion itself. He crouched by a low wall, merging with the shadows.

Checking his watch again, he saw he'd made good time. He needed to wait for the next cue from the team before he continued.

He rested his head back against the wall, staring at the stars that came and went between the clouds. He didn't want to think about the potential outcome for them all if this plan didn't succeed. They had been over every single contingency they could think of, and he had finally managed to persuade Ian to his way of thinking.

"There's no one here."

That was George's cue to get going. He braced himself and checked his surroundings before rounding the wall and aiming for the same entrance Jesse had used. He reached for the handle of the door and froze at the sound of a gun cocking behind him.

"Hands where I can see them."

George lifted his hands into the air and slowly pivoted around to face the guard who had found him. He didn't see one guard; he saw three.

"Handcuff him." The guard who had spoken kept his gun trained on George while the one to his left dropped his and came toward George. The handcuffs were cold against his skin as the man linked his hands in front of him.

"Over and out." His words were quiet.

"What did you say?" The guard handcuffing him shoved him closer to the ones holding the guns.

"Nothing."

"Received and understood." Ian's voice was quiet in his ear.

George knew Ian would've stopped the signal to George's earpiece, so hopefully it would become undetectable. He'd soon find out, he was sure.

The guard gripped his upper arm and pulled him forward. He was led through several expensively decorated corridors by the three men until they reached a wooden door. One of the men came from behind him and knocked. George didn't hear anything, but the guard opened the door and stepped inside, murmuring something to the occupant. When he stepped aside, the guard holding him dragged him forward into a spacious, furnished conservatory.

Within seconds, he had cataloged four men in suits sitting on sofas to his right, three guards around the room, a man behind a desk and Jesse.

Their eyes locked, and Jesse's widened. George saw his mouth move, but no words came out.

"Thank you for joining us, Valmonte. It's a pleasure to meet you, finally."

1 9

JESSE

He couldn't believe George was there. That hadn't been in their plan. He was supposed to be as far away from this mess as possible. What the fuck was he thinking? Because he knew George well enough to know this had been planned.

The man who had taken his heart was brought closer but not close enough to touch. George's gaze ran all over Jesse as if checking to make sure he was in one piece, and Jesse's anger softened.

"To what do I owe the pleasure of your company?"

Baker's voice was full of humor, and Jesse wasn't sure he liked the tone. He wished he was privy to the new plan. Having no idea what to expect was not his favorite pastime.

"I wanted to see how the other half lived." George's voice was cocky, and Jesse withheld his chuckle.

"And what do you think?" Baker waved his hand around.

"Not my cup of tea."

Jesse bit his lip to stop his smile. He couldn't believe George was making jokes at this point, but he appreciated the nod toward Jesse's home country.

"Well, where you're going, you don't need to worry about it. I'm sure we have something more to your tastes." Baker gave a small smile and focused his attention on the guards. "Was he searched?"

"No, sir. At the request of Mark, we brought him straight here."

The slight tightening of Baker's features was the only indication of his anger.

"Mark, please do the honors."

His kidnapper—if he could be called that when Jesse had come willingly—stepped forward and reached for the scanner another guard provided.

"Lift your arms to the front."

George did as requested, and while he was scanned for trackers, Baker continued talking, sliding papers across his desk and generally appearing to tidy up. "I will advise you, Valmonte, if I find any trackers on you, I will be taking my anger out on Mr. Flint."

A lump stopped in Jesse's throat, and he swallowed against it, choking. George's eyes narrowed on the man, but he said nothing.

"He's clean." Mark returned to his original position.

Jesse was surprised that George had no earpiece or mic on him. Usually, George would have something like that on operations like these, unless it wasn't sanctioned and he was on his own. A thought Jesse didn't want to think about.

"I don't know if you're too confident or stupid. Either way, I appreciate you making my life a little easier."

"Anything to help."

Baker's gaze locked onto George's, and an uncomfortable silence ensued. Jesse fought to keep from fidgeting on his perch. Surprisingly, he'd been kept in the same room as Baker for the last three hours. The men behind him had come and gone several times, but it was as if they were waiting for something.

Baker broke the stare and focused on the computer in front of him. At that point, the room went quiet and stayed quiet. He tried not to keep glancing over at George, but he couldn't help himself. On occasion, Jesse flicked his gaze to Mark, but he received nothing back from him. He could've been wrong about how gentle Mark had been treating him. He'd thought there was something about the man that advertised his disquiet about the situation, but he must've been wrong.

It was extremely unsettling to be sitting in complete silence, but he'd become accustomed to it during his time there.

A knock sounded, and Jesse craned his neck to watch as another guard opened the door, listened to what was said and closed it again. The guard, one a lot younger than the rest, strode over to Mark and spoke in low tones. Mark nodded, and the two of them separated, the guard returning to his position, and Mark stepped closer to Baker.

He spoke in Baker's ear, who nodded.

"I think you can tell the rest of the room, Mark." Baker arced his hand to encompass the whole room.

If Jesse hadn't been staring at Mark, he would've missed the tensing of his jaw.

"Trident has been contained in the warehouse, sir."

Jesse's heart raced at the implications, and Baker clapped his hands together. "Good, good. I think we can move from here now." Baker stood, rounding the desk, and addressed the men behind Jesse. "Thank you, gentlemen. I will be in touch within the next twenty-four hours. Remember to leave your envelopes."

The men shook hands and dropped white envelopes onto the coffee table before exiting the room, followed by a guard.

"I think it's time for a change of scenery. Mark, if you and Patrick could lead Valmonte, and Trick, you should be fine with Mr. Flint.

Jesse's upper arm was gripped tightly, and he was pulled to his feet. He peered up at the guard named Trick and cowered at the dark flash in his eyes. He wobbled a little when the guard dragged him toward where Baker waited at the door. Behind him, Jesse could hear George and the two guards following. Baker exited, the rest of them following in his wake. They wandered through several corridors, passing the room Jesse had broken into and down some stairs.

The air was cooler as they descended, and Jesse had an inkling of where they were headed. This area was not on any of the blueprints of the property for obvious reasons, but Jesse had noticed the door the other time he'd been there. The wooden steps gave way to a stone floor, and Jesse could see several doors. Baker stopped outside one and unlocked it, surprisingly, with a thumbprint. When the door was opened, Jesse's hands fisted behind him.

He was dragged into a cold area containing six cells—the kind of cell he'd seen on crime dramas where people who have been arrested wait. The difference was that these cells contained chains, which he assumed they would be locked into.

Baker stopped in the middle of the room, and both Jesse and George were held on opposite sides of the room. It was as if Baker didn't want them to touch, not even a strand of hair.

"I hope you find your accommodations to your liking. Mark, place Valmonte here and chain him up. Trick, the cell next door, please but leave Mr. Flint free and remove his handcuffs. I wouldn't want to harm Mr. Flint more than necessary before his usefulness has ended."

Trick pulled Jesse into the cell, standing by the entrance

while he unlocked the handcuffs and shoved him forward. Jesse stumbled to keep his balance, but before he could whirl around, the cell door had slammed shut.

He stayed still, not wanting to call attention to himself, watching George be restrained and his handcuffs replaced with the shackles above his head. When they finished locking him in, the two guards left the cell and locked the door.

Jesse wanted nothing more than to be in George's arms, but it was impossible.

"Okay. You have a bit of a wait while I make my decision about which gentlemen deserves you most, Mr. Flint. As for you, Valmonte, I'll decide what to do with you after I've spoken with Trident. Have a good evening."

Baker smoothed down the front of his suit jacket, smiled and exited the room. The moment the door closed, Jesse rushed over to the bars separating them.

"Are you okay? What the hell is going on?"

"Calm yourself." George's mouth morphed into what appeared to be a shushing expression but without the finger in front of his lips. Jesse frowned, not understanding until George began examining their surroundings from ceiling to floor. While George did that, Jesse looked around his cell and shuffled closer to the bars to see the ceiling outside as well. He wasn't sure how small cameras or microphones could be in this kind of place, but he was sure they could be easily hidden to give the prisoners a false sense of confidentiality. When he caught sight of a black circle, he ignored it and wandered back to George.

"I think it's safe to say they're watching and probably listening."

Jesse sighed and shook his head, resting his arms through the bar and linking his fingers on the other side. He pressed his forehead against the cold metal poles.

"This is a nightmare."

"We're fine, Jesse. Everything will be fine."

Jessie peered at George and raised his eyebrows, working his mouth in disbelief. "I'll believe it when I see it."

"Trust me."

Jesse scrutinized George's expression and received the steadfast and solid demeanor he had come to rely on.

"Okay."

"Why don't you try and get some rest. I'll keep watch." George lifted the corner of his mouth, and Jesse chuckled.

"I bet you will."

George grinned. "There's nothing I enjoy more."

"Nothing?" Jesse raised his eyebrows and licked his lips.

In the dim light, he could see George's eyes darken as they followed Jesse's tongue.

"Almost nothing."

Jesse ducked his head and stepped back. "As you wish."

He climbed onto the cot-style bed and folded the pillow in half before tucking it under his head. He stayed on his side, slightly curled to watch George without having to move. The cells were chilly, and there were no blankets for them, but he tucked his hands under the pillow and watched George until his eyes became too heavy to keep them open.

~

"JESSE. WAKE UP."

Jesse startled awake, his heart pounding from being dragged from his dream. "What?" He sat upright, rubbing his eyes as he tried to focus.

"I'm sorry you can't have more sleep. You need to be prepared."

Jesse stood and wandered over to the bars separating them, staring at George with a frown. "Prepared for what?"

"Prepared for anything." George stretched his fingers as if

they were aching, which Jesse could understand from the position he'd been in for however long they'd been down there. But when he glanced up at them, he noticed something different about the shackles, and he squinted for a closer view. He couldn't figure out what it was; he pushed it aside, thinking he was still half asleep.

"How are you feeling?"

Jesse smiled. Despite their situation, he had been able to hear George's voice when he woke. The idea made him chuckle.

"What are you laughing at?"

"I like the idea of waking up together in the morning, regardless of what separates us." He tapped against the bars, the metallic ding sounding throughout the room.

George's mouth twitched. "It seems as if nothing can keep us apart."

Jesse stared at him, memorizing every inch of his face. "I like the idea of that."

"Keep that in mind if I do something wrong. Or when."

"Are we going to get out of here?"

"Have I failed you yet?" George laughed. "Actually, don't answer that. Yes, we are getting out of here."

The door to the room opened with the clank, and Mark entered.

Jesse stared at the guard, uncertain of the reason for his appearance.

"Cameras are down, and we can talk freely, but we have two minutes, please listen. You have one hour until there will be an attempt to breach the fence line. All but five guards will be outside the mansion. Two of the remaining guards will be with Baker, one will be outside this door, and another guard will be roaming the corridors. There is also one security guard who will remain in the communication room. The distraction will give you a maximum of five minutes to get out of this room. There is nothing I can do about the guard outside or the one patrolling inside. However, I will be stationed in the communication room. This means I can only help you with keeping the cameras away from you. Follow the same route Jesse did previously. As I said, five minutes."

"How will we know?"

"The cameras will go down again for a short time, and the guard will be asked to open the door to check on you visually. When he does, it's time to move. Your mic won't work until you're outside the perimeter after that."

"Understood, and thank you."

Jesse's mouth opened, but Mark retreated from the room, slamming the door shut behind him. He stared at the closed door for several seconds before focusing on George, who shook his head. His brain was full of questions, but he knew he couldn't get any answers when there were chances of Baker seeing or hearing what was said.

"Trust me."

"Always have, always will."

"How are your arms and legs? And your ankle?"

Jesse gave a small smile. "They're all good. My ankle twinged a little when I first got here, which was why I was sitting down when you arrived, but it's settled down now."

"I might need some of your massage skills when this is over." Jesse raised his eyebrows. "My shoulders are a little tense."

There was a hidden meaning behind those words, and Jesse knew that admitting to being hurt was something George would always find difficult. "You have medical knowledge. Is a massage the best option?"

He needed to know what George would need help with without letting everyone on the other end of the cameras know.

"I'm not sure crutches would work. I'd probably break

them." He assumed George leaning on Jesse wasn't a good idea. "You might have to carry any shopping we do."

Jesse's eyes widened. He didn't know if he'd be able to hold a gun for him; he had no idea what to do with one. "I'm not sure I'm…strong enough to carry the shopping."

"It's just to carry it. If we need anything from the bag, I can grab it."

Jesse swallowed hard and nodded. His heart raced at the idea of holding a gun. "Anything else?"

"If I'm too sore, you can carry on and take the shopping home, then come back for me with the car."

Despite the seriousness of the underlying meaning of the outwardly benign conversation, Jesse smiled. "I can't believe we're talking about shopping when we're in here."

George grinned. "Planning for the future, sweetheart."

They spoke about random topics for several long minutes until the door opened, and the guard stared at them.

"All clear. Visitors safe."

Jesse snorted at the choice of words, and the guard slammed the door shut once more.

"Time to go."

"But how are we—" His words stopped when George lowered his arms from the shackles without issue. "When… How…?"

"Explanations later." George reached through the door of his cell and unlocked it with a key he somehow had, and proceeded to unlock Jesse's door.

Jesse wrapped his arms around George for a brief moment. "Right, you need to stay in your cell with the door held closed—not locked, don't worry. I'm going to bang on the door, and when the guard opens it to see what the noise was, call him to gain his attention. When he steps closer, I'll knock him out."

He inhaled deeply. "Okay." He stepped back into the cell

and held the door shut, resting his arms through the bars. "Ready."

George banged on the door and hid to the left out of the guard's sight. As expected, the guard opened the door, peering inside.

"Sorry, I need to pee. How does that happen around here?" It wasn't a lie either, but he had more important things to worry about at the moment.

"You'll have to hold it until the boss says otherwise."

"Oh, come on, man!"

The guard stepped forward. "I said, you'll ha—"

George grabbed him and knocked him into the wall, unconsciousness hitting him instantly. George rested the guard upright and removed his gun, handcuffs and radio. By the time he was done, Jesse was by his side.

"Keep hold of the radio but put it on low. I should be able to keep hold of our 'shopping.'" George smirked.

"Glad to hear it."

"Let's go."

They worked their way toward the stairs. The only sounds were the occasional report across the radio, and from what Jesse could hear, Mark had been right about everything.

"Do you know the way?"

George nodded when he peered out the door. "Yes. I followed your route on the blueprints when you were explaining everything you did."

Jesse hooked two of his fingers in the belt loop at the back of George's khakis so they wouldn't be separated.

"We have two minutes to get out of here."

"Let's do it." Jesse smiled, and they jogged down the corridors, Jesse hoping Mark kept his word and avoided them on the cameras.

When they reached the door to the outside, Jesse braced himself for an alarm, but nothing happened. George peered outside, scanning the area before fully exiting the house. Jesse pushed the door shut behind him but left a small gap.

George's forehead creased. "Why not shut it?" Although he asked the question, he didn't stop and wait for an answer, and Jesse took it as George trusting him.

"It has been known for alarms to sound when the door is closed, not when one is opened. I've learned to be cautious when it comes to things like this."

George didn't reply but led the way to the first bush to hide their escape. No words were spoken while they raced across the land toward their hopeful freedom. When they reached the fence where Jesse had first entered, it was apparent the hole had been repaired. Jesse's heart sank. He had no idea how they were going to get out of there without some sort of cutters or something.

George tucked the gun into the back of his waistband and reached for the fence closest to a cement post. He pulled at the wire, and it came away from the post with a quiet snick. Jesse's mouth opened, and George grinned at him.

"I was a SEAL, Jesse. Always be prepared."

"I thought that was the boy scouts."

"Similar concept. Come on."

Jesse slipped beneath the fencing, George following before replacing the wire with small clips that had been waiting on the ground. When George stepped back, the fence appeared intact. It would only be on a closer inspection the issue would be noticed.

"Nice job."

"Now we need to get the hell out of here. Up for a jog?"

Jesse huffed and pouted. "If I have to."

George grabbed his hand, and they ran. He had no idea how long they ran for until they heard sounds of shouting in the distance behind them.

"Our secret is out."

Jesse panted beside George. "It took them longer than I thought it would."

"Not as long as I'd hoped."

George slowed to a walk, head moving from side to side. "What are you searching for?"

"Us."

George spun around, pointing the gun into the shadows and pushing Jesse behind him. When the man stepped into view, George's stance softened, and he lowered his arms.

2 0

GEORGE

"You scared the shit out of me, Carter."

"I apologize. It wasn't my intention, but I needed to be sure you weren't followed." The Chris Hemsworth lookalike drifted closer, and George saw he was dressed completely in black, not even his dark blond hair showing from underneath the beanie. His blue eyes shone in the limited light. "Let's get you back to the compound."

"Is that the best idea right now?"

Carter nodded. "Nowhere safer. Baker is on his way down, and you need to keep up appearances."

George hadn't been privy to this part of the plan, but he could imagine what it was. He concentrated on Jesse. "How are you holding up?"

"I'm good." Jesse's gaze flicked to Carter.

"Jesse, this is Carter. Carter, Jesse."

Carter held out his hand, and George had to stop himself from slapping it away. "Nice to meet you."

"You, too."

"Let's go."

Carter marched past them, and George followed, twining his fingers with Jesse's. "Let me know if you get tired."

Jesse grinned. "Aww, you're going to carry me? That's sweet."

Carter snorted, and George's face heated, and he was glad no one could see. He rolled his eyes at Jesse and focused on their movements. They dashed across several properties before Carter slowed near a black car.

"Your chariot awaits." He held out some keys.

"Are you not coming with us?"

Carter shook his head. "I have work to do."

George didn't ask because he knew Carter wouldn't tell. "Thank you for the escort."

Carter winked at Jesse and disappeared back the way they'd come.

"Who was that?"

"A ghost."

They climbed into the car, and he drove away, keeping to the speed limits and drawing no undue attention. He knew where they were and, within fifteen minutes, was back at the gates of the Trident compound.

Once they were parked, he rested his head against the headrest and blew out a breath. Jesse's hand landed on his thigh, and George took it in his hand, squeezing.

"Are you going to explain to me why you got yourself caught when the idea was for me to stay there for a short time and gather evidence against Baker?"

George rolled his head toward him. "Plans changed."

It was Jesse's turn to roll his eyes. "Naturally, but why?"

George sighed. "Let's go inside, and we can discuss it with everyone."

"Okay, but first…"

Jesse leaned forward, fusing their lips, and George

threaded his fingers through Jesse's hair, pulling out the band that had held it back. At first, the kiss was benign—a hard press with no movement, but George needed more. He needed to feel and taste every inch of Jesse. He gripped Jesse's hair, pulling him back, and licked and nibbled at his lips. Jesse's breath shuddered from him, and George took advantage of the opening, spearing his tongue inside. He caught Jesse's moan as his tongue explored every part of his mouth, tangling with Jesse's tongue and sucking it inside his mouth. The kiss heated further, George holding Jesse in place while he devoured him. He didn't care if he was running out of air. He inhaled through his nose, not wanting to move away from him, needing to remind himself Jesse was unharmed.

Pulling Jesse closer, which wasn't easy with the design of the car, George dragged his mouth away and across his jaw to his ear, nibbling on the lobe.

"George, please."

George kissed his way down the column of Jesse's neck until he reached his collarbone. He licked and nipped at the area and sucked hard on a spot at the base of his neck. Jesse groaned and dropped his head back. George kept sucking, his eyes closing while Jesse's hands cupped the back of his head. Several long seconds later, he licked over the area, smirking when Jesse shuddered and kissed the red mark he'd left behind. Jesse was his.

"Fuck, George. We need a bed and now."

George chuckled. "Unfortunately, we can't. But soon."

Jesse whimpered when George licked over the mark and pressed another kiss on it. It wouldn't be completely visible, but he wanted his mark on Jesse. He probably should've asked first, but it was easier to ask forgiveness, or so he'd been told.

George reclaimed Jesse's lips in a softer, sensual caress,

then pulled back. He rested their foreheads together. "I'm sorry for everything you went through."

"Is this the end?"

"Hopefully. You stumbled upon an international operation, Jesse. Let's go see what's happening."

Jesse raised his eyebrows. "I did what?"

George chuckled. "Come on."

His knees were weak when he tried to climb out of the car, although George would never admit it. His shoulders ached from being held above him for so long, but they were getting better. When this was all over, he was planning a vacation. Abroad somewhere. On a large island that had English-speaking people.

Jesse rounded the car and grabbed George's hand, resting his head against his biceps. George pressed a kiss to his head as they strolled across the parking area. Before they entered the office area, Jesse stiffened.

"What's wrong?"

"Why are we here when the team has been captured?"

George smiled. "They haven't. Come on. Time to let you in on a boatload of information."

Jesse's frown was cute, and George knew he was done for. Cute? What the heck? He couldn't get it in him to care. They wandered to the war room, where he knocked and waited for the enter command before opening the door. Usually, he wouldn't have waited, but he wasn't entirely sure how much information Jesse would be given and wanted to give the team a warning to remove anything necessary.

"Welcome back, Jesse, Wash." Ian stood, rounding the table to greet them with a shake of hands and a slap on the back for George.

"Wash? I thought your nickname was Nipper?"

The men in the room laughed, and George shook his head. "It has been Nipper for as long as I've worked here.

Before, I was called Wash when I was in the Navy. Nipper was a play on a baby or young one." George smirked. "I'm assuming I've climbed the ranks a little further for them to be calling me Wash now."

"You'd assume right. With everything you've been through this past week, you've proven yourself time and again."

Ian's praise tightened George's chest, and he had to swallow against the lump in his throat. He'd never received anything similar to it before. Not even from his parents. He glanced at Jesse, who stared at him with a smile on his face.

"Let's sit. We have a ton to get through." Ian indicated for them to take a seat at the large table.

It was only when he sat, he noticed Sykes was sitting with them. "What are you doing here?"

"Earning my keep."

George raised his eyebrows but didn't ask for clarity. He was sure he'd be told soon enough.

"Okay, long story short for the moment. Jesse, you stumbled upon a huge undercover operation when you stole from Baker." Ian crossed his arms and leaned forward. "Baker has been under surveillance with the FBI for years, but no one had ever been able to gather evidence on him. There are three undercover agents within Baker's employ who have been there for three years or more."

"Mark!"

Ian nodded. "Yes. Mark has been with Baker for six years. We're hoping he's good at what he does and has enough of Baker's confidence that he would never be suspected as the one who helped get you out."

"But he was with us when the cameras went down! He might be found out. We have to help him!"

George gripped Jesse's arm. "Let's listen first, okay?" Jesse nodded.

"From what we have been told and can figure out for ourselves, there is someone behind Baker who is well hidden, and yet, no one has figured out who it is. Although, Sykes and Brody have their suspicions." Ian nodded at Brody.

Brody clicked on his computer, and several pictures came up on the wall in front of them. "We've seen multiple instances of vehicles arriving and leaving the mansion. Some are low down on the totem pole, some are higher up. So far, no one has tripped our radar, except for two potentials."

Sykes took over. "I've overheard several telephone conversations between Baker and someone he referred to as 'Sir,' but once he slipped and said, 'Castle.'" Sykes rubbed a hand over his shaven head. "I'd never heard the name before, and it wasn't until I started talking to you guys that we may have found a connection."

Brody sat forward. "Two men have slim—very slim—connections to Baker, who also have a link to Castle." He clicked again. "Ignacio Castello, a high-ranking member of a mafia family in Florida. His nickname is 'Castle' per his surname." Another click. "There is also August Castle, one of the seven City Council members of Tampa."

George's eyebrows rose. "Either a mafia member or a council member. I know which way I'd go."

Devon cleared his throat. "I would've initially as well. It seems Ignacio hasn't been seen outside of his home for several years." He held up his hand to forestall interruptions. "It doesn't mean it isn't him, but we *know* the person behind it has been to Baker's property. Now, Ignacio could easily travel there, but I'm sure someone would've noticed him."

"You're saying it's the council member?" Jesse pulled his bottom lip between his fingers.

"We can't be sure which it is." Ian sat back. "But regardless, the FBI has no evidence to point to either one of them."

"We're going to let it continue?" Jesse's voice was low and hard.

Ian shook his head. "No. We have our people checking into things as well, but we need to tread carefully because if we mess up the FBI's operation, our asses will be toast."

"You said the connections between them and Baker were slim. In what way?" Jesse leaned forward.

Brody scooted his chair closer to the computer. "Vehicles have been seen leaving the mansion and visiting Ignacio's house on a rare occasion. As in twice in the last five years. It's not much to go on."

"And August?" Jesse tilted his head.

"August and Baker went to high school together. There doesn't seem to have been any link between them after they left school."

"And there's no one else it could be?"

"Oh, there's plenty of people it could be, but nothing relates to Castle. Castle might be a red herring, but it's all we've got to go on." Ian sighed. "Jesse, did you overhear anything while you were at Baker's?"

Jesse shook his head. "Apart from the occasional murmurs from the men who were there to check me out, the room was practically silent. Baker worked on his computer, and guards came and went, usually whispering to Mark. I heard and saw nothing, which is extremely annoying since that was the whole point of me getting caught."

"It's also one of the reasons we got you out."

George's plan had been to get caught himself to allow him to be with Jesse, and if necessary, fight their way free.

"Wash was ready to come in guns blazing to get you out until we received word from a contact of ours that Mark had reached out about you. Baker had planned to keep you locked away until your new owner came to collect you. If

Mark's calculations were correct, it would have been at nine tomorrow morning."

Jesse shivered beside him, and George rested his hand on his nape, squeezing gently. "Where would I have gone?"

Ian stared at him and shook his head. "We don't know. Possibly somewhere we wouldn't have been able to find you."

George wanted to get things away from the horrible thought of what could've happened to Jesse and diverted the conversation to the original topic. "How do we figure out which of the men it could be?"

"We need to dig into their pasts: Baker's, Ignacio's and August's."

After several minutes of talking through each members' assignments, they dispersed, and George and Jesse settled into a spare office. Brody brought Jesse a computer so they could each do their own research into August. Jesse knew his way around the dark web, and it gave them an advantage of being able to have someone else look into it so Brody could focus elsewhere.

George researched the council member through the easiest method, by searching his name. "It says here August Castle has been a council member for six years and has two years left on his term. He was re-elected to serve the district. Before, he did various goodwill ambassador jobs throughout the area. He's had his time at the Chamber of Commerce and various other high-profile positions. He is fifty-nine, has a wife he's been married to for twenty-seven years and has five children, oldest is twenty-five, youngest is fifteen." George sighed. "On the surface, he appears squeaky clean."

"Yeah, on the surface..." Jesse tapped away at the computer with a speed George would never match, and George watched in fascination.

"What have you found?"

"I'm not sure." He clicked a few more times. "I'm

examining their school records to see if they had anything in common other than being at the same school."

"What, you mean like clubs or something?" Jesse nodded. "You can find that information? It was like thirty-five years ago."

"Yeah, it's not easy because a lot of stuff isn't digitized. But sometimes you'll get lucky because people are always reminiscing about their time at school and often add photos of yearbooks and memorabilia and such like." Jesse shrugged. "It's not always foolproof."

"You amaze me." A flush colored Jesse's cheeks, and he shrugged again, obviously embarrassed. George dropped a kiss onto his heated cheek and went back to his own computer, smiling. He pulled up some photos of August Castle, checking to see who he interacted with at events throughout the years. Nothing showed up as untoward. At least until he stared into the face of a man he knew well.

"Shit."

"What?" Jesse leaned over to see George's screen. "Who's that?"

George swallowed. "My father."

"Your father knows August Castle?"

"Apparently."

"How?"

George frowned down at the table as a memory resurfaced. "Fuck, no." He typed away until he found his father's school—the same as August Castle and Robert Baker. "Shit. All three of them went to the same school."

"I doubt your father has anything to do with this. It's a coincidence." Jesse rested his hand on George's arm.

"I have to tell Ian." George stood, his heart racing at the implications. He whirled back to Jesse. "What if he's involved?"

Jesse strolled over to him and wrapped his arms around

his waist, resting his cheek on George's chest. "If he is, we'll deal with it."

George closed his eyes and dropped his cheek to the top of Jesse's head. "Thank you."

Jesse lifted his head and smiled, and George was helpless to stop from kissing him. It was brief and chaste, but he felt it to his toes. "I better go."

"And I'll keep checking." Jesse grinned.

George took several deep breaths as he made his way down the corridor to Ian's office and knocked.

"Come in."

He opened the door. "I found something."

"Do we need the rest of the team?" Ian tilted his head.

"Not yet."

Ian waved for him to enter, and George shut the door behind him. "What's wrong?"

"The school connection between August and Baker… we've been studying it. I've found another person who was at the school at the same time."

"Who?"

"My father."

Ian's eyebrows rose. "It doesn't mean anything."

"I know, but I thought you might want to get someone else on this. I've been scanning photographs of events to see who August interacted with, and that was where I saw my father. Jesse is investigating any school clubs or events they may have had in common."

Ian narrowed his eyes. "I doubt your father has anything to do with it, but let's cover all our bases. I'll get Jake to check into it." George nodded. "Don't worry about it. Finish your trail like you were before. List and check out anyone who is a regular at the events. It won't hurt to have more avenues to study."

George sighed. "All right." He rose and retraced his steps, finding Jesse half-standing while typing.

"You're back! I've found something!"

George braced one hand on the table and the other on the back of Jesse's chair. "What?"

"August and Robert were both inducted into the same club for three years."

"What club?"

"Cum Laude Society."

"What's that?"

"Staff choose certain students who have reached a specific grade point average. Only a percentage of the students can be inducted. It's a prestigious honor."

"It will no doubt look good on August's resume."

"But does it link them any further?" Jesse's shoulders lowered.

"No idea. Keep searching. See if there is any mention or indication that their lives crossed again at any point after high school."

"What did Ian say?"

"He's getting Jake to tackle it."

Jesse rested his head on George's shoulder for a brief second and went back to work. George couldn't think about his father now. It would destroy him if he found out his father had anything to do with this fiasco.

21

JESSE

"There's movement at Baker's mansion."

Brody stuck his head through the door, and George and Jesse scrambled to follow him into the war room. On the screen was a video of several cars arriving at the property. Jesse and George had been free for three hours, and there didn't seem to have been any repercussions about their escape. Not that they could see, anyway.

"What's going on?"

Several men exited the cars and strode straight into the house.

"Who are they?"

"No idea. I'm trying to do facial recognition. Oh, shit. Boss-man, you have the FBI on the line."

Ian closed his eyes. "Transfer it to my office." He left the room while the rest of the team, including Sykes, watched what was going on.

"Sykes, do you recognize any of them?"

He shook his head. "But I didn't get to see many of the visitors. I did the grunt work. I wasn't as high up as Mark is."

"It can't be the men who were coming to collect Jesse because they are way early. It's only 3:00 A.M."

"Where are we getting this video from anyway?"

"A…friend." Brody smirked.

Jesse itched to get back to checking his leads, and he excused himself and sat down in front of the computer, picking up where he left off. He'd found nothing in the first years after August and Baker had left school. Nothing was showing any connection or interaction between them. August went on to University, and Baker started an apprenticeship with an antique company, which he eventually bought.

Jesse dug deeper into the years before Baker sold his company. He had no idea how long he'd been working when he stilled and blinked. Rubbing his eyes, he re-read the article, and his eyes widened.

"George!" He raised his voice, hoping the man would hear him, which he did.

"What?" He wasn't the only person who came.

"Check this and tell me I'm reading this right."

George dropped into the seat beside him. "'*Stolen artifact returned to the owner. After four months of searching, August Castle, a local hero due to his charity work, received information that the statue, which had been stolen from his home here in Tampa, had been found. Robert Baker, of Baker Antiquities, personally returned the artifact to its rightful owner after someone tried to sell it to him. The seller was arrested, questioned and summarily charged with stealing the expensive item several months prior.*'"

"When was this?" Brody was half out the door as he asked.

"Twelve years ago."

"It sits well in the timeline. He sold his business *eleven* years ago," Brody called.

"Sounds like too much of a coincidence to me." George squeezed the back of Jesse's neck.

"I might be able to find out more information if you would allow me to call Rio." Jesse knew it was a long shot, but it didn't hurt to ask.

George frowned. "Who's Rio?"

Jesse glanced at him and raised his eyebrows. "Did I never tell you about Rio?" George shook his head. "He used to be my boss, from when I did this with others instead of alone. He has access to many aspects of the dark web, although you didn't hear it from me."

"We'll have to run it past Ian."

"I already have. He says it's fine." Brody returned to the room, carrying his computer.

Jesse raised his eyebrows. "Are you sure?"

Brody nodded. "Yeah, go ahead."

Jesse reached for the phone he held out but hesitated. "He might not be happy I'm bringing him into this."

"The worst he could do is say he won't help." George stared at him, a small smile on his face.

Jesse stared at the phone, dialed and lifted it to his ear.

"Who is this?" The voice was deep and hard.

"It's Robin."

"Fuck, Robin! Where the fuck have you been? I've been fucking worried about you! And you know I don't fucking care about anybody!"

Jesse grinned and shook his head. He knew when Rio was worried because he swore ten times more than usual. "Good to hear from you, too, Drake." Drake was his code name when they were talking on an unsecured line. Jesse hadn't asked Brody whether they were or not, and he wanted to be careful.

"Fuck you. What trouble have you gotten yourself into now?"

Jesse chuckled. "I'm the epitome of angelic, Drake. I have no troubles, only inconsequential bumps in the road." He gave his code phrase to let Rio know it was truly him and he was safe.

"Yeah, there's my English rose. What's wrong?"

"I'd like some information if you can."

"Go." Straight to the point, as always.

"Robert Baker. August Castle."

"Fuck, man. You're in deep shit."

Jesse's heart raced, and he locked gazes with George. None of them could hear Rio's side of the conversation, but he needed George's strength for what Rio was no doubt about to tell him.

"I don't need to do much investigating because Robert Baker is the worst of the worst. Stay away from him, Robin."

"Too little, too late."

"Fuck. As for August Castle, he's squeaky clean."

"How do you know that without researching?"

Rio laughed. "Because it's his alter-ego who's a shitstorm."

"His what?"

"Alter-ego. August Castle is the most perfect man, husband, father, councilor, neighbor, and so on, on the face of the planet. However, Kale Lunasa is a well-known leader in the black market."

"They're the same person?"

"Yes."

"How do you know?"

"How do you think I know? This is my job, Robin."

"Can you get me evidence to show the correlation?"

"Potentially." There was a warning in his tone.

"The FBI is involved at this end, Drake. It needs to end now."

He waited while Rio thought about his options. Jesse had no guarantee Rio would help, but it would put Rio in the best light if he did. If anyone found out, Rio's business would be affected.

"I'll see what I can do."

"We don't have long."

"How long?"

"An hour?"

"Fuck, Robin."

The line went dead, and Jesse snorted.

"What did he say?"

"He's going to see what information he can find to prove August Castle is a leader in the black market."

"What? Nothing is showing any kind of link."

"Search Kale Lunasa."

Brody tapped away at his computer for several minutes before glancing at Jesse with wide eyes. "What the actual fuck?"

The rest of the team crowded around the laptop before Ian entered the room. "Let's go to the war room instead of all trying to fit in here. We have stuff to talk about."

Once they were all seated, Ian explained about his conversation with the FBI. "They're at a loss of how to proceed. They don't have enough evidence to do anything about Baker."

"Jesus Christ. You would've thought with some of their men being at the place for six years, they would have *something* at least." Jake shook his head.

"Jesse did well." Brody winked in his direction.

"What did you find?" Ian stared at him, as did all the other members of the team, and his cheeks heated.

"He contacted his old boss, Rio. Go on, fill them in." George nudged him and gave a small smile.

Jesse inhaled deeply and explained what Rio had told him and that Rio would call back within the hour with more information and, hopefully, some evidence to prove August Castle was indeed Kale Lunasa.

"The name itself is a small indicator." Brody tapped away, bringing up a screen on the wall. "Kale is the Turkish translation of 'castle,' and Lunasa is the Irish translation of 'August.'"

"Why make it so easy for someone to link them?" Nick's confusion was evident.

"Was it easy? We didn't think to do it." Ian leaned his chin on his fist.

"Sykes, what are your thoughts on this?"

The man leaned forward, resting his arms on the table. "As far as I'm concerned, nothing is impossible. I can't confirm anything because, as I said earlier, I did the grunt work."

"And there's nothing else you heard that might point to this being correct?"

"No. I've been trying to recall as much information as I've heard, but nothing else stands out."

Ian nodded, tapping his fingers on the top of the table. "Okay. Keep checking. See what we can find." He stood, marching to the door.

"What did the FBI want?"

Jesse heard Devon ask the question when they exited but didn't hear the reply.

Jesse and George retreated to the office they were using and continued their investigations.

"How come Sykes is in on this now?" Despite the words he used, what he wanted to know was why Sykes was being trusted when he'd tried to kill them.

George's forehead furrowed. "To be honest, I have no idea. I trust Ian. If he thinks Sykes should be there, he should."

"Hmm." Jesse wasn't so sure, but he refrained from arguing. It wasn't his company.

He focused on the more recent years, trying to find any interconnecting points between Baker and August.

"Jesse! Get in here!"

He scraped the chair back and jogged down the corridor to where Brody held out a phone.

"Hello?"

"Robin. I have something." Rio's voice sent a thrill of excitement through Jesse.

"What is it?"

"Do you have a place I can send the info?"

"Hold on." He put the phone on mute and glanced at Brody. "Do you have an address or something I can give Rio to send the information to?"

"Sure." Brody typed something out and twisted the screen so Jesse could see.

"Here." He told Rio the address, and the line went dead. Jesse rolled his eyes. "Saying goodbye wouldn't hurt you, Drake." He sighed. "He's sending something over."

"He has." Brody's eyebrows drew together. "Wow, he's thorough."

Jesse checked out some of the information, and his eyes widened. "Is this what we need?"

"I think so."

"You don't sound sure." Jesse glanced at Brody.

He pursed his lips. "It's too clean," he mumbled, typing something.

Jesse didn't interrupt, waiting for Brody to talk. A hand on his shoulder made him jump, and he spun around to George.

"Sorry!"

"Definitely a fucking bell." Jesse huffed a breath. "What's up?"

"Do you want a drink?"

"Yeah, water would be great." George pressed a kiss to his forehead and left.

"You make a good team."

Brody's voice had him spinning back to the man. "What?"

"You and Wash. You'd be good together."

"Yeah, no. I'm going back home after all this has finished."

"Shame."

Jesse frowned but didn't say anything else. "Is the information any good?"

"Yeah. We have enough here to give the FBI and send August and Baker to jail for many years."

Jesse narrowed his gaze. "Why are you not enthusiastic about it?"

Brody shook his head but gave a half-hearted smile. "No reason. Let's go tell Ian and the rest."

They wandered along the corridor to the war room, where several of the men were already talking. Jake and Nick were sitting side by side, chatting, while Sykes was on the opposite side with his computer. Devon was on the phone.

"I'm going to get Ian. I'll be back in a minute." Brody wandered off, and George entered with a tray of drinks.

"Here's yours." He held out a glass of water, and Jesse took it gratefully, draining half the glass in one go. He had been thirsty.

"Okay. Let's go through everything we have before we decide what we're going to do with it." Ian sat.

They went through every detail each of them had retrieved before moving on to what Rio had found. Brody brought the information up on the screen and talked it through. Despite having noticed Brody's initial hesitation when he went through it, Jesse was confident about Rio's ability to wade through the crap to find the gold. He believed this was what they needed to nail Baker and August before he could go home.

The thought had butterflies fluttering in his stomach, and he glanced at George. What would he do about them? Was there a "them" after all this had finished? Or did it have an expiration date?

"I think this is enough to send to the FBI. Let me give my contact a call and lay it all out. We can go from there. Good work, guys. Relax for a bit, and I'll catch you up once I've spoken to them." Ian left the room with Brody following them.

Jesse sat back in his chair and let out a deep breath.

"You okay?"

He glanced at George and smiled. "Yeah. It would be nice for this to be the end. I don't want to be watching over my shoulder for the rest of my life."

"Yeah, it wouldn't be conducive to a happy life."

"Are you going home after all this is done, Jesse? Or have you found a new home?" Jake grinned.

Jesse snorted. "I'm British, born and raised. I think I'd be a fish out of water here."

"You've done well from where I'm standing."

"I want to go to New York when this is done, but Jake thinks it's a tourist trap." Nick crossed his arms over his chest.

"Sykes? You went to New York, didn't you? After you got out of the Navy. What was it like there?" George asked.

"Busy, loud, constantly on the go." Sykes chuckled. "I had enough of that in the Navy."

Devon glanced at him. "What made you go there?"

"I wanted to see what if New York was a better option for me regarding my health."

"And was it?" Devon raised his eyebrows.

"It wasn't my cup of tea." Sykes winked at Jesse.

Jesse grinned, but his insides curdled. Listening to the rest of the team banter back and forth, he pushed down his panic and tried to join in until Ian returned. Jesse needed to speak to George alone.

"They're going to investigate and take action as they see fit. They won't tell me any more than that, but I'm sure there is someone who can give us a bit more information later should we need to know." Ian blew out a breath. "Right, everyone. Get some rest. We'll see what happens when we wake up in a few hours."

Chairs scraped and conversation rose while everyone grabbed their things and returned them to their rightful places before exiting. Jesse stayed close to George, not wanting to be alone at that moment in time.

"I need a quick word with Ian. You head to my room, and I'll be there soon."

"No, it's okay. I can wait for you."

"No, get some rest. I won't be long."

"I need to—"

George silenced him with a melting kiss, and Jesse's arguments floated away.

"Get some sleep." George pushed him in the direction of the bunkrooms. He had shown Jesse which one was his a couple of hours earlier in case he'd wanted to sleep.

Jesse blew out a breath as George disappeared down the hallway. He pinched his bottom lip between his fingers as he trailed to the room George often used when he was there. Opening the door, Jesse stepped over the threshold before he was shoved forward, and the door closed behind him.

He attempted to spin around but was pushed against the wall with a hand covering his mouth.

"I wondered whether it was too much of a clue. I knew you'd figured it out the minute I said it. Why didn't you tell the rest of them? Why wait?"

Jesse couldn't answer.

"We're going to go out to the parking lot as if we're bosom buddies now. If anyone asks, you're getting the dirt on George from his long-time friend. Understand?"

Jesse nodded as best he could.

"Do anything to give this away, and all I have to do is press one button on my phone, and your parents and Linc are dead."

Tears pricked at the corner of his eyes, but he refused to let them go. He blinked rapidly, trying to clear them. The pressure on his back eased, and he stepped back, turning to face Sykes.

"Why?"

"If you can't get a job done properly, do it yourself. That's my motto. And what better way to see how an operation works than to be part of the grunt work itself? This business has been my livelihood for too many years now for it to be taken down by a petty thief who thinks he's better than everyone else." Sykes jerked his head. "Move."

They strode down the hallway to the exit, Jesse not seeing anyone, which he wasn't surprised about when they'd been given time for themselves. He had hoped someone—anyone —would come out of a room and see them and question what was happening, but no one did.

His heart raced, and his palms sweated as he inhaled the fresh air of the morning, the sunlight beginning to lighten the horizon while stars twinkled above them.

"This way."

He followed Sykes's instructions to the black car he and George had returned in, and the lights flashed as it unlocked.

"Get inside."

"Jesse! Where are you going?"

His heart jumped when he heard George's voice, more so

when he heard a gun cock. He glanced to the side to see Sykes pointing a gun at George.

"I didn't think you'd figured it out; otherwise, you would've been with us on this trip." Sykes shrugged. "Never mind. I need the thief, but you? Not so much."

Sykes tightened his finger around the trigger. Seconds later, a gunshot sounded, and Jesse flinched, closing his eyes, tears leaking.

22

GEORGE

George took stock of his body, expecting to feel pain, but there was nothing. He glanced at Sykes as the man dropped to the ground, blood pooling around his head. Seeing the man he'd thought of as one of his best friends laying dead was difficult despite knowing it needed to happen. He swallowed hard and transferred his gaze to Jesse, who stood with his eyes tightly closed, shoulders curled.

"Jesse?" Was he hit? What had Sykes done to him in the few minutes it had taken George to explain the situation to Ian and Devon and figure out Jesse wasn't waiting in the bunkroom like he'd asked him to? He stepped closer. "Jesse?"

"No, no. Please, god, no."

Jesse's mutterings reached George's ears. He slid his hand onto Jesse's shoulder, tightening his grip when Jesse flinched violently.

"Jesse? What's wrong?" George visually checked him over and, seeing no injuries, exhaled roughly. "It's over, Jesse."

The door behind him slammed open, and George whirled around, double-checking it was his team and no one else.

"Fuck. How did you manage that, Wash? I didn't realize

you had a gun on you." Jake raised his eyebrows as he stared at Sykes's body.

"I didn't."

Holding onto Jesse's shoulder, he glanced around them, not seeing anything out of the ordinary.

"I know who did. All's good." Ian stepped closer. "How is Jesse?"

George shook his head, his hands trembling. He was a corpsman for god's sake, he knew what he was doing, but when it came to someone he cared about, all his training went out of the window. "Not good. No injuries I can see. He's in shock, I think."

Ian drifted to a stop in front of Jesse and ducked down to see his face. "Has he opened his eyes yet?"

"No."

Ian lifted Jesse's chin with the side of his hand. "Jesse? It's Ian. Sykes is gone. Open your eyes for me. You're safe now."

"He killed him." Jesse's voice was scratchy. "I couldn't stop it. He killed him."

Ian narrowed his gaze. "Hold him, George," he mumbled. George slid his arms around Jesse, who didn't protest but didn't acknowledge it in any way.

Jesse's whole body tensed, his breathing stopped, his pulse pounded. After several seconds, where George had started to become concerned about him not breathing, Jesse shakily inhaled. "George."

"Yes, sweetheart."

Jesse flinched again, but he faced George with his eyes closed. "George."

"Open your eyes for me, sweetheart. Let me see those beautiful hazel eyes." George didn't care if he sounded like a sap in front of Trident. He needed Jesse to know how much he meant to him. No matter what happened from here on out, he was with Jesse, be it in America or the UK or somewhere else Jesse decided they needed to be, he would be there.

Jesse's eyes flickered open, and he studied George's face for a long moment before bursting into tears and turning into George's chest. George closed his eyes, let out a breath and held him tightly, nuzzling his face into Jesse's hair.

"We'll be inside. You'll be safe out here." Ian squeezed his shoulder.

George listened for the receding footsteps until they disappeared, and all was silent, except for the usual nature sounds. "God, Jesse. I'm sorry. So sorry. I should never have left you alone as soon as I'd figured out who it was."

He couldn't believe he had been so stupid. Sykes had fooled him, lulling them into a false sense of security. George questioned every interaction he'd ever had with Sykes and knew there would probably be red flag warnings littered all over their conversations and meetings, even if he discounted the ones since George had started working with Trident.

"How did you know?" Jesse's question was barely audible.

George sighed and pulled back, resting their foreheads together. "Two reasons. Something niggled at me after he'd mentioned my father several times as if he knew Father would be implicated when we saw the photos. Sykes seemed to want to rub salt into the wound, and not just today either. It had always been something he spoke about with me. I never understood his fascination."

"What else?"

"Cup of tea." George kissed Jesse's forehead, cupping his face and staring into his red-rimmed eyes. "We only ever mentioned your liking of tea when the team was around, and Sykes was locked away. There's no way he could've heard it. Yes, he could've made an educated guess with you being from Britain, but using the exact turn of phrase I did at Baker's?" George shook his head. "Too coincidental."

"I didn't think you'd picked up on it." Jesse sighed.

"I thought you'd be fine for the few minutes it took me to explain to Ian, but you were gone by the time I got to the bunkroom."

"Sykes followed me and took me straight away."

George pulled him close again and closed his eyes, pressing his lips to Jesse's head. "I'm sorry."

"I thought he'd shot you." Jesse's voice trembled. "I thought if I opened my eyes, I'd see you lying on the ground." His breath hitched. "I'm sorry if it's too much for you, George, but I love you. I don't care what I have to do to keep you, but please, god, don't leave me alone."

Jesse's tears soaked into George's T-shirt, and George's own trickled down his cheeks. "Fuck. I love you, too, my little thief."

George lifted Jesse's head and kissed him, leaving no uncertainty between them.

A throat cleared behind them, and George tore his mouth away to glare over his shoulder at Nick, who grinned. "Boss-man needs you both."

George sighed. "Let's get this over with, and we can go and relax somewhere quieter than here."

They wandered toward the building, arms around each other, both studiously avoiding the red stain on the ground. George was glad Jesse didn't have to see Sykes's body, although knowing his boyfriend, he was a blood-thirsty individual on occasion, and the man would probably have kicked him.

They joined the team in the war room, and George raised his eyebrows at the presence of Carter. Then he understood.

"Thank you." George nodded to the man, who inclined his head and continued to drink his coffee, a small smile playing around his lips.

"Who are you thanking?" Jesse asked.

"I'll explain later if it's not mentioned here," George murmured in Jesse's ear.

They took seats next to one another, neither willing to relinquish the other's hand yet; Jesse's were trembling.

Ian wandered to the front of the room. "Carter has some information for us."

Carter slurped his drink, reclining in his seat. "Robert Baker was arrested an hour ago, as were several of his men. We were able to gain access to his computer, which had always been kept by his side until you two arrived." Carter gazed at George and Jesse.

"What do you mean?"

"Baker had never been anywhere without his laptop being on his person. As far as anyone was concerned, he slept with it under his pillow." Carter rolled his eyes. "A bit overkill if you ask me, but...anyway, whenever he went anywhere, it went with him."

George's eyes widened. "When he took us to the cells."

Carter nodded. "Yes. After six years of the FBI trying, he finally slipped up, and their man was able to do his job and get access. They were able to link him to years' worth of bad stuff."

"What about Ignacio Castello and August Castle?" Jesse leaned forward.

"Ignacio Castello is nothing more than what he seems on paper. He's a mafia member, nothing more, nothing less. As for August Castle, he would've been a scapegoat. Sykes set him up as if he was the one behind it all. The name Kale Lunasa was exactly what Sykes wanted him to be...a red herring. He'd chosen it on purpose. August Castle is exactly what he appears to be."

"How do you know this?" George stared at him, his head not wanting to trust as easily as he used to.

Carter quirked his mouth. "Baker had figured out who

Sykes was. He had evidence on his laptop. It was why he'd given Mark the go-ahead to kill him. Baker hoped he would become the head honcho once Sykes was out of the picture."

"Was that why you were here?"

"I did my job." Carter's response and gaze were steadfast, and George knew he could trust the man. He'd had limited interactions with him before, but he trusted his instincts and believed him.

"How did Sykes know about what was said at the mansion when he was here?" Jesse asked.

"He was wearing a tiny earpiece, invisible at a glance. He had been listening in on the mansion." Brody shook his head. "Bit weird if you ask me."

George rubbed a hand over his face, and Jesse squeezed his hand. He smiled across at him.

"Right, you two. Get some rest. You're on leave for the next week, except to go over your statements and whatever else the FBI will need from you." Ian gave a half-smile and jerked his head toward the door.

"I wouldn't wait in case he changes his mind." Brody chuckled from across the table.

"Understood." George stood, pulling Jesse with him. "What car can I borrow?" He caught the keys Nick threw at him and nodded in thanks.

George dragged Jesse down the corridor to the sounds of laughter from his team behind them and Jesse at his side. "I only have small legs, George. Slow down."

George grinned and picked Jesse up in a fireman's hold, striding for the exit. He avoided the area of the incident and raced to Nick's car, unlocking it with a touch of a button. Bending his knees, he allowed Jesse to slide from his shoulder until they were standing together once more.

"Where to?" Jesse lifted his head and smiled.

"My place."

George opened the door, waiting until Jesse slid in before closing it behind him, and dashed around to the other side. He drove away from the compound, eager to get Jesse to himself after far too long of not being able to touch him like he wanted to. He wasn't sure how long he could hold back.

The journey was made in silence and without any kind of physical contact because George was sure he'd pull over and devour the man beside him if he did. When he pulled into his parking spot, he climbed out and rounded the car, opening the door for Jesse.

"The first time won't be gentle." He stared at Jesse while he mumbled the words, his cheeks heating at being so exposed.

"It doesn't need to be."

George grabbed Jesse's hand and dragged him to his apartment. His blood heated, and there were so many images of what he wanted to do with Jesse, he could barely stumble along without falling flat on his face.

Unlocking the door, he crossed the threshold and stepped away from Jesse. "If you want to do anything, like inspect the apartment, or have something to eat, or whatever, you need to do it now."

His voice was hoarse and strained, and his gaze followed Jesse's movements as the man stepped closer.

"Nothing but you. The rest can wait."

George slammed him back against the wall, cupping the back of his head before it made contact to stave off a concussion. His lips feasted on Jesse's mouth, taking every groan, every breath, every whimper into him to keep and remember later. He slid his hands down to Jesse's hem, yanking the T-shirt off with barely a breath between their lips leaving and meeting again.

Jesse's nails gripped at George's back, and George arched toward him, growling deep in his chest at the bite of pain but wanting more. Jesse bunched his T-shirt up, pulling it higher and higher until George pulled away again to get rid of the offending item.

Their heated skin touched, and Jesse gasped into George's mouth, George taking the opportunity to sink his tongue into Jesse's mouth and explore.

George kicked off his shoes, dropping them somewhere nearby as Jesse's hands traveled along his torso, lower and lower, until he skimmed across George's waistband. The clink of his belt and the nudge of Jesse's hands had George hardening further in his trousers. His cock found some relief when Jesse opened the front of his khakis and curled a hand around his shaft.

"Fuck." He licked his lips, staring into Jesse's eyes, mouth open on a shaky breath.

George skated his hands around Jesse's back and underneath the waistband of his trousers, cupping Jesse's ass cheeks in his hands and molding them, pulling them apart to tease his hole with the stretch to come and pressing them together again.

Jesse's hand tightened on his cock while Jesse's hips thrust against George's thigh. George released his ass despite Jesse's denial and pushed his khakis off, throwing them somewhere behind him. He dropped to his knees, his lips finding purchase on Jesse's stomach and following the hills and valleys, swirling his tongue around Jesse's belly button.

He unfastened Jesse's pants, dragging both the trousers and briefs off Jesse's exquisite body while Jesse toed off his shoes. As soon as Jesse stood naked before him, George wrapped his hand around Jesse's cock, stroking slowly and watching a pearl of fluid appear at the tip. His mouth watered. He leaned down and lapped it up, groaning at the taste.

George's eyes closed, and he needed more. He sank down, taking Jesse into his throat and swallowing hard.

"Jesus!"

George stared at Jesse's flushed face, his boyfriend's eyes rolling and fluttering as George sucked as much liquid as Jesse would give him. When Jesse pushed against his shoulders and shuddered, George pulled off and stood, hiking Jesse's legs around his waist. He stumbled across the room, dropped into an armchair with Jesse straddling him and resumed kissing him.

Their cocks slid against each other when they shifted, trying to find some friction, but it wasn't enough. It was never enough. George needed everything Jesse could give him.

He reached to the side, fumbling for the small drawer in the table next to the chair and grabbed the lube and condoms he stored there for this reason—he'd never needed them before.

Jesse pulled at George's boxers, and George lifted his hips so Jesse could work them down, freeing his shaft for Jesse's overheated hand. George dropped his head back against the chair while Jesse expertly worked him into a frenzy. His eyes crossed when Jesse twisted his hand at the tip, catching the sensitive nerves on the underside and drawing a grunt from him.

He palmed the tube, squirting some gel onto his fingers and reaching behind Jesse to press against his entrance. Their mouths found each other again, and George's tongue mimicked his fingers, sliding deep, then withdrawing before sliding deeper, repeatedly.

"Fuck, please, George. I need you inside me."

He made Jesse wait, his pleading becoming incoherent mumblings while George made sure he was prepared enough for him. He rolled a condom on, slicking it well. Lifting Jesse, he held his cock at the younger man's pucker.

"Take me." At least that was what George meant to say. He had no idea if what he said was words or noises, but either way, Jesse lowered himself, inch by inch, bracing his hands on George's shoulders.

George stared at Jesse as he took every bit inside, pausing when he was fully seated. He cupped Jesse's jaw, pressing sweet, chaste kisses to his mouth before Jesse writhed on him, and he had no choice but to heed his call. Jesse lifted and dropped over and over, reaching for the climax barreling toward them both.

"More! Fuck, George. I need more!"

George took Jesse's weight and hammered into him from below, sweat sliding down his skin.

"It's not enough!" Jesse's whines broke the last of George's restraint, and he stood, gripping Jesse tight. He staggered the short distance to the couch, tripping over something on the floor and landing on top of Jesse. He barely stopped to reposition them before he lined himself up and slammed home.

"Yes! Fuck, yes!"

Jesse's nail dug into his shoulders when George drove forward. He held Jesse's legs wider, gripping his hips and giving him everything. Jesse's mumbling continued into a fever pitch of nonsensical words until George encircled his shaft and stroked.

"Ah!"

Jesse's release painted his stomach, and the rhythmic clenching of his ass took George over the edge with a bellow. He rested his forehead against Jesse's chest as he held him tightly.

"When can…we do that…again?" Jesse's words were interspersed with panting.

George snorted and lifted his head. "After sustenance."

He kissed Jesse sweetly, softly and with a reverence he had never expected to give anyone. "I love you." He stared into Jesse's eyes, watching as tears filled them and leaked over the edge.

"I love you."

2 3

JESSE

Despite their declarations of love, Jesse pondered their relationship during the few days that followed, where they spent time with the FBI, answering questions, with Trident, filling them in on what they'd missed, and with each other, tearing their clothes off.

He'd been away from home for long enough, and he needed to get back, but he was reluctant to bring the subject up with George. He didn't want to ruin their time together, but it couldn't be ignored.

His parents had called him the previous evening, wanting to know when he would be back in the country and demanding an explanation of why he refused to talk to his friend Oliver. Jesse knew he would have some explaining to do when he saw them, but he needed to have a cover story first. His parents had no idea what his job entailed except that he was hired to find items of value. As far as he was concerned, it was all they needed to know.

Rio had also contacted him when news arrived of Baker and Kale Lunasa's business going down. Of course, Jesse couldn't tell him anything on the record, but they had their own code; therefore, Rio knew the basics. It was another face-to-face conversation he would need to have shortly.

Jesse wasn't disillusioned enough to believe it was the end of the black-market dealers. By chopping off one head, another always took its place.

"What has you worried?"

Warm, strong arms encased him as he stared out of the window of the apartment at the darkening evening sky. He would miss the apartment because it had become a haven to him, something hiding them away from everything outside of the walls.

"I need to go home soon."

George pressed a kiss to where his neck met his shoulder, and a delightful shiver slithered down Jesse's spine. "I know. Can it wait another week? I have a few loose ends to tidy up, then we can arrange flights."

Jesse twisted in his arms, sliding his hands around George's back and raising his eyebrows at the slogan on his T-shirt: *Some days, the supply of curse words is unable to meet my demands.* "We?"

George grinned. "You can't get rid of me." George frowned. "Unless you don't want me to come with you."

Jesse silenced him with a kiss, which wasn't easy when he was smiling so much. "I'd love for you to come with me, but we need to talk about where we go from here. You live in America. I live in the UK. How is this going to work?"

George sighed and tucked Jesse under his chin, holding him close. "I don't know. We'll sit down and decide what we want, and I can speak with Ian and see what we can come up with. We could split the time between the two places or something." He shrugged. "I don't know."

Jesse's heart eased some at George's words. He wasn't

convinced they could figure it out, but at least they were both willing to try.

"I have to see whether the vase is there. I spoke to my client, and he understands the delay, but I'd feel better if I could finish this job."

George leaned back, cupping Jesse's face. "All right. I'll come with you. Do you want to go now?"

"I doubt they would be open at this time of night."

George smirked. "We have our ways."

Jesse shook his head and shrugged. "Why not? May as well get it over and done with."

"Okay. Let me call the guys, and you get ready." He left a chaste kiss on Jesse's lips and pulled his phone from his pocket as he strode away. "Hey, Boss-man. We're going—"

George's voice got quieter the further he went, and Jesse stared after him, smiling. The man was full of contradictions, most of which had been taught by his father, unfortunately. Captain Valmonte could do with a cuff around his head to knock some sense into him as far as Jesse was concerned. The man never cared for George; that much was evident in their interactions.

Jesse brushed George's father aside and drifted to the bedroom, wanting to change into something better fitting for retrieving the vase than sweats. He pulled a pair of black khakis from his bag and slid them on, adding a black long-sleeved T-shirt to the ensemble. He didn't want to go full-on ops mode because it would appear more suspicious than going to a storage locker in the middle of the night. He snorted and shook his head. They should've waited until tomorrow.

"Jake is starting out ahead of us to scope the area, and Boomer and Devon will be there as backup in case we have any unwanted visitors."

"You shouldn't have got them out of bed."

"They weren't in bed, and they were more than happy to help. I think they want this finished as much as we do." George pulled a shirt over the top of his T-shirt.

"Why do you cover those up?"

George glanced down at his T-shirt and paused, his forehead creasing. "Habit." He didn't move for a moment, then slid the shirt back off, leaving him in the slogan T-shirt. "I did it to annoy my father but didn't want to push too far. He was happy enough the slogans weren't visible."

"I love them. Although, I could think of a few more quotes we could add."

George raised his eyebrows. "Oh, yeah?"

"Those would be for the apartment only." Jesse winked and smirked.

George laughed. "Do I want to know?"

"Probably not. I'll surprise you."

"Come on, Robin. Let's finish this."

He held out his hand, and Jesse grabbed onto it as a lifeline. Everything felt more bearable when George was with him and wasn't that amusing when Jesse had prided himself on not needing anyone in his life for the past nine years.

The journey to the storage locker was quiet except for the radio, which alternated between music and the news about Baker. When they arrived, they saw Boomer and Devon leaning against a car, and they strode over to them.

"Sorry for getting you up at this time of night." Jesse gave a small smile.

Devon waved a hand. "No problem. Let's go see if it's there."

"I doubt it will be."

Jesse led the way to the door, smiling at the clerk when he

opened the main door for them. Devon spoke to the man for a moment, and they continued toward locker 367. Jesse hadn't requested a large locker because he hadn't planned on needing to fill it with anything but the vase.

He fished the key from his pocket and stopped in front of it.

"Wait. Let's check to see if the lock has been messed with first." Boomer stepped forward while the rest of them shuffled back, giving him space to work.

"This was why we brought Boomer." A whisper of sound floated into his ear.

"All clear."

Boomer waved Jesse forward. He unlocked the door and hesitantly pulled it open. When nothing happened, he let out a breath of air he'd been holding. Crossing the threshold, he came to a standstill, his heart racing.

The vase stood front and center where he had left it. Beside it was a black canvas bag.

"What's wrong?" The heat of George's body released some of Jesse's tension.

"This wasn't with the vase when I put it in here."

"What? The bag?"

Jesse nodded. "I put the vase in here, nothing else."

Boomer stepped past them, approaching the two items. Jesse, George and Devon stayed still until Boomer gave another confirmation of no explosives. He whistled and stood from his crouch, having opened the zip on the bag when he checked it out.

"What?"

"You might want to read this."

Jesse trailed closer, his breath leaving him in a rush and his stomach churning as he saw the amount of money the bag held.

"There's a note." Boomer held out a piece of paper, which Jesse took tentatively.

For your inconvenience or for your charity, whichever you prefer. M

"M? Mark?" Jesse glanced at George, who shrugged.

"Possibly." George took the paper and scanned it, passing it to Devon when he'd finished. "How much do you think there is, Boomer?"

"I'd say half a million, easy. Probably more."

"Why would he put it here? Is he trying to frame me for something?" Jesse's heart raced at the implications of being caught with this amount of money.

"I doubt it. Carter vouched for Mark—if it is him—and I trust him." Devon lowered his eyebrows, staring at the paper. "I would take it at face value. Whoever it was probably looted Baker's house safe before the feds could get to it. Fitting, in my opinion."

"Can I use this money when there is so much blood on it?" He didn't mean physical blood either. This money had been made through the black market for many unsavory things.

George stepped forward, sliding an arm around Jesse's shoulder. "I think it would be a fitting end to Baker's reign— or Sykes's reign. Having the blood money used for good...I think whoever was hurt with this money would be happy it was used to help others. But that's my opinion."

He'd never thought of it like that.

Half a million could help many people.

～

THE FLIGHT HOME had been long because Jesse had been jittery and nervous. Not about bringing George to meet his parents, but because he didn't know how to explain everything to them. And now, as they shuffled toward the exit and to where Linc was supposed to be waiting for them, he was no closer to the answer.

"Jesse!"

Linc's voice had him smiling regardless of his inner turmoil. He dropped his bag when Linc wrapped his arms around him and held him tight. Tears pricked at his eyes when he thought of what could've happened.

"I can't believe how long you were gone. Did you manage to do some sightseeing?" Linc pulled back, glanced over Jesse's shoulder and back to him again. "Except for the obvious." He smirked, tilting his head in George's direction.

Jesse slapped his chest, laughing. "You're so juvenile."

"Ah, but you love me." He held out his hand to George. "Nice to finally meet you."

"You, too."

They shook, and Jesse was surprised there didn't seem to be any male posturing going on.

"Come on. Let's get you guys settled back home."

"Is my home in one piece?" Jesse asked Linc with a grin as he pulled into traffic.

"Nah, I burnt it down."

Jesse snorted. "I wouldn't put it past you."

"Hey! Is that any way to talk to your best friend?"

"Yes."

Linc punched his shoulder, and Jesse laughed.

"You could've brought a friend with you, George. Don't you have any single friends who might want an English—"

"Delinquent?" Jesse finished.

"I could stop the car and let you walk, you know." Linc side-eyed him.

He was glad to be home. The conversation continued with Linc, bringing George out of his usual reserved nature into a more relaxed one. They spoke about George's T-shirt collection, including his chosen slogan for the day: *If my jokes offend you: 1. I'm sorry. 2. It won't happen again. 3. 1 & 2 are both lies. 4. You're a fool.* George hadn't been sure if it was the right one, but Jesse told him it was perfect.

Jesse's parents would either love George or hate him, but Jesse had come to the conclusion, he didn't care. He loved his parents and always would, but he no longer needed their permission or validation. If his trip to Florida had done nothing else, it had caused him to see even more how precious life was, and he was done trying to be the perfect son when they didn't care enough to grieve with him.

Linc pulled up in the driveway of Jesse's parents' house and idled the car. "Are you sure you don't want me to come in as well?"

Jesse shook his head. "We'll be fine. We'll see you at home in a couple of hours."

Linc nodded. "I'll take your bags. Ring me if you need anything."

"Will do. Thanks."

Jesse climbed out of the car. When he'd left for America, he'd parked his car in his parents' garage because there wasn't anywhere safe to leave it at his and Linc's apartment. At least if things went downhill, they could get out of there.

A warm hand rested against his lower back, and he leaned into it. "We'll be fine."

"I know. They're not—"

"You've met my father, Jesse. We have each other. No one can take it away from us unless we let them."

Jesse frowned at him. "When did you get so wise?"

"Must've happened somewhere across the Atlantic."

He snorted. "Come on." He grabbed George's hand and opened the front door, calling out a greeting.

His mother entered the hallway, her face brightening when she saw him. "Jesse! I wasn't expecting to see you today." She enveloped him in a hug, which he wasn't expecting.

"I thought we'd come for a visit before we head home and sleep off the jetlag." It wasn't the reason, but it would do as an explanation. His mother glanced to his side, raising her eyebrows. "Mum, this is George, my boyfriend. George, Felicity Flint."

"Mrs. Flint, nice to meet you."

"And you." She shook his hand and glanced at Jesse. "Why is this the first I'm hearing about a boyfriend?" She cocked her eyebrow. Jesse's cheeks colored—damn pale skin—and he ducked his head. His mother chuckled. "He's easy to rile up. I love your T-shirt, by the way, George. You'll fit in well with Jesse and his friends."

Jesse stared at her, open-mouthed. She closed his mouth with her hand. "What...?" He shook his head.

Her expression closed up, and she frowned at the floor. She squeezed her hands in front of her. "I've made many mistakes over the past few years, Jesse. I didn't realize how much pressure we'd put on you and how little love you received from us until you were gone for far longer than usual. Without any contact from you, I felt like I'd lost both my sons. I'd taken your presence at face value, and I, of all people, should understand life is short." She reached forward, grabbing Jesse's hands. "I am *so* sorry for everything we've put you through."

Jesse stared at her, disbelieving of the words she spoke.

"He does understand." George wrapped an arm around his waist. "He knows exactly what you've been through because he went through it as well. Unfortunately, you weren't there for him as much as he was for you. It's damaged your relationship, Mrs. Flint, but it's not unrepairable. Trust me."

Tears trickled down Jesse's cheek, and he threw his arms around his mother.

"I'm sorry, sweetheart. So sorry."

He lost track of time while he held his mother and cried for everything they'd lost. When he pulled back, he found his father standing by their side, talking in low voices with George. George nodded and smiled, conversing back, but he had his hand on Jesse's back, keeping them linked to ensure Jesse didn't feel alone.

"This was not what I was expecting when I returned." He gave a small laugh.

His father stepped closer. "You know I've never been as emotional as you and your mother, but I am sorry for what happened. It took a stronger man than me to point out what I was pushing away." He glanced at George, then back to Jesse. "Keep hold of him, Jesse. He's a keeper despite his awful taste in T-shirts." Jesse snorted, and his father squeezed his shoulder. "Come on, let's get some tea."

"We'll be there in a minute." Jesse waited until they had left the hallway before rounding on George. "You spoke to my father?"

George gave a lopsided smile. "If I say yes, are you going to hit me?"

"No."

George nodded. "I called them a couple of days ago and spoke to them. They know a little more about your job, but not that you," he lowered his voice, "*steal* anything. They know what happens to the majority of your money. I'm sorry if I crossed a line."

Jesse pressed his forehead to George's chest, holding back

his tears at the thoughtfulness of the man in front of him. "Thank you. I never expected this. It's...the greatest gift ever."

George pressed a kiss to the top of his head. "You're welcome, although I didn't do much."

Jesse lifted his head. "You gave me back my family, and with you here, I have more than I could've ever hoped for."

He lifted into his toes and fused their lips, trying to show George exactly what he meant to him.

2 4

JESSE

Seven months later . . .

"There's someone here who would like to see you."

Jesse twisted his head in the direction of the voice and frowned. "Who would want to see me here?"

In the seven months since he had been through hell with Baker and Sykes, he and George had been trying to find the best solution to their location problem. It was only when Linc suggested he and Jesse team up for their new business venture and take it across the pond that Jesse knew where his heart lay, and it was by George's side, no matter where in the world they were.

With Jesse's parents' help, they had created Beau's Beauties, a charity that raised money for people who struggled under the weight of the financial burden of medical bills. They had undertaken several fundraisers already despite only being up and running for the past three months, and they had plenty more planned.

"I think you'll want to see them."

Jesse saved his work, closed the lid of his laptop and

followed Nick through the hallway until they reached Ian's office. Nick knocked, standing to the side after he'd opened the door. Jesse stepped forward and froze.

"How are you, Jesse?"

All Jesse could do was stare at the man who had put his own safety on the line for him and George. "Mark? What are you doing here? Not that I'm not happy and all, but I thought you were undercover?"

Mark grinned, the expression making him appear younger. "I've done all I can do there now. I'm out. I wanted to check on you and make sure they're treating you right." He glanced to the side with a smirk.

"I'm sure if we weren't, George would have something to say about it." Ian leaned back in his chair.

"Yes, I heard you two were still together. I'm glad. I saw the sparks when you were at the mansion. Hold onto that. It doesn't come around often." A flicker of emotion, almost wistfulness, tightened Mark's face, but it was gone before Jesse was sure he'd seen it.

"I'm glad you're out. It couldn't have been easy living that life for as long as you did."

Mark's smile faded. "It wasn't, but you did what we'd tried to do for years, and for that, I owe you a debt. If you ever need anything, let me know."

"No, you don't have to—"

"I know I don't have to, but I want to. There's no telling how long I could've been undercover there before we found a way in. Despite what you did being accidental, it blew the case wide open." Mark stepped forward and held out his hand. "Thank you."

Jesse shook hands with him, overwhelmed with emotion. Since he'd been with George, his sarcastic front didn't appear as much as it used to, but his emotions were all over the place because he wasn't used to dealing with them. He didn't mind, but it threw him when he felt like crying some days…for no reason.

"I see you've created a charity. I'm happy you were able to do it."

"A guardian angel made it possible." Would Mark understand the underlying meaning of the phrase? "What are you doing now?"

Mark chuckled and grimaced. "I'm on desk duty for a short time while I get my bearings back in the real world. My therapist is having a great time trying to decipher all the shit in my head."

"I know the feeling." At Mark's questioning gaze, he explained, "I'm seeing a counselor to help with everything that happened this year and with my family issues. I'm glad. It's helping."

Mark nodded. "Anyway, I should leave you to your work. Please, call on me if you need anything at all."

"Thanks."

Mark shook hands with Ian and exited the room. Jesse blew out a breath. "That was not a meeting I'd been expecting. Ever."

"Mark's a good man from what I've been told. Way more than the FBI deserves." Ian stared at the door.

Jesse chuckled. "You just want him to work on your team."

Ian laughed and stood. "Damn right. He'd be an asset."

Jesse couldn't deny it. He had a feeling Mark had something in his past he needed to work through before he would make any life-changing decisions.

"Are you coming to the club tonight?"

They wandered toward the war room, where George and the team waited for a meeting. As Jesse was not part of Trident as such, he wasn't allowed in some of the meetings, but he had been given access to George's office to work when George was around. Other times, he either stayed at home or worked at Linc's new apartment. They had yet to decide on an office location for the charity.

Jesse pursed his lips. "I'm not sure. I'll speak to George. I don't know if it's my kind of thing."

Ian held his hands up. "It's not a problem, Jesse. You don't have to come, but I know you've been asking questions about it, and the best way to understand is to visit. As I've told you, there is a guest pass for you should you wish to have a tour. But only if and when you're ready."

"Thanks."

They stopped outside the war room, and Ian entered. Jesse waved at George and pivoted away, stopping when an arm snaked around his waist. He spun back and claimed George's mouth before pushing him away.

"Go before you get into trouble." He couldn't contain his smile.

"Yes, sir."

George grinned at him before he closed the door, and Jesse chuckled, hoping his life never changed.

❧

GEORGE

George waited for the meeting to start, licking his lips and tasting Jesse on them. His life had changed so much in the last few months, and all of it was for the better. Once Jesse had decided on moving to Tampa, George had quickly offered his apartment as Jesse's new home. Jesse hadn't been sure, to begin with, because it had been quick, but George's argument had been if they were to find themselves incompatible after all, moving in together would make it quicker to find out.

They'd found a small apartment nearby for Linc, and Jesse had been assured by his best friend that if things went wrong, he'd have a place with Linc if he needed it.

So far, everything was going well. George was proud of everything Jesse had accomplished since he'd relocated. The charity received more recognition every week.

"Wash?"

George refocused his attention on the meeting. "Sorry."

Ian handed him a slip of paper, which he unfolded.

Your father has been on the phone again. He wants a meeting between the three of us. Let me know what you want to do.

George blew out a breath and refolded the paper, slipping it into his pocket. He met Ian's gaze and nodded once. Ian returned the nod and refocused on the team. George pushed everything else aside while he did his job. His father could wait.

When the meeting ended, George went to find Jesse. He was focused on his laptop while talking to Linc, and George stared at him for a moment, marveling at the person who had changed his life for the better.

"Linc! Leave the poor woman alone and do your job!"

George snorted, giving away his presence, and Jesse smiled over at him. Linc had found a woman he liked who worked within one of the catering companies the charity used for some of their events. The woman—Rosa— appeared as interested in Linc, but neither would ask the other out on a date. They chatted and flirted and stared longingly at each other, but neither would take the first step.

"Right. I'm hanging up now. I have work to do."

Jesse hung up and shook his head. "That man is a menace.

We're going to have to push them together so they will stop mooning over each other. Any ideas on how to do it?"

George cleared his throat. "Why not book them a table at a restaurant and tell each of them they are having a meeting with you. When they get there, you can call them and let them know the dinner is on us." Jesse raised his eyebrows. "It's cheaper than this pining."

Jesse laughed. "We can try if nothing else."

George leaned down, resting his hands on Jesse's chair and nuzzling his nose down Jesse's neck and to the area he loved the best. He pressed a couple of kisses on his warm skin, then pulled away. "Are you ready to head home?"

"Definitely. Give me five minutes to finish this off."

George knew it would be longer than five minutes, but he didn't care. He'd wait as long as he needed. He sat in his chair and pulled out his phone a second before it rang.

"Ian?"

"George, can you come to the office, please?" Ian's tone indicated exactly what this was about. He closed his eyes and agreed.

"What's wrong?"

"Father's here."

"What? Why?"

"Why does he ever come here? To check up on me as usual."

Jesse closed his laptop with a bang and stood. "Well, let's go see him."

"You don't have to come, Jesse."

"I know. Come on."

George withheld a smile at the show of bossiness Jesse gave. It wasn't often he saw it, but he knew it came out whenever George's parents were involved. He followed Jesse down the corridor to Ian's office. He knocked and waited for Ian to invite them in.

"Ah, there you are. Come on in." Ian didn't seem shocked Jesse was with him if the quirk at the corner of his mouth was any indication.

"George. Ian has been filling me in on your time here. I'm glad things are going well." His father barely glanced at his boyfriend, choosing to ignore him as usual. George was a little tired of it.

"I'm enjoying working here. I wouldn't want to be anywhere else."

"What are your expectations for him, Lieutenant? Does he need to aim for any kind of promotion?"

Ian leaned forward, linking his fingers over his paperwork, and opened his mouth, but Jesse beat him to it.

"Why does he need to? He's told you he enjoys working here. Shouldn't any potential advancement of his career be his choice, not yours?"

His father's mouth firmed when he gazed at Jesse. "I am interested in what my son could make of himself. You should be interested in such a thing as well."

"Why?"

Captain Valmonte frowned. "If he is the sole source of income for your…family, he needs to make good choices."

"He's not. So shouldn't the choices be his?"

"He's not what?"

It was like watching a tennis match, but George couldn't help except admire Jesse's gall of facing off with his father.

"The sole source of income. And regardless of whether he is or not, it's not your concern. You have no say in George's career path. As you admitted yourself, he and I are family now. His choices are no longer at your whim."

His father's face darkened, and George could see him vibrating. He refused to allow Jesse to take him on alone. "He's right, Father. Please stop harassing Ian with these attempts to drag me up the ladder. I'm happy where I am, and if I ever feel like I'm not, I will speak with Ian about it myself."

"I'm trying to help you, George. I want what's best—"

"No, you want what's best for your image, Captain Valmonte. If you knew anything about your son, you would realize exactly how worthy he is of being your son. Instead of focusing on his faults, start seeing his strengths as I do." Jesse pivoted toward George and dropped to one knee, pulling a box out of his pocket. "Everything I said is true. You're worth more than anything I can think, and I would love to spend my life with you. I know it's quick, but I love you. Will you marry me?"

"Fuck, yes!" George laughed and wrapped his arms around Jesse, kissing him soundly. Jesse slid the ring on his finger.

"I hope this will be a long engagement." His father's voice indicated exactly what he thought of what had happened.

Jesse pulled out of George's arms and glared at his father. He strode to the door, opened it, advertising exactly what he expected his father to do. "It will be as long or as short as we deem necessary."

"Are you going to let him talk to me like that, George?" His father stood in front of him, and he finally saw him as the man he was: trying to finish his dreams through George, seeing him as a pawn instead of a son, and he was done with it.

George swallowed and, without hesitation, nodded. "Yes. Your presence is no longer required…Captain."

There and then, he drew the line, choosing Jesse and Trident instead of those who continually belittled him. Unless his father changed, George did not need the negativity in his life any longer.

Captain Valmonte glared at the three of them and stormed off.

"Well, that was a turn up for the books." Ian rubbed a hand over his face, then stood, striding over to the two of them. "Congratulations."

"Thank you."

"Sorry for taking over your office and meeting. I didn't mean to." Jesse grimaced.

"You're more than welcome to deal with him. I'd had enough and was about to tell him so. But you doing it made it all the sweeter." Ian chuckled.

"It's time to go home." George slid his arm around Jesse's shoulders and squeezed. "And by the way, it's not too quick. I've told you before, the sooner we figure stuff out, the better."

Jesse grinned and kissed him.

"I'm leaving. Do not do anything in my office that I will need to have uncontaminated. Understood?"

George pulled away, laughing. "Yes, sir."

"Come on. Let's go home."

Home. The place where all his dreams came true.

WOULD you like to read my books before anyone else? You can sign up for Steamy Delights, a membership subscription service, and gain early access to chapters from my work-in-progresses, exclusive bonus content, and more. I have four tiers available: Contemporary, Kink & Daddy, Taboo & Dark, and Club Royal Bonus. See which one grabs your fancy.

And for a taste of the free short story you get if you sign up for my newsletter...

FREE!

JASON DOESN'T HAVE the strength to fight his stepfather for a happy life, so, to stop the man from turning his fists and words to his younger siblings, he takes the brunt of his anger himself. He vows to get those children away from him as soon as possible. Then, when there is one bruise too many for his best friend's eyes, they come up with a plan for a fake boyfriend for Jason—someone who's really a bodyguard.

DARIUS DOESN'T GET ASKED to the royal family's domain often, but he doesn't say no when he is. Being asked to be a fake boyfriend is far from usual, but he's happy to do it if it means he gets to spend time—and protect—the man he can't stop staring at. When things don't quite go the way Jason hopes, Darius offers another option. One that might backfire. But with Darius at his side, Jason finds more strength than he ever thought possible.

AND MAYBE, he might've found the one person who could give him his happily ever after.

THIS IS an MM bodyguard romance that spans both the Club Royal and Guarding Royalty series.

GET this book FREE here

BOOKS BY ELOUISE EAST

Guarding Royalty

Protecting his Past

Protecting his Heart

Protecting his Secrets

Club Royal

Royal Firsts

Rogue Royal

Secretive Royal

Grieving Royal

Disowned Royal

Trained Royal

Awakened Royal

Commanding Royal

Illuminate Matchmaking

Ignite

Blaze

Kindle

Scorch

Boys, Daddies, Snuggles & More

Need Him

Trust Him

Daddy

Love Me, Daddy

Soothe Me, Daddy

Spoil Me, Daddy

The Complete Daddy Series

<u>Love in Flames</u>

Fight Fire with Fire

Out of the Frying Pan

Smokescreen

Breathing Fire

Love in Flames Collection

<u>Crush</u>

Love Conquers

Instant Desire

Primary Seduction

Deep Down

A Crush for Christmas

Life Support

Covert Strength

Love Scene

Lawful Attraction

Crush Volume 1

Crush Volume 2

Crush Volume 3

<u>**Just A Little Crush**</u>

First Kiss
He's Behind You
A Special Love

<u>**Standalone**</u>

Treehouse Whispers
Star-Crossed
Protecting the Thief
Sizzling Chauffeur
A Home for Barney
Mattie

<u>**Elouise R East (taboo)**</u>

Dark & Divergent

Forbidden Temptation
Too Many Secrets: A Life of Secrets
Too Many Secrets: The Lake House

Collide

When Fantasies Collide
When Dreams Collide
When Pleasures Collide
When Cravings Collide
When Hungers Collide

Dark

Defying Sanity

Stronger Together

ABOUT ELOUISE EAST

Elouise East writes sweet and steamy connections in gay romance. She also touches on taboo stories under the name Elouise R East.

Books that tell the stories where friendship and family are the focal point - be it blood family or chosen - are very important to her. That's why she includes a variety of personalities, talents, ages, situations and abilities as she believes a story or character needs. She wants her characters to be real, to be relatable, to be free to have whatever views they tell her they have. And trust her, most of the time, she does not have *any* say in the matter!

Her characters come to life on the page for her as well as her readers. Their stories unfold in front of her as she writes, and she has very little input into how they want to be shown. Just like real life, the lives of her characters change with every choice, every interaction and every conversation. And she wouldn't have it any other way.

She writes books that are emotionally realistic, even if liberties are taken with other aspects of the stories. She doesn't know any other way to write. It comes from deep inside.

Who is she? A single parent to two children living in the UK. An avid reader who still tries to devour every book she can get her hands on. A student of learning about any subject that takes her fancy. An author of books she would read herself. And a romantic at heart who loves anything cheesy.

Who's joining her on her journey?

Stalk her here… ;-)
Website : https://elouiseeast.com
Newsletter : https://elouiseeast.com/newsletter
All links : https://elouiseeast.com/links

Also by

Samantha Cole

***Denotes titles/series that are only available on select digital sites. Paperbacks and audiobooks are available on most book sites.

THE TRIDENT SECURITY SERIES

Leather & Lace

His Angel

Waiting For Him

Not Negotiable: A Novella

Topping The Alpha

Watching From the Shadows

Whiskey Tribute: A Novella

Tickle His Fancy

No Way in Hell: A Steel Corp/Trident Security Crossover (co-authored with J.B. Havens)

Absolving His Sins

Option Number Three: A Novella

Salvaging His Soul

Trident Security Field Manual

Torn In Half: A Novella

***HEELS, RHYMES, & NURSERY CRIMES SERIES

Her Sleuth

Largo Ridge Series
Cold Feet

*****Antelope Rock Series**
(co-authored with J.B. Havens)
Wannabe in Wyoming
Wistful in Wyoming

Award-Winning Standalone Books
The Road to Solace
Scattered Moments in Time: A Collection of Short Stories & More

Standalone Books
Sweet Revenge

*****The Bid on Love Series**
(with 7 other authors!)
Going, Going, Gone: Book 2

*****The Collective: Season Two**
(with 7 other authors!)
Angst: Book 7

*****Special Collections**
Trident Security Series: Volume I
Trident Security Series: Volume II
Trident Security Series: Volume III
Trident Security Series: Volume IV
Trident Security Series: Volume V

Trident Security Series: Volume VI

Trident Security Series: Volume VI

USA Today Bestselling Author and Award-Winning Author Samantha Cole is a retired policewoman and former paramedic. Using her life experiences and training, she strives to find the perfect mix of suspense and romance for her readers to enjoy.

Awards:

> *Wannabe in Wyoming* (co-authored by J.B. Havens) won the bronze medal in the 2021 Readers' Favorite Awards in the General Romance category.

> *Scattered Moments in Time* won the gold medal in the 2020 Readers' Favorite Awards in the Fiction Anthology category.

> *The Road to Solace* (formerly *The Friar*), won the silver medal in the 2017 Readers' Favorite Awards in the Contemporary Romance category.

Samantha has over thirty-five books published throughout several different series, as well as a few standalone novels. A full list can be found on her website.

Sexy Six-Pack's Sirens Group on Facebook
Website: www.samanthacoleauthor.com
Newsletter: www.geni.us/SCNews

facebook.com/SamanthaColeAuthor
instagram.com/samanthacoleauthor
bookbub.com/profile/samantha-a-cole
goodreads.com/SamanthaCole
amazon.com/Samantha-A-Cole/e/B00X53K3X8

www.ingramcontent.com/pod-product-compliance
Lightning Source LLC
Chambersburg PA
CBHW070602170726

48291CB00003B/671